Every family has skeletons in the closet. But the sorcerous Crafter family has magic, mayhem, mystery, and more! Meet . . .

The Crafters

CHRISTOPHER STASHEFF conjures up a tale of alchemists who hate witches — and the witches who love them.

ROBERT SHECKLEY reveals how raising children can be confused with raising demons.

ESTHER FRIESNER learns that monsters and humans make strange bedfellows.

RU EMERSON follows a bewitching young girl who's trying to follow in her mother's enchanted footsteps.

KATHERINE KURTZ summons a tall grey-eyed stranger for heroic things-to-come.

MORGAN LLYWELYN serves up a beggar's banquet of magic and science... and everything in between!

This enchanting new shared-world anthology series also includes stories by **JODY LYNN NYE** * **JUDITH R. CONLY** * **ANNA O'CONNELL AND DOUG HOUSEMAN** * **WENDY WHEELER**

THE CRAFTERS

**Edited by CHRISTOPHER STASHEFF
and BILL FAWCETT**

ACE BOOKS, NEW YORK

This book is an Ace original edition,
and has never been previously published.

THE CRAFTERS

An Ace Book / published by arrangement with
Bill Fawcett & Associates

PRINTING HISTORY
Ace edition / December 1991

ISBN: 0-441-12130-6

CONTENTS

PROLOGUE

Jeffrey Ambrose Crafter opened the worn leather envelope slowly, almost reverently. Although the pages it contained were only copies, he handled them as though they were the actual handwritten documents. The originals, the diaries and manuscripts, some frayed and worn, mended time after time, were in safekeeping with a Crafter cousin wealthy enough to afford a museum-quality storage system. Still, to Jeffrey, even these copies, the record of ten generations of his family, were his heritage, precious in duplicate.

Next, he pulled the frayed drawstring on the deep-blue velvet bag, and spilled the contents on the bed. A small ruby, a silver button, scraps of cloth, a broken piece of glass, pebbles and twigs—these too were his legacy.

He moved the only chair in the room close to the bed and sat contemplating the odds and ends, the papers and pieces of apparent debris. Outside, snow fell steadily, and furred and booted figures plodded their way through the square. The room was warm, however, if not cozy. Crafter had engaged it over a week before, and in that week had sat, as he now sat, many times.

He was a Crafter. He had, in his lifetime, used the particular abilities that this gave him in the service of his country. He was a special agent, an operative, a spy. Whatever term might be applied, he was very good at what he did.

But the fact that he was a Crafter had also given him a damnable foresight. He had come to realize, along with other members of his far-flung family, that the current course of world history was a dire one, that the precarious balance of power would soon tip toward disaster. Unless *something* was done.

So he had come here, to this small hotel in the center of Moscow, with a plan in mind, a dangerous, desperate plan. He was assailed by doubts. What if the spell he would dare to attempt failed and brought about the very Armageddon he was trying to prevent? And what right had he, or any other Crafter, to use the powers they possessed to manipulate others? How far was it possible and proper for a Crafter to go in interfering with the lives of those around them?

For days such questions had plagued him. He walked the snowy streets of the city, ate sparingly, and sat with his heritage and the memory of his father's voice, counseling him to allow others, always, to live their own lives and think their own thoughts without magical interference. A basic law of the family.

But these were extraordinary times and extraordinary circumstances. Jeffrey knew that the time had come for him to make a decision. The practice cantrips of the last week now had to give way to a difficult and risky conjurgation. He hoped to find—no, he knew he *must* find—in a final contemplation of the artifacts of his family's past the strength of will and conviction to do what must be done. For the smallest flicker of doubt, and the spell *would* fail. . . .

He breathed deeply, and picked up the shard of glass, translucent and irregular. With the glass in his hand, Jeffrey Ambrose Crafter began to search the past. . . .

THE CRAFTER FAMILY

**Amer and Samona Crafter
married 1682**

| Arabella (Amy) (b 1684) m Andrew Greene | Jacob (b 1685) | Ahijah (b 1687) m Dorcas Weaver | Margarethe (b 1693) m Robert Singer | Samuel (b 1696) m Faith Bethany Weaver | Cynthie (b 1705) |

Lucinda *m* Jacob Levy
(b 1717)

THE ALCHEMIST AND THE WITCH

by Christopher Stasheff

The wind howled around the log cottage, straining at the eaves and rattling the shutters and the door. It made the pine trees that were gathered around the cottage moan and sway. It pushed at the chinking between the logs, then swirled up to test the shingles of the roof. Finally, it swept panting down the chimney.

Inside the cottage, Amer heard it and turned to close the flue. The wind struck against the metal plates and stopped in surprise, then began to rattle and beat at them. Finally it gave up and turned back up the chimney, shrieking with anger.

Amer looked up as he heard it. He sighed, shook his head, and clucked his tongue, thinking that the wind would never learn. He finished the seam of the brass tube he was working on and laid down his torch.

"Master," said Willow, "wha'cha makin'?"

She was a globe of light in a large glass jar. If you looked closely, you could see, within the globe, a diminutive, very dainty, humanoid form, but only in rough outline.

"A blowpipe, Willow." Amer looked the tube over carefully. He was a good-looking man, but overly solemn for one in his early thirties.

"Wha'cha gonna blow through it?"

"Air." Amer puffed through the pipe, checking to see that

1

there were no leaks. Outside, the wind heard him and swept against the cracks and crevices of the cottage with a blast of redoubled fury at a being who dared mimic it. But Amer paid it no heed.

"Well, of course you're gonna blow air through it," Willow said, disgusted. "What else is there to blow? What I want to know is, 'Why?' "

"To make glassware." Amer went over to the hearth for a look at the kettle of liquid glass that was bubbling thickly over the flames. He found the fireplace filled with smoke from the glowing coals and opened the flue to let it out.

With a joyful shriek, the wind bounded down the chimney again. A second later, it came tumbling back out, coughing and spluttering with the smoke.

"Oh, I like glass!" the ball of light sang.

"It *is* attractive, isn't it?" Amer closed the flue and dipped the pipe into the glass. He lifted out a lump of the amorphous mass and began to blow gently into the pipe, swinging it in slow, cautious circles. Gradually the glass took the form of a globe.

"It's magic!" Willow breathed.

"No, just practice." Amer shook the pipe, and the globe slipped to the side. Then, with a wooden forceps, he drew it away, so that the narrowing tube of glass connected globe and pipe. He broke the tube and placed the finished object on a pile of sand on the floor, to cool.

"It's pretty," Willow said doubtfully, "but what *is* it?"

"An alembic," Amer said. "It's for boiling solutions and channeling their fumes where I want them to go." He dipped the pipe into the glass again, and soon, test tubes, flasks, beakers, and all the rest of the paraphernalia so vital to the alchemist had joined the retort on the sand pile.

"Oh, they're lovely!" the ball of light enthused. "But why are you making so many?"

"Because I have to replace all my apparatus," Amer explained. "The goodfolk of Salem town made that necessary."

The citizens of Salem had, with great civic zeal, destroyed all Amer's glassware in the process of razing his house. Due to the unselfish dedication of the goodfolk of the town, Amer had lost everything—laboratory, wardrobe, notebooks, and dwelling—which ten years of work and wonder had won from the New England wilderness. Barely escaping with his life, he had found his way at once to this hidden spot deep within the mountain forest, and in defiance of the rain and wind which had until then been undisputed masters of the forest, built a small house of logs and reproduced as well as possible his lost notebooks.

There was more to do, of course. There was always more to do.

Taking up a knife and a stick of wood, Amer went to the armchair by the fireplace, sat down, and began to whittle.

"*Now* wha'cha makin'?"

"A model of a human skeleton, Willow." Amer made a careful scrape along the tiny wooden bone with his carving knife, held back the piece to evaluate it, compared it with the drawings in Galen's text on anatomy beside him, and nodded, satisfied. He put it down and took up the next roughly cut blocky bone and began to whittle its details.

"Wha'cha makin' *that* for?"

"To better understand human anatomy, my dear."

"Why in firedamp do you want to understand *that*?"

Amer smiled. "So I can write a book about it."

A miniature skull began to grow out of the wood under his knife. On the table at his elbow lay a diminutive rib cage, a pelvis, and an assortment of other bones. There was also a large stack of drawings and pages, all written in the alchemist's hand. Amer was preparing his own text on anatomy.

"Oh," said the ball of light, "I'm writin' a book, too. I'm gonna call it *Bizarre Behavior of the Bipedal Beast*."

"Indeed!" Amer looked up from his work. "And where are you finding your information?"

"From watching *you*. You're about as bizarre as they come. Let's see . . . 'makes little skeletons . . . ' "

Amer smiled, wondering what his little captive was using for pen and ink—or paper, for that matter. He, of course, had never heard of electricity, let alone the concept of rearranging electrical charges that store her words. "You're not exactly a conformist yourself. Will-o'-the-wisps aren't supposed to write books, you know."

"Must be the company I keep."

"*Touché.*" Amer smiled. "I am a trifle eccentric, I suppose."

"No 'suppose' about it. You do a *lot* of things people aren't supposed to do."

"Do I really!"

"Uh-huh." The ball of light bobbed. "Like, for one thing, they're not supposed to go messing around with smelly ol' potions and things. They're *also* not supposed to catch will-o'-the-wisps and keep 'em in bottles!"

"Beakers," Amer corrected automatically. "You wouldn't want me to be lonely, would you?"

"Yeah," the will-o'-the-wisp said pensively. "That's another thing people aren't supposed to do."

"What? Be lonely?"

"Uh-huh," said Willow. "They're supposed to live in towns, or maybe farmhouses, with other people—but not high up on mountainsides, all alone."

"Well, yes," Amer conceded. "I must admit that's true. But the people of Salem didn't want me there, Willow."

"Aw, I'll bet they did. You just *think* they didn't."

"No," Amer said, frowning, "I'm afraid they made their opinion quite clear. They burned my house and notebooks, and broke my instruments. I barely escaped with my life."

"No!" Willow said, shocked.

"Why, yes," said Amer mildly.

"But why, Master?"

"Because," said Amer, "Samona told them I was a warlock." He frowned. "Actually, I don't think they'd have taken action on her unsupported word—she's never been terribly well-liked, except by the young men, and then in the worst possible way. She must have had some help, some others telling the goodfolk that I had made a pact with Satan."

"Master!" Willow gasped. "You didn't, did you?"

"Of course not, Willow. I'm an alchemist, not a warlock."

The will-o'-the-wisp sounded puzzled. "What's the difference?"

"A warlock gains magical powers by selling his soul to the Devil," Amer explained. "An alchemist gains magical results by studying the phenomena of nature and mind."

"By how?" The will-o'-the-wisp was totally at a loss.

"By constructing logical generalizations encompassing ever more natural and supernatural phenomena."

"If you say so." But the will-o'-the-wisp sounded doubtful. "You sure you're safe here, though?"

"Oh, yes," Amer murmured. "Quite safe."

For Amer had done more than merely rebuild. He had set an elaborate network of traps and warning devices around his cottage in a wide circle, for it was highly possible that the good colonists would not rest until they had hunted him down and burned him at the stake.

"It is possible," he told Willow, "that the Salem folk may still be pursuing me. I'm quite certain that Samona, at least, will not rest until she has settled with me."

"But who *is* this Samona? And why'd she say you're a whosiwhatsis if you're not?"

"Samona," said Amer, "is a very beautiful young witch who lives in Salem—only they don't know she's a witch. And she told them I was a warlock because she hates me."

"Hates *you*?" Willow demanded, incredulous.

"Hates me," Amer confirmed. Not that he had ever done anything to Samona that should cause her to hate him; indeed, he was supremely indifferent to any being that walked on two feet, and especially so to those who wore skirts. Samona despised him for this; but then, she held the whole colony in contempt for similar reasons.

And this Amer could never understand, for though Samona loathed the Puritans for their reserve, she was herself extremely reticent, so much so that more than a few of the stern young men still bore the scars of her fingernails for their boyhood audacity in paying her a courtly compliment.

"Why does she hate you, Master?"

Amer made a guess. "Because she hates all men."

"Well—yeah, I can understand that. But why you especially?"

"Because my magic is just as powerful as hers."

"But that's no reason to hate you!"

"That's just the way women are, Willow." Amer sighed.

"Aw, it is not!" Willow said stoutly. "I'm not, and I'm a woman!"

"That's different," Amer explained. "You're a will-o'-the-wisp."

"What woman isn't?" Willow returned. "There's gotta be another reason why she hates you, Master."

"Well, there is, really. You see, she sold her soul to the Devil, and I didn't."

Notwithstanding his refusal to sell his soul, Amer had garnered more knowledge of magic through his experiments than Samona had gained through her pact with Satan. "I think we were both born with the ability to work magic, actually—it was just a matter of learning how. She thought she paid a much lower tuition than I, but she's begun to realize that the bill will come due eventually, and will be rather exorbitant. Mine took longer, but is paid in full as it goes."

"Oh." That gave the will-o'-the-wisp pause.

"No wonder she hates you."

Amer looked up, surprised. "I don't see any logic in it. . . ."

"That's all right, Master," Willow assured him. "There isn't any."

"Then it is absolutely necessary that I keep an eye on her." Amer put down the tiny bone and went back to the hearth. He placed the new glassware on a tray and took it over to a keg-spigot he had hammered into one of the logs that formed the wall. He twisted the handle, and clear, sparkling water gushed out, though the spigot met only solid wood within the log. It was fed by a clear mountain stream, a mile away; the alchemist had learned well from his research.

He washed the new glassware with water and sand, then

set it up on metal stands on a bench that ran the full length of the wall. He lost no time in setting an alembic bubbling merrily into a cooling tube with a beaker at its end, to collect the distillate.

While he waited for the beaker to fill, he turned to another workbench, one that bore racks of vials, another alembic, several glass tubes, and a small crucible. It was backed by shelves of jars and boxes, each carefully labelled. Amer took another, larger beaker, filled it with water, and set it over an elaborately carved alcohol lamp. Then the alchemist began to ladle powders into a beaker. "Let's see . . . green pepper . . . sugar . . . cinnamon . . ."

"Sounds good, Master."

" . . . powdered batwings . . ."

"Gaaaaaack!"

"Oil of ambergris . . ."

"Uh, Master . . ."

"Eye of eagle . . ."

"Master . . ."

"Monosodium glutamate . . ."

"M-A-A-A-STER!"

"Oh." Amer looked up, blinking. "Yes, Willow?"

"Wha'cha makin'!?!"

"Making?" Amer looked down at the frothy liquid in his beaker. "A far-sight potion, Willow."

"A what?"

"A far-sight potion. So I can watch Samona, wherever she is."

Willow gasped. "You're a peepin' Tom?"

"Willow!" Amer remonstrated, scandalized. "I am merely performing a vital mission of strategic reconnaissance."

"That's what I said. Wha'cha wanna look at her for, anyway?"

"I'm afraid it's necessary," Amer said, thin-lipped. He peered into the beaker. "You see, she's always trying to find some way to enslave me."

"Enslave *you?* What's she want to do *that* for?"

"Because she's a woman."

"*That's* no reason," Willow maintained.

"Samona thinks it is," Amer explained. "As I've said, she hates all men."

"And you most of all, 'cause you're not a warlock?"

"For that," Amer said judiciously, "and because I'm the only man she can't enslave with her magic."

"Why's that?"

"Because *I've* got magic, too."

Willow sounded puzzled. "I thought you said you weren't a witch."

"Warlock," Amer corrected absently. "That's the male equivalent. And no, I'm not. I'm an alchemist."

"Same thing."

"Not at all." Amer sighed, striving for patience and trying to find a slightly different way to explain something he'd already explicated. "A witch gets her power from the Devil. But an alchemist gets his magic by working experiments."

"Gotta get this down," Willow muttered. "Chapter Four: Magic, Male and Female . . . Now—you're an alchemist?"

"That's right."

"And she's a witch?"

"Mmm-hmm."

"And that's why she hates you?"

Amer looked up, startled. "You know, Willow, you may have something there. If I got my magic from the Devil, she probably wouldn't even notice me."

"Why not?" The will-o'-the-wisp was totally perplexed.

"That, my dear," said Amer, "is one of the peculiarities of the female mind."

"You mean," said Willow, "you don't know."

"Precisely."

A gentle bubbling announced that the beaker was ready. Amer recited an incantation and peered into the fluid. "Now let me see . . ." He found it filled with a swirling of unearthly colors. He sighed patiently and muttered a refinement of the earlier spell—with no results. He tried a second and a third spell, and then, losing patience, slapped the side of the beaker. Instantly the colors swirled together, stretched and wriggled, and snapped into focus in the form of Samona.

She was dressed in a low-cut, red velvet gown with a high Elizabethan collar that framed her head in a scarlet halo. The bodice was molded to her as though it had been born on her and had grown as she had grown, narrowing as her waist had narrowed and flaring out into the skirt as her hips had become wider and fuller, curving softly, and then sweeping up in a futile attempt to hide her high, swelling breasts. But where cloth had failed, long shimmering hair had succeeded, flowing down to hide her in soft, luxuriant black waves. Her face was smooth, gently tinted, with slanting black eyes and wide, full, blood-red lips.

All this Amer noted, and had noted every day of his childhood and youth almost without knowing it. She'd changed her eyebrows again, and the mahogany highlights were back in her hair.

"Still so easily bored," he murmured, staring into the beaker.

"Not you, Master!"

"No, no! Samona."

"Master! You really shouldn't!"

"Fo," Amer said, frowning at what he saw. "I think I should."

For the miniature Samona's hands were moving lightly and quickly among the bottles on the shelves alongside her fireplace, measuring their contents into a small cauldron that boiled and chortled softly over an unearthly green flame. She stirred the brew, dropped in a pinch of a white, glittering powder, and stood counting her pulse-beats as she watched the thickening liquid.

"What's she doing, Master?"

"I thought you said spying was wrong, Willow."

"Well, yes, but gossip is another matter. Tell me!"

Amer smiled. "She's making a potion, too. But what kind? Let's see . . . she's using essence of sweet zephyrs . . . powdered tears . . . rhadlakum. . . . What can it be?"

"That's what I was wonderin'," Willow muttered.

"My heavens!" Amer looked up, eyes wide. "Another aphrodisiac!"

In the beaker, the miniature Samona, judging the time to

be right, swung the cauldron off the flame, let it stand for a few minutes, and then skimmed the surface with a ladle and poured the skimmings into a small vial. She held it up to the light; it glittered with ruby liquid, steaming. Her eyes glowed; she eyed the vial with a smug smile, then began to laugh.

Suddenly, there was a flash of green light, and she was gone.

Amer stood looking into the beaker for a few seconds more.

"What is it, Master?" Willow cried. "Master? Master!"

For Amer had taken a clean beaker and started pulling powders off the shelves.

"What kind of potion is an aphro-whatever?" Willow demanded.

"An aphrodisiac, Willow."

"What's *it* for?"

"Me, I'm afraid."

"No, no! I mean, what does it *do*?"

"Stra-a-a-a-ange things," Amer said.

"Like what?"

"Well," said Amer, and "well," again. Then, "It will, uh . . . make me, uh . . . like her."

"Wonderful! Then you'll be friends again?"

"Well, something like that, yes."

"Master," the will-o'-the-wisp accused, "you're not bein' honest with me."

"Very well, Willow." Amer sighed, looking up from his work for a moment. "An aphrodisiac makes a man desire a woman carnally. And the particular kinds that Samona brews are also love philtres."

"A love filter? What's it do, take the love out of the carnal-whatever?"

"Desire. And no, a 'philtre' adds love in to where it wasn't before."

"That doesn't make much sense to me."

"Nor to me, either," Amer confessed. "But here's the manner of it: if she can trick me into drinking that potion, I'll become her slave."

"I thought you said her magic didn't work on you."

"It hasn't—so far. And only because I counter her spells and potions with my own. But there is always the possibility that she might be able to concoct a *new* potion that *would* work on me."

"So what're *you* doin'?"

"Making an anti-aphrodisiac, Willow."

"A *what*?"

"A protective drug," Amer explained. "It will ward me from the effects of her potion. Let's see . . . where did I put the saltpeter?"

"But," said Willow, "don't you *want* to fall in love with her?"

"Willow," said Amer, "don't ask embarrassing questions."

"But I don't understand."

"That makes two of us."

"Why does she want to make you like her?"

"Because she's a woman."

"No, no! I mean, besides that!"

"Willow," Amer said between his teeth, "it is not tactful to remind a scholar of just how much he doesn't know."

"Well, I'm sorry! Y' know, this whole thing seems really silly to me. She mixes a potion so you'll fall in love with her, and you mix one so you won't. You could save a lot of time and trouble if neither of you mixed the potions."

"Very true," Amer agreed. "Unfortunately, Samona doesn't see it that way."

"Why not?"

"Well . . . I suppose it's that if she can't enslave me one way, she'll try another."

"And an aphro-whatsis will do that?"

"It's a good start," Amer allowed.

"I don't understand," said the poor, confused will-o'-the-wisp.

"I only wish I did!" Amer said fervently. "Let's see . . . wormwood . . . a pinch of gall . . . wolfbane . . ."

"Love potions." Willow was engraving in her book of energy impulses. "Protective drugs . . . Wait till Harvard hears about this!" She spoke of the College that had been established for many years.

Amer gave the potion a final stir, lifted it to his lips, and drank it off in a single draft. His face twisted in a wry grimace; he coughed, and came up smiling. "There! I'm safe!"

A tone, so low that it was more felt than heard, filled the room. Willow vibrated with panic, but Amer breathed, "Just in time."

"Good afternoon, Amer," murmured a low, husky voice.

"Good afternoon, Samona." Amer noted that her tones were deeper and fuller than usual, sending a shiver through his system; he reminded himself that his potion needed a few more minutes to take its full effect.

She came over to the side of his chair, and the flowing skirts clung to her as she came.

"You aren't very polite," she said. "A host usually offers his guest some refreshment after a long journey."

"Of course," Amer said. "Forgive me." He rose and took a decanter and two glasses from the mantel. "Will amontillado do?"

"Quite well," Samona said, and a smiled flickered for an instant over her lips. It lasted no longer than the tick of a watch, but that was long enough for Amer to be certain it had been there.

He filled the glasses and gave her one. "To your power— may it increase."

"Hypocrite!" she said. "Toast something else, Amer, for you know as well as I that I'll never be stronger than I am now."

"Oh, come," Amer said. "You're young yet."

"Yes, but I've reached my peak. You're young, too, Amer, but somehow your power keeps growing. I should know, I've been trying to defeat you long enough."

"Oh, now, Samona!" Amer protested. "You mustn't give up so easily! You might win yet, you know."

"Indeed? It doesn't seem very likely."

"Don't believe her, Master!" Willow whispered, just behind his back. "Remember her potion!"

That jarred Amer out of his shock. "Yes! Well, uh, Samona—I'm glad to see you've finally given up chasing a will-o'-the-wisp."

Someone cleared a miniature throat behind his back.

"I beg your pardon, Willow," Amer hissed out of the corner of his mouth.

Samona didn't notice; she had turned away, pacing toward the hearth. "You're right, Amer. I've become wise in the hard school of frustration. I know when I'm beaten."

"Surely . . ."

"No," she said, bowing her head forlornly, "I've come to admit defeat, Amer."

For a moment he panicked, thinking she meant it. But then he remembered the fleeting, gloating smile as he poured the wine, and said, "Well, I'm glad to see that you've finally become wise, Samona. It's not good for you to keep wearing yourself out getting nowhere."

"So I've learned," she said with a touch of bitterness. "No, I've come for a truce. And to prove that I mean you well, I've brought news of danger."

"Danger? From whom?"

"From Death."

Amer smiled. "There's always danger of that, Samona."

"You don't understand." Samona turned away impatiently.

"I'm willing to learn."

"Yes, and eager, too, I know," she said, bitter again. But she smoothed her face with a smile. "Then learn, scholar, that in this eldritch world we inhabit, Death is not a force, but a being."

"Fantastic . . ."

"But real enough, for us." Samona turned to face him again. "Death doesn't come in the usual way when he comes for a witch. He comes in person, and you may never know he's there until you feel the cold, damp bones of his hand clutching your shoulder."

"Come now," Amer said. "Surely, with all your powers, you could invent some sort of protection for yourselves."

"True," she said, "but if we ever relax for so much as a

second, he is upon us. If we forget ourselves in our delight with our own cleverness, if we lose our heads in glee as we watch a victim shudder, we will almost certainly feel the chill on our shoulders and feel it creep to our hearts, and will hear a cry of triumph as we sink to the depths of Hell." She stood gazing at the fire, pale and trembling, as though she could see the hollow eyes of Death staring at her.

"But if Death is always lying in wait, as you say," said Amer, softly, "how is it that you have never thought it necessary to speak of him until now?"

"Because he struck among us last night," Samona said in a hushed, almost strangled voice. "This morning Goody Coister was found sitting in the old rocking chair in front of her fireplace. She was stone dead." Samona's eyes reflected the fire burning quietly on the hearth. "I saw her myself," she whispered. "You could still see the marks of his fingers on her shoulder."

"Goody Coister?" Amer whispered in shock and disbelief.

Samona smiled with malicious satisfaction. "Yes, Goody Coister, that virtuous old hag. That venerable symbol of New England purity. Shall I tell you how many bastards she and old Moggard have spawned?"

"Moggard?"

"Yes, Moggard. Warlock-General of New England and Vice-Chairman of the Universal Brotherhood of Sorcerers. He begat quite a few on the old biddy—not that any of them lived to know of it, of course." For a moment, Samona seemed sad and forlorn.

"But Goody Cloister taught me my catechism!"

"Of course. The worst ones always look to be the most respectable. Shall I tell you about Sexton Karrier?"

Amer shuddered. "Please don't."

Samona's eyes gleamed, and her smile deepened with satisfaction. She turned away, and when she turned back to face Amer again she looked quietly humble once more.

"Ah, well," she said, "I just wanted to warn you. Come, Amer, fill my glass again, and let's drink to friendship."

Amer shook off the mood of apprehension and forced a smile. He nodded and took the decanter from the mantelpiece and poured them each a glass. "As red as your lips, my dear, and as sparkling as your eyes."

"Gallant," she noted, and lifted her glass. "To our truce."

"*Pax nobiscum*," Amer said, and drank.

Samona nearly choked on her wine. "Please!" she said between splutters, "must you use Church language?"

"I'm sorry," Amer said. "Really I am." He patted her back gently.

"Don't touch me!" she screamed, and turned on him like a cornered vixen. For a moment, Amer could have sworn that he saw the Devil looking out at him from her midnight eyes.

But she regained her composure immediately. "I'm sorry, Amer. But you know I could never bear to be touched. And it's become worse since I . . . joined the coven."

"Yes, quite so." Amer had a brief, nightmarish vision of what her initiation must have been like, and how much of herself she had lost. He shuddered. "I'd forgotten. My apologies."

"Accepted," she said, looking up at him, and, "Oh, Hell!" in a slightly reverent tone. "I've spilt my wine all over you."

"That's all right," Amer said, recovering himself with equal rapidity. "I've plenty more. Would you care for another glass?"

"Yes, please," she said. She put her hand to her forehead. "Yes, I—I think I need it."

"Why, you're pale," he said.

"No, I'm all right," she said. "It's nothing."

"Sit down," Amer said, pushing an armchair toward her. She all but fell into it. He picked up a notebook and fanned her gently.

"Just a moment's rest . . ."

"There, there," Amer soothed. "Too much excitement, that's all . . ."

"Yes. I—I'm fine now. Thank you."

Amer put the notebook down, took Samona's glass to the

mantel, and filled it from the decanter. He knelt and gave it to her.

But as she took it, he noticed a ring on her hand, a ring with an exceptionally large stone—a huge emerald with a deep, almost liquid lustre. In all the time he had known her Amer had never seen Samona wear such a ring. "What a beautiful gem!"

"I—I'm glad you like it, Amer." Her eyes were wide with surprise and—was it alarm?

"That—uh—friend I've heard you speak of . . . Lucretia . . . ?"

"Yes, it was a present from her."

He smiled sadly as he looked at it.

"Amer . . ."

"Yes, of course." He tore his gaze away and went over to a cabinet that stood next to the table on which Willow rested. "You'll need something stronger than wine."

As soon as he'd turned away, Samona sat up, pressed the stone out of its setting with feverish haste, and emptied the drop of potion it contained into his glass of wine.

"Master," Willow hissed, "she's pouring something into your wineglass."

"I thought she would," Amer muttered. "Fortunate that I didn't drink it all."

"Aren't you worried?"

"No, not especially, Willow. Let me see . . . I suppose I've given her enough time. . . ."

Only just; Samona had scarcely replaced the stone and fallen back into the chair before Amer returned.

He took a glass from the mantel and filled it from the bottle of whiskey he'd taken out of the cabinet. "Here." He pressed it into her hand, which trembled as she brought the glass to her lips. Amer took his wineglass from the table and raised it, wondering what kind of spell the potion was supposed to cast over him. "To your quick recovery," he said, and downed it.

Samona watched him out of the corner of her eye and muttered a short incantation as he drank. Then she leaned back in the armchair and sipped her whiskey slowly, waiting for the potion to take effect. Beneath the dark waves of hair that covered them, her breasts rose and fell softly with her breathing, and Amer was shocked when he realized that he'd been wondering just what the low-cut gown would reveal if she wore her hair back over her shoulders.

Finally Samona set down her glass, took a deep breath, bit her lip, and said, "Amer, I—I don't feel too well. Would you see how my pulse is?"

"Certainly," Amer said, and he took her wrist, frankly puzzled as to what she was up to. He probed for the large vein, probed again, and frowned. "I can't seem to find it."

"I never seem to be able to, either," she said, "not there. See if you can feel my heartbeat." She slid his hand under the heavy black tresses, and Amer found that the gown was cut very low indeed.

For a moment he was stunned, completely at a loss. Then, with a sort of numb amazement, he realized the purpose of the potion, and began to be very glad he'd taken the antidote. For one way or another, Samona meant to have his soul. He would play along to see if she had more tricks prepared.

Amer caressed her, slowly moving his hand to part the rich black waves and stroke them away to her shoulders; then he let his hand slide over the swelling softness of her. He felt her shiver under his touch. He knelt and watched her cream-white breasts as they rose and fell, straining against their velvet prison.

Then he looked at her face, and it was dead white. He realized with a shock that he was the first ever to touch her with tenderness, and that her trembling was not from passion alone. Finally, with a sense of awe, he realized her courage.

Then she looked at him with fear in her eyes, and her trembling lips parted softly. He slid his free hand to her back, between her shoulders, and pressed her to him. Their lips met in moist sweetness.

They broke apart, and he pulled her head down onto his shoulder. "So," he said, with wonder, "that's what it's like. . . ."

"What . . . ?" Samona half-gasped.

"Your scapula," Amer breathed. "It articulates with your clavicle by ligament! And I thought it was connected by cartilage. . . ."

For a moment, Samona sat very, very still.

Then she was out of the chair and over against the wall with a wildcat's scream. "Take your hands off me and get away from me, you tin-bellied machine!" She clasped at the wall behind her with fingers hooked into claws, glaring at him and hissing, "I wish you were in Hell!" And, for a moment, Amer could have sworn he saw hellfire in her eyes.

Then a cloud of green smoke exploded. When it cleared, she had vanished.

"Thank Heaven!" Willow sighed. "Master, she's gone!"

But Amer only stared at the place where she had been, murmuring, "Strange . . . strange, very strange . . ."

"What, Master?"

"My emotions, Willow."

"Why, Master?" the will-o'-the-wisp cried in alarm. "What's wrong?"

"I must write this down," Amer hurried to his writing desk and snatched up a quill. "It's priceless information . . . I'll probably never have the same experience again."

"I'll say!" Willow said fervently. "But what's the matter?"

"Well, Willow . . ."

"Now, now, Master, you've had a nasty shock. Just lie down and relax. You've had a hard day. I'll write it down for you." Willow prepared to make alterations in the electrical potentials within her.

Amer took her at her word, going over to the narrow cot against the wall and lying back, head pillowed on a horsehair cushion. "It started when she told me that she'd come to declare a truce. . . ."

"Just let it flow, Master," the will-o'-the-wisp said, oozing sympathy.

"She looked up at me, and her eyes looked so innocent, and she seemed so submissive . . . "

"Mm-hmmm."

" . . . and she said she'd come to surrender. . . ."

"Yes, Master . . ."

"And, well, Willow, for just a moment there, I felt *panic*!"

"Really!"

"And, Willow—that *worries* me . . ."

The wind swept around the cottage, infuriated at being balked. But it was gaining strength, because other winds were coming, ushered by the towering black clouds that drifted from the west, obscuring the moon. The wind welcomed its kin, and together they tore at the cabin, howling and tearing. Then a great black cloud arrived and broke open a drum of rain, with a huge crack of thunder. Torrents gushed down, lashing the little cabin, and the winds howled in glee.

Inside, Amer slept on in blissful but disturbing dreams, unheeding of the winds. Enraged, they redoubled their force. Still Amer slept—until Willow came to attention, startled. She listened, was sure she'd heard right, and called, "Master! Wake up!"

It came again, from the door—a knocking.

"Master! Wake up! There's someone here!"

"What? Here? Where?" Amer lifted his head, dull with sleep.

"At the door!"

"Here?" Amer stared at the portal.

It shook as the knocking sounded again, louder and quicker.

"Oh, my heavens! And at this hour of the night!" Amer shoved himself out of bed, shuddering as his feet touched the cold boards, shoved them into slippers, and stood. He shuffled over to the door as the pounding came gain, insistent, impatient. "Patience, please! Patience! I'm coming!" Finally, he pulled out the bar.

The door slammed open, and the wind howled in triumph, whirling toward the doorway—and swooping away as something blocked it from entering. It howled in frustration, but a flash of lightning drowned it out with a huge clap of thunder—and showed Amer the robed and hooded silhouette standing in his doorway.

The alchemist froze. Then he turned to catch up his dressing gown and don it. Knotting the sash, he turned back to the doorway.

"Please excuse my appearance," he said, "but I must admit that I was not expecting you."

"That's perfectly all right," the figure said. "Very few ever do."

Amer frowned. "I hope I'm not being too presumptuous," he said, "but would it be too much trouble for you to tell me who you are, and what you've come here for?"

"Not at all," the figure said, and, in sepulchral tones, "My name is Death, and I've come for you."

Amer raised his eyebrows.

"Indeed?" he said, and then, a little taken aback, "Well, I—I'm quite honored."

But then, recovering himself, he saw that Death still stood outside the door.

"Oh, my heavens!" he cried, "you must think me terribly rude. Come in out of the rain, won't you?"

Somewhat puzzled, Death stepped into the cabin, and Amer pushed the door shut behind him. The wind screamed as the door shut on it, then howled and battered against the door in rage. But Amer dropped the oaken bar into its brackets, then turned and went over to the fireplace to throw on another log. "Come stand by the hearth and dry yourself. May I get you a drink?"

"Why, yes," Death said, pleasantly surprised. "Wormwood, if you have it."

"Of course," said Amer, taking another decanter from the mantel. He filled a glass and handed it to Death, then poured one for himself. Reaching up, he took a vial from the mantelpiece, shook a little of the fine, chickory-scented powder it contained over the stool, and muttered a short, unintelligible phrase. The outline of the stool blurred, then began to stretch and bulge as though it were alive. Within thirty seconds, it had assumed the shape of a high-backed wing chair. It sprouted cushions, which grew and blossomed into a luxuriant golden velvet. The outlines hardened again, and a soft, comfortably padded armchair stood by the hearth.

"Sit down, won't you?" Amer said.

Death didn't answer. He stood staring at the armchair. At last he cleared his throat and said, in a businesslike tone, "Yes. This brings me to the matter about which I came, Master Amer."

"Please sit down," Amer said. "It pains me to see a guest standing."

"No, thank you," Death said. "My cloak isn't quite dry yet. But about this—ah—strange gift of yours, Master Amer."

"How rude of me!" Amer said. "Please forgive me. Being freshly wakened, I'm afraid I'm not thinking very clearly." He turned to a closet in the wall near the workbench and drew out a leather laboratory coat. "Please put this on and let your wet cloak hang by the fire."

"No, thank you," Death said, a little hastily. "However, it *is* getting rather warm, and I must admit that I'm beginning to feel like a steamed chestnut." He opened his hood and the front of his cloak, and Amer stared, fascinated. For Death's head was a skull, and his body was a complete, articulated skeleton.

"Excuse me," Amer said, "but would you mind holding your arm straight out to the side?"

Death frowned. "Like this?"

"Yes, exactly." Amer picked up a notebook and pen and began drawing. "Now, would you move your arm in a circle? Yes, that's fine. You see, I'm in the midst of an investigation of the relationship between the scapula and the bones of the upper arm, and . . ."

"Please!" Death drew his cloak tightly about himself and turned away, and the white skull became suffused with a touch of pink.

"Oh, curse me!" Amer cried, and his face turned bright magenta. "When I become absorbed in an investigation, sir, I'm apt to forget everything else, including my manners. I beg your forgiveness."

"That's quite all right," Death said, turning back to him. "We all have our faults. But if you're really sorry, Master Amer, you may prove it at the price of a little more wormwood."

"Certainly, certainly," Amer said, filling Death's glass again. "Are you sure you won't sit down?"

"No, thank you," Death said. "But perhaps you should. I'm afraid I have some rather unpleasant news for you."

"Oh!" Amer sank into the armchair Samona had occupied earlier in the day. "Unpleasant news? What would it be?"

"Well," Death cleared his throat and began to pace to and fro in front of the fireplace, skeletal hands clasped behind his back. "Well," he said, "I'm afraid this may seem rather ungrateful in view of your excellent hospitality, but—well, duty is duty, and . . . Certainly you're aware, Master Amer, that none of us can live forever."

"Yes," said Amer, smiling blithely but blankly.

"Well . . . that's how it is," Death said, with a note of exasperation in his voice. "We must all die sometime, and . . . well . . . Confound it, Amer, now's your time."

Amer sat in a stunned silence for a minute, and then, in a hollow voice, he said, "I see . . ."

"Master!" Willow wailed. "What're we gonna *do*?"

"Well, Willow," Amer said slowly, "it would seem as though you're finally going to have your freedom."

"Oh, I don't want it, I don't want it! Not at *that* price!"

"Well . . . I'm sorry, old man," Death said gruffly, "but what must be, must be."

"Oh, that's all right, that's all right," Amer said, staring at the fire with an unwavering gaze. "But . . . isn't that strange?"

"What?"

"Samona. For some reason, all I can think is that I should have kissed Samona—just once, without my protection drug. I never did, you know." He turned and looked, frowning, at Death. "Now, why should I be thinking of that?"

A tear formed at the edge of the skull's hollow eye and rolled down the hard white cheekbone. "Come, come, let's have done with it quickly! Give me your hand."

Amer ignored the outstretched, bony fingers, and his eyes began to wander aimlessly around the room. "But I've so much left to do. . . ."

"So said Caesar when I came for him, and so said Peter and so said Charlemagne. Come, cease torturing yourself!"

Amer's wandering gaze fell on the miniature bones he had carved earlier in the day. The look of intelligence returned slowly to his eyes as, very carefully, he lifted the model bone-pile into his lap. He took a roll of fine wire from the table and began to string the little skeleton together.

"Just let me finish this," he said. "Just one more work completed—then I'll go."

"All right, but be quick," Death said, drawing back his hand. There was a note of relief in his voice.

He began to pace the floor again. "If you'd just had sense enough to keep your fingers out of magic, none of this would be necessary."

"Why, what's wrong with magic?" Amer fixed the collarbone in place.

"It's not the magic, it's the way you go about getting it that ruffles the boys upstairs."

Amer looked up. Death spun toward him and pointed an accusing finger. "You could at least have had the good sense to guard your door! Your master would have given you as many spells as you wanted for the express purpose of keeping me out!"

Amer smiled sadly and shook his head. "But I don't have a master."

"It's complete and utter carelessness! If you—*What* did you say?"

"I don't have a master."

"Indeed! And I suppose you're not a sorcerer?"

"Quite right—I'm not." Amer threaded the pelvis onto the spine.

"Oh?" said Death. "Then how did you come by your magic?"

"I was born with it, I think. In fact, I'm growing increasingly certain that every magic-user is conceived with the talent for it. You either have it, or you don't—but if you do, the raw ability isn't enough; you have to learn how to use it." He warmed to his subject. "That's all the witches and warlocks in the neighborhood gain by their pact with the Devil—instruction. Of course, there are many who have no power whatsoever; Satan and the older witches merely delude them into believing they're able to work magic." He frowned, gazing off into space. "I've learned, in the last few years, that there are holy men in the East who know how to work wonders, though that's not the main purpose of their study—and they do teach those who truly wish to cultivate the life of the spirit. So their magic is gained by spiritual advancement, without condemning their souls to eternal agony in the afterlife. But I knew nothing of them, when I wished to learn."

"Then where did you find your teacher?" Death demanded.

"I taught myself," Amer said, stringing up a femur. "I learned by investigation and hard thought. I experimented until I found the rules by which the world operates. I win my own knowledge, sir. I don't beg."

"Rules?" Death snapped. "What sort of rules?"

"Oh, there are many of them—the principle of equivalence, for example: for every effect you work, you will always have to pay in one way or another. Or the principle of similarity, which makes it possible for me to do something to someone—say, removing a wart—just by doing the same thing to a model of that person, once I've learned how to focus my thoughts properly. That's really just an application of a larger principle, actually—a sort of rule of symbolism: 'The symbol *is* the thing it represents,' in some metaphysical way I haven't discovered yet. I've reason to believe there are other worlds, other universes, in which the rules of magic don't apply—in which the symbol is *not* the thing, for example."

"Fantasy," Death snapped.

"For us, yes. But we are no doubt fantasies for them. In this world in which an alchemist can talk to Death, the laws of magic work well enough."

Death eyed him warily. "You haven't sold your soul, then?"

"Not in the least," Amer said. "*Invictus.*"

Death paced the hearth for a long time, wrapped in thought. Amer was twisting the last toe into place when the skull spoke again.

"It may be," he said. "But I've heard the story before, and it's almost always a lie. I'm afraid you'll have to come with me, after all."

Amer smiled sadly. "Perhaps I shouldn't have been so hospitable," he said. "Then you might have been willing to give me the benefit of the doubt." He twisted a loop of wire around the little skeleton's leg and laid it on the table.

"Perhaps," Death said, "though I'm not worried about bribery—I'm immune to it. But come, you've finished your plaything. The time's come."

"Not quite," Amer said, twisting the other end of the wire around the table leg. He took the vial of powder from his dressing-gown pocket and sprinkled it over the model.

"Milyochim sloh Yachim," he said.

"What?"

"Milyochim sloh Yachim," Amer said again (repeated obligingly).

"What does that mean?" Death said.

"Well, for all practical purposes," Amer said, "it means you can't move from that spot."

"I don't know how you expect to convince me that you're not a sorcerer," Death said, "if you keep on materializing liqueurs that way."

"Oh, I'm not really materializing them." The alchemist snapped his fingers, and a flask of absinthe appeared on the table. "I'm transporting them. There's a spirits merchant in Boston, you see, who keeps finding bottles missing from his stock."

"Thief!" Death accused.

"Not at all; he finds gold wherever there's a bottle missing. You've noticed that I always place a nugget on the table before I transport the bottle?"

"And it disappears." Death gave him a severe stare. "I was wondering about that."

"The mass of the bottle must be replaced with an equivalent mass," Amer explained. "I suppose I could use stone, but it's much more honest to use gold. I believe he makes quite a profit on the transaction."

"I should think so. But where do you find the gold?"

"I dig it up—after I've dowsed for it, of course."

"Where did you learn dowsing?" Death demanded.

"It came naturally," Amer explained. "I was very young when I began to notice that hazel twigs twitched when I held them—perhaps three years old."

"And you will *still* have me believe your powers have nothing of the supernatural about them?"

"For that matter," Amer countered, "how do you expect me to believe that you're supernatural when you continue to consume such vast quantities?"

"Bah," Death said. "We've only had a couple of drinks."

"Uh-uh!" the will-o'-the-wisp slurred. "I been keepin' track!"

"And partaking, too." Death turned to Amer. "So that was why you poured the brandy into that beaker."

"Even a will-o'-the-wisp needs fuel. . . ."

"Your fifth glass of cointreau was emptied three hours ago," Willow said brightly if blearily. "Since then you've downed six glasses of chartreuse, four of cognac, and four of absinthe—right now, you're starting your fifth."

"Willow," said Death, "you have missed your calling. You would have made an excellent conscience."

"And to top it all," the alchemist said, "you're not the slightest bit tipsy."

"Naturally not," Death said.

"Don't you mean 'supernaturally not'?"

"I meant what I said." Death set down his glass. "Would it be natural for Death to become intoxicated?"

"Is it natural for Death to be a connoisseur of fine liqueurs?"

"Certainly, as long as I'm not affected by them. In fact, I've quite an affinity for spirits. But come, Master Amer,"

Death said, "pour me another absinthe, for we stand in great danger of becoming philosophical just now."

"My heavens! We must prevent *that* at all costs!" Amer filled Death's glass again. The Pale Horseman sipped the liqueur and settled back in his chair with a satisfied sigh.

"You know, Master Amer," he said, "I'm beginning to like you quite well."

"That's not surprising," Amer said.

Death looked at him sharply. "Sorcerer," he said, in a tone of great severity, "have you been casting more spells in my direction?"

"Oh, no! Nothing of the sort," Amer said. "It's merely that absinthe makes the heart grow fonder."

"I'll overlook that remark," Death said, "if you'll fill my glass again. But wormwood this time."

"Try it with some juniper-flavored gin." Amer poured three measures into a glass.

"I notice that you are showing no more effects of your drinking than I do," Death noted.

"Mashter'zh on'y had two shnifterzh o' brandy," Willow slurred.

"I haven't much tolerance," Amer confessed. He followed the gin with a dash of wormwood, and handed it to his guest.

Death tasted a drop. "Not bad." He tasted another. "In fact, it's quite good. Is this your own invention, Master Amer?"

"It is," Amer said, very pleased.

"What do you call it?"

"Well, I named it for the saint on whose day I first tried the mixture."

"And that was . . . ?"

"Saint Martin's Day."

"It appears to be excellent," said a fat, rasping voice. "May I have some?"

"Why, certainly," said Amer. He had poured the wormwood into the glass before it occurred to him to wonder where the voice had come from.

He turned and saw an enormously fat man dressed in a

huge black cape and conical, flat-topped, broad-brimmed hat with a tarnished brass buckle. His whole face seemed to sag, giving him the mournful appearance of a bloodhound. But the sadness of his face was belied by his mouth, which curved in a wide grin of insane glee.

"Amer," said another voice, a feminine one. "May I introduce you to Master Moggard, Warlock-General of New England and Vice-Chairman of the Universal Brotherhood of Sorcerers."

Amer turned and saw Samona standing nearby, the glow of victory in her eyes.

"Who is it?" said Death, for he sat facing the fireplace in a high-backed wing chair, and Samona and the sorcerer were behind him.

"Samona and a—um—friend," Amer said, looking at Death. "They seem to have . . ." But he stopped there, for he saw pits of fire at the back of the skull's hollow eyes.

"Master Moggard," Samona said, "this is Amer, the man of whom I told you."

Moggard waddled forward, holding out a stubby, hairy paw. "Charmed," he croaked.

"I'm glad you are," Amer murmured, rising to grasp the acid-stained appendage.

"No, no," Moggard said. "Not *I*. It's you who are charmed—or will be shortly."

"Indeed?" Amer said, freeing himself of the warlock's clammy grasp. He turned and poured the juniper gin into the glass with the wormwood. Turning again, he placed it in Moggard's hand.

"Would you care for something, Samona?"

"I believe I would," she said.

"Amontillado?"

"Of course."

Moggard waddled about the cabin, inspecting apparatus, thumbing through notebooks, examining powders. He turned back to them as Amer was handing Samona her glass.

"Excellent, excellent," he said, rolling up to them. "You have a superb laboratory, Master Amer."

"Thank you," Amer said, bowing in acknowledgment of the compliment. He remained wary.

Moggard turned to the bookshelf and leafed through another notebook. "Yes, indeed! You have amassed an amazing deal of knowledge, Master Amer." Then, thoughtfully, "Perhaps a bit too much."

"Oh?" said Amer. "May I ask exactly how I am to interpret that statement?

Moggard sighed—or rather, wheezed—as he replaced the volume.

"You are not, if I am correct, a member of the Brotherhood, Master Amer?"

"The Brotherhood?"

"That is to say, you have gathered your knowledge with no other—ah—'being's' help?"

"Certainly. I have extracted all of it by myself." Amer's voice rang with a note of pride.

"Ah. So I feared," Moggard said. "I am sure, Master Amer, that you can appreciate our predicament. We cannot have a man practicing without—ah—having been initiated."

Amer's gaze sharpened. "I wasn't aware you had any jurisdiction over the situation."

"Not technically, perhaps." Moggard's smile turned toothy. "But we have ways of influencing affairs, for people who disagree with us. For example, I'm certain you have realized that your expulsion from Salem was not purely spontaneous."

Amer frowned. "That the goodfolk did not originate the notion of my being a warlock? I was aware Samona had put the idea into their heads. . . ."

"But you also must have realized that a female, so young and with so little influence, would not have sufficed to arouse so fierce a movement." Moggard crowded closer. "No, no, she had a great deal of support from some very influential citizens, very influential."

"Such as . . . Goody Coister? And Sexton Karrier?"

"Them, yes." Moggard nodded vigorously. "And others—there were several others, all substantial citizens."

"And all members of your coven."

"Not mine, no; my coven is elsewhere. But of the Salem coven, yes. We did wish it to be lethal . . ."

Samona looked up, shocked.

" . . . so that the problem you represent would have had a final solution—but unfortunately, you were too adroit for the mob."

"The action was ill-considered." Amer frowned. "It will rebound on you—not immediately, perhaps, but it will rebound."

"Oh, I think you underestimate us—as we underestimated you. No, the knowledge and skill you have demonstrated make you a problem of great significance."

"Why, thank you!"

"I assure you, though it is a compliment, it is also a statement of menace—so you will understand that we must revoke your powers."

Amer smiled slowly. "May I ask how you propose to accomplish this?"

Moggard pursed his blubber lips thoughtfully. Then he said, "It's somewhat irregular, but a man of your ability merits the courtesy."

Meaning, Amer realized, that Moggard hoped to frighten Amer out of his dedication to God and goodness, and add both him and his powers to the coven.

Grinning again, Moggard said, "Master Amer, all your powers are based on knowledge of certain laws which your investigations have revealed, are they not?"

"They are."

"Then I am certain you realize what the consequences would be if these laws were suspended in a certain area, and if that area were to surround you, rather like a cloud, no matter where you were to go."

The smile faded from Amer's lips. "You have the power to do this?"

"Yes, my—ah—superior has arranged it for me."

"And of course you would not hesitate to use it."

"Of course." Moggard's grin widened. "Unless, of course, you were to apply for membership in the Brotherhood."

"I see." Amer's voice was calm, but his face was white. He turned away and looked at the fire in the grate. "And if I don't choose to apply, you will cancel my powers by suspending all natural and supernatural laws within my immediate area."

"That is correct."

"The forces that hold the tiniest bits of matter together would lose their hold—and everything about me would turn to dust."

"To a dust so fine that we could not see it," the warlock agreed.

"Including food."

"Ah, I see you have grasped the essence of the situation," Moggard chortled.

"In short, if I refuse to sell my soul, I die by slow starvation.

"Indeed you would! Admirable perception, sir! Really, you delight me."

"Starve!" Samona turned to the warlock sharply. She was white-faced, and her lips trembled as she spoke. "No, Moggard! You said you would do no more than make him powerless!"

"True, my dear, but at that time I had no idea that he had garnered so much— ah—wisdom."

"I'll not let you harm him!"

A new glint appeared in Moggard's eye, and he waddled up to her with a rapt, fascinated stare.

"Oh, do try to stop me, my dear!" he gurgled. "Such an act would make you liable to discipline"—and his voice dropped to a low, giggling tone—"of my choosing."

Samona backed away from him, revolted and trembling. Giggling, Moggard followed her.

"Let her be!" Amer shouted, brandishing the poker.

Moggard spun, and then he waddled up to Amer, and his giggling became almost hysterical.

"So you, too, wish a display of my powers?"

Amer fell back. A bony hand shot out and closed round his wrist. He stared down into the flaming eyes of Death.

"Loose me!" Death said in a low, angry voice. "Loose

me and I'll rid you of him forever!"

Amer stared at Death, and then he looked up at Samona, pressed blanched and trembling against the wall. He shook his head slowly.

"Are you a fool?" Death hissed. Then, in a tone of mild disgust, "Don't worry, these two have convinced me you're no sorcerer."

Amer just shook his head again.

"Why?" Death's voice was hoarse with rage. But then he realized that Amer was looking at the witch, not the warlock. He sat back in his chair, glowering at the alchemist.

"I see," he said bitterly. "Thus are men made powerless. I'd thought better of you than that, Amer."

"Come, sir!" Moggard gurgled. "Will you sign your name in our—ah— 'captain's' book? Or will you die?"

Cold determination crystallized within Amer. He stood straight and tall, giving the sorcerer a stony glance. "I have never had any dealings with the Devil, Master Moggard, and I will not have any now—even at the cost of my life."

"As you will, then," Moggard giggled, and his voice had the sound of twigs crackling in a fire. He stretched out his paw and spoke a polysyllable that was mostly consonants, and Amer saw the objects around him dissolve as all laws, natural and supernatural, ceased. In a few seconds everything near him was powder.

Including the miniature skeleton, the wire, and the table— and with them, the spell that held Death bound.

Death shot to his feet, and the skeleton hand closed on Moggard's neck. The sorcerer turned to stare into the flaming eye sockets, and his face had scarcely registered his horror before he fainted.

"You see what comes of cowardice, Amer," Death said. "Had you loosed me when I asked, I might have spared your witch for you. But now she too must come with me." And he stalked toward Samona.

"Wait!" Amer shouted. "Give her a chance. Can't you spare her if she gives up her witchcraft?"

Death halted. He fixed his blazing stare on Samona.

"Your absinthe was good," he said. "This one time I'll be clement."

Amer breathed a sigh of relief.

"Come then, she-devil," Death said. "Which will it be? Life or damnation?"

Samona looked from Death to Amer and back again, and then she stood away from the wall and straightened her back.

"I don't have much choice, do I?" she said, and the look she threw at Amer was pure hate. "Yes, I renounce the darkness."

"Well enough!" Death turned and stalked to the door, dragging Moggard along like a rag doll. He paused with his hand on the latch and turned to Amer.

"Farewell, alchemist. You've won your witch. But I wish you luck, for you've made a bad bargain." And Death threw open the door and in two long strides was lost in the stormy night. The cabin returned to normal, but only for seconds. Then the wind shrieked in joy and tore into the cabin.

It raced around the room, overturning furniture, smashing glassware, and triumphantly hurling notebooks into the fire. It fanned the flames and howled with glee.

Amer fought his way to the door and shoved it closed. The wind screamed in rage as the door pinched it off, and blasted the cabin with the finest imprecations in its vocabulary as the alchemist shot the bolt.

Amer leaned against the door, catching his breath. Then, with a smile which, considering the smiler, could be judged as sizzling, he turned to Samona. But the smiled faded and Amer fell back against the door as he looked at her, for the wind had blown her hair back over her shoulders, and Amer suddenly became acutely aware of her femininity.

Samona frowned, puzzled—Amer had never behaved in such fashion before.

"Wha'sa matter?" Willow asked.

"My protection drug," Amer gasped. "It wore off an hour ago!"

Then Samona realized her advantage. She advanced on him relentlessly, with a smile on her lips and victory in her eyes, and she pulled his mouth down to hers and kissed him very thoroughly.

And in her arms we must leave our friend Amer, for he has finally been completely and very capably bewitched.

OF ART AND SCIENCE

by Judith R. Conly

The Art of magic, Crafter's joy,
From Nature's passion takes its part,
The spirit's talents to employ,
And celebrates the gifted heart.

Yet purest Art, the Crafter's flame,
Allowed to blaze without control,
Much like the fires of Hell, can maim,
Can char the kindler to the soul.

Science of magic, Crafter's pride,
Calls laws of Nature to its aid,
And, using reason as its guide,
Treads patterned paths by logic laid.

Yet strictest Science, Crafter's rule,
Can claim emotion as its price,
And intellect, if kept too cool,
Might wither feeling with its ice.

Holding but one, the Crafter's bane,
Works contrary to Nature's way.
Unbalanced strivings, all in vain,
Bring darkness to midsummer's day.

Yet blending both, the Crafter's goal,
Achieves the harmony required
To form from parts a balanced whole
And spells both reasoned and inspired.

Anno Domini 1684

A CUP
OF CHAOS

by **Wendy Wheeler**

Samona sat putting up her hair by the light that filtered through the waxed parchment window. The dark wisps around her face were dry, but the heavy ringlets stayed a little damp. Amer loved her hair—at least, at night, in bed, he did. In daylight hours, he was a different man altogether, rarely noticing any of the things she wore to please him.

Samona slipped another comb into her coiled braid and sighed. Amer Crafter. Her husband—finally. So many years, so many mistakes.

Her reverie was interrupted by a vigorous knocking at the door of their log cottage. Knowing that Amer would take care of it, Samona took her time fastening a fresh collar onto her blue dress.

She came out the bedroom doorway to find her husband sitting in his chair, a piece of parchment in his hands. Beside him stood three men, merchantmen from the look of their rough clothes. Like Amer, none of the men wore wigs or powder. The biggest, a fellow with a long, lugubrious face and frizz of orange ponytail, was speaking.

" . . . and as we're men of peace, with a good proposition in hand, Goodman Crafter, here we are to parley with ye. Ye'll see that there charter to scavenge for buried treasure is signed by King Willie hisself, all nice 'n' legal like. Allowing as we give the king his one-fifth part—oh, pardon, ma'am."

"My wife, Samona Crafter," said Amer, his blue eyes never leaving the paper. "Samona, this is Master Caleb Brown, a retired seaman, he says. And here are his partners, Frederick Churcher and—?"

"Seth Markham," said the third man, small and swarthy with pox-marked skin. "And very pleased to meet ye, Goody Crafter."

"It's needing a dowser we are, ma'am," said Brown. "We've had it confirmed that Peggity Hank Barlo's bunch buried an iron pot filled with gold bullion and Spanish pistoles along a certain inlet of the Schuylkill River—"

"—and the witches of these parts are of no use on such a project," added Churcher, a slope-shouldered man with nervous movements. "We heard your husband was the best 'cunning man' along the coast, so we come to ask him to take a short voyage with us on the *Fortunate Osgood,* docked just there in Boston harbor."

A thrill went up Samona's spine to hear men talk so casually of treasure. What little money she and Amer had came mostly from the white magic Amer did for the people of the Salem countryside: removing the coven's curses, dowsing for wells, some medicinal and magical remedies. But it wasn't much—it wasn't much at all. "This, then, is a paying voyage?" she asked in her most businesslike voice.

Brown rubbed his chin. "Well, we 'us thinking, maybe a small deposit now, but then one-twentieth of whatever we find. And it looks certain to make us wealthy men, missus, that it does."

Oh, one-twentieth, thought Samona. As if in response, she felt a small flutter in her belly. Before she could say a word, however, Amer rolled up the parchment and handed it back to Caleb Brown.

"No, gentlemen. I'm sorry for you to make the trip for naught, but I won't be able to help you with the dowsing."

"But—?" said Samona.

"One-tenth," said dark little Markham. "And not a bit more."

"No," said Amer again. His lips were set in a straight line. He rose and ushered the men out the door.

Samona stood in the middle of the room, fists clenched, and watched them go. She knew she was glowering in the way Amer hated, but she couldn't help herself. "Amer," she said in a low voice. "That could have made us rich. What were you thinking about?"

Amer had obviously already dismissed the event in his mind. He ambled over to his worktable, where the beakers and bottles of his alchemical experiments bubbled merrily. "I know what I'm doing, Wife," he said mildly. "Those were no gentlemen, and I mistrusted the feel of their paper."

"The feel of their paper?" Samona's voice began to rise. She took a breath. "You naysay a possible fortune over the feel of a paper? Amer, you make no sense!"

He gave her a speaking look. "You know how I dislike arguing, Samona. Let's talk no more on this."

She bit her lip and turned away, thinking that here it was again. How could he burn so cold when she flamed so hot? *He doesn't really love you,* said the sly, familiar voice in her heart. *The courtship, the marriage, all a result of that love philtre you tricked him into drinking.* Oh, how she cursed this uncertainty. *Especially now,* she said silently, her hand on her still-flat belly. *Especially now.*

An arm went around her waist. "Hist, now, Samona," said Amer, giving her a rare daytime hug. "Have you noticed that when we argue, it's always about money? A good alchemist strives to be free of all vices, but especially from the sins of greed and covetousness. I don't concern myself with material wealth, for I won't be able to find the Philosopher's Stone as long as I do."

"Ah, your Philosopher's Stone," said Samona, smiling in spite of herself. The way Amer spoke of it, it was to him like the Holy Grail to the crusades. A Panacea for all ills, a Door to Immortality, the Catalyst to turn any metal, no matter how leprous, into its Pure Soul State—back to unblemished gold.

"Yes, the Stone," said Amer. He drew her over to the table. "Come see what I obtained yesterday. Such a rare find, I could scarcely credit it." He ran his hands reverently over a large, leather-bound book. "See? A complete and unabridged de Brahms. The Latin is more arcane than what I'm accustomed to, but already I see a formula that has me all afire. Listen to this: *Prepare three Athanors, each capacious to hold three Pounds—*"

"Athanors?" said Samona.

"A certain kind of crucible." He bent his head back to the book. "And then you generate in each athanor a certain Earth by putting in each a cup of Chaos. Chaos is the primeval matter I was telling you about, Samona."

"The source of the four elements in their original combined state, I remember," said Samona. She turned back the leaf to read the front cover. "How did you pay the tradesman for this book?"

"Oh." Amer shrugged, but watched Samona from the corner of his eye. "I gave him the silver from our cache."

Samona straightened. "You spent our cache! Oh, Husband! I begged you not to; we must save that aside. We'll— we'll have need of it someday." She felt tears in her eyes. Of all times for him to be so profligate!

" 'Tis all right, Samona. We can replace it in good time. Why, you yourself are getting quite excellent at rhabdomancy. You could find a bit of silver, or even some gold ore, did you put your mind to it." Amer had made Samona her own dowsing rod, fine hazelwood with a quicksilver core.

"Nay, Husband," said Samona, biting off each word. Disappointment had left a huge hole where her heart used to be. "I know I lost all my powers when I renounced my witchcraft for you. This prattle of my Talent is suspect and only meant to indulge me. How could I ever approach the skill of a man who can read intentions merely by the feel of a paper?"

As she flounced off to the bedroom, Amer called after her, "You do have real Talent, you know, Samona. It's true."

Once in the bedroom with the door closed, Samona lifted a certain floorboard. She took out the crockery urn nestled in a small cavity beneath it. The urn was light, so light. She loosened the lid to stare awhile at the tiny collection of ore nuggets. She felt again the tiny flutter in her belly. Someone must tend to the needs of this family, she told herself.

At last Samona stood and went to the mirror hanging above the washbasin. She pulled her heavy braid from its pins. *I can take care of this myself,* she thought. *Why, I did the witch's initiation, didn't I? I'm a brave woman, a woman ripe for adventure.*

Nevertheless, she closed her eyes at the first snip of the scissors.

The *Fortunate Osgood* was a likely looking square-masted three-rigger about eighty feet long. Samona found the boatswain buying provisions at the shipping dock and asked him to take her aboard. He cast a doubtful eye on her, and Samona was afraid he could see right through her brother's old breeches, coat, and hose that she wore. She was glad she'd taken the precaution of binding down her breasts with a swath of linen.

"Aye, lad, I'll be going back in a quarter hour or so. You got business on the ship?"

Samona had practiced lowering her already husky voice. "Master Caleb Brown and his partners will be glad to meet up with me, I reckon." *Hurry, man!* she said to herself. Her note to Amer was purposefully vague, but he could have ways of finding her before the boat sailed. Amer was always surprising her.

"Oh, Brown." The boatswain spit against a wall. "Wait, then."

Once on the shore boat, he put the oars in the rowlocks and seemed more disposed to talk to her. "Look sharp, lad. You ain't a lubber, are ye? What'd you say your name was?"

"Sam—Samuel, sir. Samuel Goldman." There, that could be a lucky name! She'd come back as the Gold Woman, she just knew it.

"Well, Sammie, you'll soon meet the finest merchant ship on either side of the Atlantic. Captain Buttons mans a trim ship, he does."

Samona was tugging at her short ponytail, trying to get it out of her collar. "Captain Buttons?"

"Captain John Baldridge, a good old salt, even if he does relish his fancy dress a bit too much. An honest man, and fair."

In a moment, they were alongside and Samona had scrambled up the rope ladder and was on deck. The boatswain called out, and, before she knew it, there stood big red-haired Caleb Brown before her. She stepped forward and shook his hand.

"Samuel Goldman, sir. My sister is Master Crafter's wife. She told me you had need of a cunning man, so here I am."

Brown looked her askance. "Aye, it's a cunning man we need, not a cunning boy. How old are ye, lad? Thirteen? Fourteen?"

"Check his whiskers, Caleb!" called Master Churcher, also on deck. "If he's over twelve, I'm a Dutchman!"

Samona drew herself up, glad she'd brushed a little ash on her chin and upper lip. "Don't you know anything about the powers of a cunning man? Why, I could grandfather you all two times over, but why should I look it, eh? It takes a good deal of Talent to keep your appearance as young as this. Thought I'd join you on your wee adventure, but if I've got to be explaining every little trick of my trade, well—"

"Nay, wait." This was little Markham, who came up on the forecastle, squinting. He was followed by a heavyset man in spotless breeches and a periwig, whose blue greatcoat was festooned with much trim and many buttons. Samona noticed many more men now hanging from the rigging and capstan bars. "Caleb, the captain and I've been talking," said Markham. "He's a reasonable man and asks no more than a one-fifth portion to take us along that bay we seek." He put a hand on Samona's shoulder. "I say we let the blackamoor give the boy a test."

"Aye, King James!" Samona heard mutters. "Call up the Blackbird!" Caleb Brown hollered down into the hold, "Jimbo! King James! On deck, you heathen!"

Samona heard a heavy tread on the galley stairs, then up came the biggest man she'd ever seen, nearly seven feet tall.

He wore clean hose, well-cut breeches, a pristine white shirt. He was black as night, with one gold earring and tricorne hat. "You call me for a reason, Master Caleb?" Even his voice was big and deep and dark, with an accent Samona had never heard before.

Brown, tall as he was, seemed to shrink a little as the black man loomed over him. "Samuel Goldman, this here is our magic man from the West Indies. He's got such royal ways, he earned hisself the name of the last King but one. King James, or Jimbo to those what know him."

Samona strode forward again, hand out. "Pleased to meet you, I'm sure, Master James." King James looked surprised, but took Samona's hand in his huge one. Samona heard the crew chuckling, and looked over to see the man in the greatcoat sputtering. Oh, she understood, this was the captain, and she should've taken his hand first. "Captain Baldridge," she remembered. "And it's an honor to set foot on your fine ship, sir." Belatedly, she shook his hand.

"Now Jimbo," said Markham, "hasn't the power to find what's buried. He has magic of a whole other sort." Samona heard Brown and Churcher snort at this. "But we think he'll know enough to test your cunning ways. How 'bout it, Jimbo? What'll the boy dowse for?"

"Hmmm." King James rubbed his chin, then gave Samona an oddly gentle look. "We must see if Master Goldman be knowing the scent of silver too, I think. My pardon, Captain, but I must borrow from your finery." King James reached over and plucked an ornate silver button from the captain's coat with no more effort than one would pluck a berry. The captain opened his mouth to speak, then thought better of it. "A handkerchief over the boy's eyes," instructed King James.

Before she knew what was happening, Samona was blindfolded. She stood there patiently, hearing King James's heavy tread across the decking, the muffled snickers of the men. Finally the handkerchief was lifted.

"Dowse away, Master Goldman," sneered Caleb Brown.

Samona reached into the heavy cloth bag she had slung across her shoulders. Amer had found her a good sturdy branch of the hazel tree, one that made an almost perfect Y. He'd peeled the bark so that the branch gleamed white. The rod was heavier than it looked, the core being hollowed out, filled with quicksilver, and plugged up again.

She licked her lips and took a breath. Yes, she did all right when dowsing for wells—often Amer took her along to verify his own work. But she'd never tried it for anything else. . . . "I'll take another of the captain's silver buttons in hand," she said, "to help me concentrate my Talent on the invisibles. And Captain Baldridge, you must step away, please. The many silver buttons still on your coat may prove too attractive."

She waited while King James plucked another button, the captain then going to stand on the poop deck. Once Samona had the silver button, she held the two branches of the rod with the tail of the Y pointing up. A silence fell on deck. Samona cast about, turning in a complete circle, and watching the hazel branch all the while.

Suddenly the rod gave a quiver. Samona let out her breath.

She continued to turn slowly. She found that even before the divining rod twitched, she felt a shiver of something run up her arms. Caleb Brown leaned against the cathead wall, continuing to grin sardonically at her efforts. For some reason, Samona's eyes kept being drawn to that long face, that mass of red hair. And when she felt the tiny tickle on her palms as she faced him, she knew there was a reason.

Without saying another word, she walked purposefully toward him. His smile fell away as the rod bucked in her hand, seeming to flip upside down. Then it flipped back up for all the world like a rearing horse. Samona put the rod to one hand and reached the other hand up to Brown's frizzy ponytail. Sure enough, she felt a pellet of something wedged in his hair. She pulled it out and held it up for all to view.

"As nimble a trick as ever I saw," breathed Churcher. He took the button and handed it back to the captain. "I'd say we found ourselves a good little dowser. One-twentieth part will be your share, Master Goldman, same as I offered your sister's husband."

"Aye, then, we'll take the lad aboard," said the captain. "And none too soon, for the tide's up."

Samona sighed and relaxed, accepting the congratulatory claps on her back with what she hoped was masculine aplomb. A woman ripe for adventure, she told herself again. Yes, indeed!

That night, in the bunk they'd given her with the other men in the forecastle, shivering in the chill though she was still fully dressed, hearing the snores and smelling the rumbullion on their breath, she curled protectively around her belly and said it to herself again. *Ripe for adventure. Ripe for adventure.*

" . . . because the brother of my mother was a *bokor*," said King James to Samona. "So it run in my blood, that I be a priest of the *voudan* religion." They were taking their ease on deck. In the three days of voyaging along the coast toward the mouth of the Delaware, Samona and King James had spent many hours together.

"My friend Amer told me you have a strange religion in the West Indies, one where blood is scattered across pictures in the sand," she said.

King James nodded his big head. "Yes, we feed the spirit ancestors, the deities—what we call *lous*—with dried food and rum. Sometimes we kill a chicken or goat for them too. Only the faithful can invoke the *loa*. We call on them for protection, for healing, for learning the future."

"Hmmm." Samona resisted the urge to shiver. "Aren't you protected by that little bag you wear?"

"Oh, yes," King James pulled the leather thong from around his neck. "The *ouanga* bag has powerful things in it, things to ward off accidents and disease."

Samona looked out across the water. "Maybe your 'wangu' bag will help us find the treasure," she said. She turned back when she heard King James sigh.

"We got a duppy there," she heard him mutter, wondering what that was. Then he looked up and met her eyes. "Not everything a *bokor* does is for good. Sometimes . . . sometimes we got to make a scary thing, a bad spell. There is ways to do that, too. You got your cunning man powers. You take care to make a protection for you, whatever you do. You understand my words? Make a protection for you."

"Jimbo, get below deck and rest up for tonight," said Caleb Brown, suddenly appearing before them. "Freddy will act as sailing master and bring us to a safe anchorage on our inlet under cover of dark." At Samona's quizzical look, he explained. " 'Twouldn't do to allow the scavengers to see us too close now, would it?"

After the *bokor* and Brown had left, Captain Baldridge walked up to Samona. "Terrible thing, that. The trading for those of our own species can never be agreeable to the eyes of Divine Justice, says I. To sell men like beasts is an unholy thing."

"What are you saying? King James is a *slave?*" Samona asked, aghast.

"Aye, the property of that Master Brown. Ah well," said the captain. "We'll be running to ground around dusk, and your party is to go ashore a few hours later. Good luck with your hunt. I do admit a one-fifth interest makes my good wishes all the more warm."

Samona nodded as he walked off. She added it up in her head: one-fifth for the captain, one-fifth for the king, one-twentieth for her. That left a little over half for the three partners to share. They must be expecting a great windfall, thought Samona.

She was dozing in her bunk when she felt a hand on her shoulder. King James's deep voice urged her to get up. As she sat a moment yawning, he opened his *ouanga* bag, removed something, and handed it to her. She held it up in the lantern light.

"What's this?" It was a smooth cabochon stone, almost black in the dim light.

"It's a bloodstone, for protection," King James whispered. "I think maybe it will drive away the duppy—"

"Hurry yourselves," called Markham from nearby.

A short while later, as she sat in the jolly-boat and stowed the shovels and pickaxes being handed to her, Samona felt the sweat begin to trickle down her back even though the

in
When
Brown and th
ded, grinning in t
the smooth bloodstone

"Away we go, gentlemen,
off for a holiday.

They were soon aground on the swamp, boat
scudding to a stop in two feet of water. They ed,
and loaded with their lanterns and tools and rop they
tramped on up past the low bluffs, through the willows
and stunted pine trees. Brown called everyone to a halt.
"Take this in your hand and be testing your powers on
it, Master Goldman," he said. He handed Samona a piece
of eight, its silver edges roughly cut.

"Is this one similar to the coins we'll find in the treasure
pot?" she asked. She blinked as the three partners guffawed
in a coarse way.

"Similar, no," said Brown. "It's from the exact same lot
that was buried, so it should be a good marker for ye.
We'll let you take the lead now. Best ye take out your
dowsing rod."

As Samona began to draw the hazel branch from beneath
her coat, Markham held his lantern high and watched her
face. "And once you've located the thing, don't go a-rushing
right up to it," he told her. "That's why we brought Jimbo
along. He's got him a pocket full of his voodoo nails, so
he can drive a magic circle in the ground around it, keep
the treasure from trying to escape."

"Have—have you done this before?" asked Samona. She
was thinking how safe the *Fortunate Osgood* suddenly
seemed.

"Well, we can say this," said Caleb Brown. "Third time's
the charm, isn't it, boys?" The three men began to laugh.
Samona saw King James staring at her with dark, sad eyes.

this done." ... Samona breathed a ... ...k, then. An irresistible tugging ...d, the men and their lanterns following ... The pull was so strong, she broke into a slow ...wn hollered at her to slow down. Samona ignored ...t was all she could do to hold the rod in her hands. ...en suddenly the dowsing rod twisted abruptly and flew off in a sideways direction.

"What's wrong, then?" panted Churcher, catching up.

"I—I don't know," said Samona. "My rod's never done that before." She found it in a thicket and took it in both hands again. Again it flew off, this time in the opposite direction. "I don't think it's leading me anymore," she said. "There must be something about this treasure my dowsing won't find."

"Well, snatch it up, boy!" cried Markham. "Dammit, men. And didn't we know that a voodoo curse was liable to fly back on us? Didn't Peggity Hank hisself warn us? Blast that Jimbo for the wild rogue he is. A treasure's no good if'n you can't claim it back!"

"Oh! Oh!" Samona began to moan. This was worse than she'd imagined. "You were pirates with Peggity Hank Barlo, weren't you? This is your own treasure we're hunting, isn't it?"

"Aye, we'd have had to tell you soon enough," growled Brown. "There's a pot full of coins and gold all right. We buried it here and had Jimbo put his voodoo curse on the pot to protect it. But something's come along that we never invited and keeps moving the blasted thing around. Jimbo can't even tell us what it is—"

"I told you; it's a duppy," said King James. Even in the lantern light, Samona could see the sweat standing out on his forehead. "You got a demon spirit and he's taken over that pot. Can't do nothing with him 'less I know his *loa*."

"Well, we got you to dowse and Jimbo to drive them nails in, so this time we got us a chance of catching it, whatever it is," said Brown. "Go on; get your rod."

Samona put the rod inside her shirt, where it continued to twitch and quiver against her skin. "No, I—I can't—" she began. Then she saw the shadows on the faces of the three men and wondered how she ever thought them merchants. They were murderers; it was plain to see now. She could only try to give them what they wanted and hope they let her live. "I'll have to try it without my rod," she said. As she squinted her eyes and held out her arms palms first, the men stepped away from her.

Yes, she felt that tickling in her hands, the thrill of something moving up her arms. It was strong and she was easily able to follow the pull. She didn't need to run this time, however, and led the men steadily into the thickets and trees.

The ground around them began to change. Samona saw strange piles of what looked like sand and cornmeal, nubs of yellow candles around strange designs sprinkled with something dark. They passed by stones piled in odd, unnatural rings. These too seemed to be marked with something dark and wet. Finally they came to a barren patch of ground, open to the sky. In the middle of this circle was a hideous gnarled tree, with branches that looked like arms flung up to the sky in agony, an arrangement of holes on the trunk resembling eyes and a shrieking mouth. White chips of rock lay scattered about it.

Samona's tingling hands and arms led her straight toward the tree. Now she wanted to stop, pirate escort or no, but she couldn't. The pull of the tree was too strong; she couldn't fight it. She heard the muffled curses of the men behind her, and could tell by the abrupt darkness that they and their lanterns had hung back. Still she stumbled toward the tree, seeing, even in the dim light now, that the white chips weren't rock at all but dozens and dozens of small bones.

"Get the bloodstone!" she heard King James cry in an agonized voice. "Quick, Sammie, save yourself!"

But she couldn't move her arms at all; they were locked rigid in front of her. And all in a moment she was standing before the tree, a tree so tall it would loom over King James. And now she saw that the branches really were arms and the hole in the bark really was a mouth.

And the earth goblin looked at Samona with satisfaction in its fearsome face and wrapped its hard, twisted arms around her and pulled her deep into the ground.

Samona dreamed that she slept too near the fire. She shrugged and turned over, but found the other side of the hearth cold and wet. She shrugged and turned over again. . . .

"What is it turning itself for? asks I," growled a voice in her ear. "Like a grub in the ground, it is. Tasty grub worm."

With a gasp, Samona came awake. Inches away was the most hideous face she'd ever seen. Bulging forehead, huge yellow eyes, gaping mouth with dozens and dozens of sharp teeth. "O Abiding Grace, King of Glory, God Whose Name is Love," she began to chatter, certain here was Hell and this was Old Nick himself. "Protect this sinner in the hour of her need—"

"Oh, now it prays." The thing reached out a long and ropy arm. It took Samona roughly by the chin. "Listen, children, how it babbles. Listen and learn."

Samona jerked her head away and saw she was in a tiny cave, barely big enough for two. The light she saw by came from some glowing moss that crept along the cracks of the rock wall. Small patches of the same stuff shone from the folds and fissures in the creature's face and body. Now that she'd pulled away, Samona could see the thing had legs as well as arms. Its feet were huge and twisted, with toenails like claws. Its naked torso was dominated by a distended belly.

A goblin, Samona decided, remembering some drawings in Amer's books. "I thought—I thought there was a tree—" she said.

The goblin cackled. " 'Tis my own fine glamour it saw. Big tree, just a tree. Then along comes yon fat fox, up runs juicy squirrel, and it's snap, snap, snap with my teeth I does."

Samona's jaw trembled so, she could hardly ask, "Are— are you going to eat me, then?" *Oh, Amer, I love you truly*, she thought. *I wish I'd been sure of your love before I died.*

"It?" The thing prodded Samona's arm. "Plump thing. Maybe tasty? Nay, I took it for one of them rousty men come to steal me babies' gold. Now that it's in me den, I smell it true and know a certain thing about it so it never could be meal for me." The goblin spread its big hand across Samona's belly in a most familiar way. "Babies of its own soon, I warrant."

Samona blinked. Even Amer didn't know yet she was pregnant; she'd not known how to tell him. "Yes, I—I am with child," she said. She saw the goblin holding its other hand on its own round stomach. "And you're a mother, too? Babies soon for you?"

"Aye, babies soon for me." The creature ducked its head in a coy gesture. "Fine, strong babies there will be. Soon, very soon. A good mother am I, finding such a lovely pot of ore for my children. And with such a smell about it! Iron pot, silver coins, goldy bars—all with tasty magic laid upon it. Such lucky children to have such fare to feed upon and grow strong."

"You—you *are* an excellent mother," said Samona. She licked her lips and shifted away a little in the dirt. She placed her hand in what felt like mud, and pulled back, disgusted. Yet nothing, she found, was clinging to her hand. "So the treasure makes your babies strong? Do they eat it?"

The goblin rested both arms on its knees and leaned forward. "Aye, a baby of the earthfolk must have pure ore for its first meal, the purer the better for its nourishment. Me mam fed me first on a vein of copper so sweet me teeth still taste it." It smacked its lips.

Samona moved a little farther away, then jumped aside with a gasp. This time she would have sworn she sat in a fire, but she saw no flame on the dark, loose earth of the cave floor. "What *is* this dirt? First it's wet, then it's burning—"

The goblin nodded. "Brought it with me, for me babies, I did. 'Twill be a comfort to them in their first hours. True Earth, it is, with all the powers together, afore it settles into fire and air and suchlike. A good floor for me den, too."

Samona scooped up a handful of the stuff, feeling it wet yet dry, hot yet chill, heavy yet light, all at once. It seemed like dark earth, except for the glimmers of color shining from the blackness. So Amer's theories were true; there was such a thing as Chaos. Would she ever get to tell him?

"I—I've been preparing for my baby, too," she said. "Back in my own home, far away from here. A wee cradle, some swaddling clothes, things like that. I'll need to get back home before it's born. . . ."

"Oh, aye. I'll let it go, then." The goblin patted Samona's abdomen again. It took a moment before Samona realized it wasn't patting her belly this time, but something higher up. "And it has its own ore for its child, doesn't it? Lovely quicksilver for a lucky babe."

With a start, Samona remembered her dowsing rod and brought it out of her shirt. "This? Do you like it?" The goblin nodded, its huge yellow eyes looking yearningly at the hazel branch. Samona's brain whirled. Nearby was that pot of treasure; surely the goblin's babies didn't need it all. And if Samona brought back, oh, even a pocketful or two of silver pistoles or gold bullion, that would be enough to keep them secure when the baby came. She'd just opened her mouth to suggest the trade, when she felt the damp/dry ground against her calf. And before she knew what she did, Samona blurted out, "I'll trade you the tasty quicksilver inside this rod for a little of this True Earth."

The goblin inhaled between its sharp teeth with a long hiss. It took the dowsing rod from Samona almost reverently. "Trade done, says I. And what a fine baby 'twill be that eats its first meal of quicksilver!"

Samona unrolled the rough scarf she'd used as a man's cravat, piled some of the earth in it, tied the ends up, and put it under her belt. Her hands shook as she did so, and her brain screamed that she was a fool, asking for dirt with all that treasure nearby. But her heart guided her now and it said to trust Amer, so she did this for him.

The goblin had pried out the wood plug in the hazel rod. It sniffed the mercury and grunted in satisfaction. Then suddenly it curled in on itself and gave a groan.

"Are you all right?" Samona put her hand on its shoulder.

"Birthing time soon," it said. "Best be going now. Reach a hand up through yon crack and feel the tree root. It'll lead up to the surface." The goblin turned on its side, stretched out its great hands and burrowed through the cave wall, the rock seeming to slide around its body. Within a moment, it was gone.

Samona sat in the small cave, dazed and bewildered. Finally she began to feel around the cracks and crevices in the rocky ceiling. Sure enough, one hole was larger than the others, big enough for her to put her head and shoulders into. She felt a long, gnarled thing and recognized a root. Taking a deep breath, she crawled up inside the hole, following the root through pitch blackness and chill rock until she felt loose dirt powdering down on top of her head. She pushed the dirt away and broke through a tangle of young roots and turf to the surface.

It wasn't until she was all the way out that she heard the shouting. Glimmers of light came through the trees not too far away, so Samona slid from shadow to shadow to see what was happening.

There in the illumination of the three lanterns, she saw Caleb Brown and Seth Markham tying her husband's wrists together. King James sat on a log nearby, his head in his hands.

"Amer!" Samona barely breathed, shocked beyond comprehension. As if he heard her, Amer's head came up. Samona saw twigs in his hair and a trickle of blood running down one temple.

" . . . don't think to ever see Sammie again," Caleb was saying. "Right sprightly for such a young 'un, but he didn't have the power to protect hisself. Nay, Goodman Crafter, we'll depend on you to overcome that demon tree."

Amer's eyes narrowed in concentration. "My brother-in-law, you say? Eaten by a demon tree?"

"How—?" Samona breathed again, still stunned at the turn of events. A hand clamped her shoulder and spun her around. Frederick Churcher goggled at her for a moment with eyes only slightly smaller than the goblin's, then let out a bellow.

"Hark! Young Sammie's back! Here 'tis!" He took Samona by the shoulder, and thrust her into the circle of illumination. Brown and Markham looked at her as if they'd seen a ghost. Amer's look of overriding relief was replaced by one of confusion as he noticed her clothes. "Found him lurking in the bushes," said Churcher.

"Good now!" said Brown. "With Sammie to guide us again, the pot's as good as ourn. Did ye parley with that demon, then, Sammie? You onto its tricks?"

"Forget the treasure. I was lucky to escape the one time," said Samona, trying for a masterful tone. "And I must needs hear how my—my sister's husband came to find me."

"Oh, he's a clever one," said Markham, tiny eyes shining. "Said he remembered which river, then dowsed for ye using something powerful you'd left behind. From some law of magic, he said—"

"The Law of Contagion, Sammie," said Amer in an even tone. "From the item you left wrapped in the chest drawer." Samona's hand went automatically to what remained of her chopped-off braid. "I was confused over your message and worried for you. I wore out three horses getting here."

"Oh, Amer." Samona couldn't throw her arms around his neck in front of these men, but she hoped her face spoke the words she could not.

Caleb Brown watched her reaction, then pulled a flintlock pistol from beneath his coat. "Look at the true brotherly affection 'atween 'em, boys. Pity to shoot a musket ball into Goodman Crafter, all because of you not helping where help's needed, Sammie. Don't hang a leg, then. Find us that treasure pot and use your wiles to trick it away from that demon."

Amer set his jaw and shook his head ever so slightly. Samona tried for a rebellious retort to Brown, but no words came. Then she heard a mighty groan that seemed to rise out of the ground itself. She started and looked down, but none of the others reacted, not even Amer. King James's face was wreathed in a smile, so obviously happy over Samona's rescue that nothing else mattered.

"Go on, now." Markham gave Samona a rough push.

More groans seemed to shake the ground, but still no one else heard them. Samona looked deep into Amer's eyes. He was a good actor, but she could tell he truly had no knowledge of the sounds. *Imagine that,* she thought, *I hear something Amer doesn't.* She shrugged. "I can point the treasure out again, certainly. And I've left the demon in a much distracted state. But you must promise to release my brother-in-law and me once I've helped you." She gave them one last chance to deal fairly with her.

"Call us speckle-shirted dogs if we don't, and that's a promise," said Brown. Samona saw him leer at Churcher. She would waste no more pity on them.

"Come along, then." Samona paced until she found the center of the moans and cries, which she'd identified as the female sounds of birth. "Put your pegs around this circle, King James," she called. At the most, the nails would provide some goblin baby with a nourishing meal of iron. "This is where you must dig, and soon, boys. The demon won't be busy in my little trap for long.

"Leave the cunning man tied to that tree," ordered Brown. "Jimbo, after you drive in the nails, you commence with those yellow candles and sand pictures of yo'rn. Don't you run off, young Sammie, until we get the pot out nice 'n' proper." They waited a moment for King James's ritual, then began to dig with zeal. Samona stood biting her lip, hearing the moans get louder and faster. Every now and then, Brown would flourish his pistol at her and at Amer, just to intimidate them.

Then, finally, came a musical clang as a shovel hit metal. The three men bellowed in victory, flinging dirt even faster. The lid of a huge black cauldron was uncovered. Brown put down his pistol and slid down into the hole. He grasped the knob and heaved, grunting. The lid came up and he tossed it aside. Then he looked down and began to howl with glee.

"It's here! It's here! It's a beauty thing, boys, just like we remembered. Here's good times, hot rum and a good fling, all for the asking!" Markham and Churcher jumped down into the hole also, shrieking and grabbing at the coins and bullion.

Samona felt a pang when she saw the treasure pot. So much silver and gold! How close she'd come to having some of her own. Then she realized the goblin's groans had stopped. Samona cocked her head and heard instead a sort of satisfied crooning hum.

King James was performing his ablutions on the far side of the circle. Samona sidled slowly around until she stood close enough to catch his eye. "You have a knife, King James?" she said softly. He nodded and pulled a small dagger from his belt. "Then hie you over to my brother there and cut his ropes. And get ready to run fast as you ever have. I'll make sure you earn your freedom for this, King."

Caleb Brown's flintlock pistol lay a few feet away. Samona judged the distance, looking for some sort of telltale movement in the dirt. She thought she saw something stir along the walls of the hole. Quick as a rabbit, she dashed over and grabbed the gun, then ran back to the trees.

Caleb saw her movement and looked around. "Not thinking o' tramping, are ye, Master Sammie? Seth, take out your pistol and show Sammie here how we fire it." Markham gave an evil grin and reached inside his coat.

At that moment, the ground around the hole came alive with clawed hands and feet. Bulging heads with yellow eyes crested the dirt, swarming around the treasure pot and its contents. Samona saw jaws crunch the silver coin and gold nuggets, then turn to the men in the hole as if seeking a fleshier meal.

Brown, Markham, and Churcher began to scream in pain and fear, but claws wrapped around their legs kept them from escaping. A goblin bit Markham on the shoulder before he could finish drawing his gun. Drops of blood began to spatter the sand, and more blood dripped on the contents of the treasure pot, which were now half gone.

Samona put Brown's gun inside her shirt, and ran toward the shore, hands over her ears to stop the gurgling cries of the pirates. Thumps and crashes behind her made her spin around, but it was only King James and Amer, their faces as grim in the bright moonlight as she was sure her own face was. They didn't stop running until they reached the marshy shore of the Schuylkill River.

Amer and King James stayed as quiet as they could rowing the jolly-boat up to the *Osgood* because of what King James had told them. Two more of Peggity Hank's crew, it turned out, were left behind on the ship to 'do some mischief.' Sure enough, when King scrambled first up the ladder, a gruff voice called, "And ye've got it, then? Peggity Hank's load? Caleb there behind ye?" Samona could hear thumps and cries coming from the stern of the ship.

"Right behind me," said King James smoothly, as Samona had instructed him, then put his dagger to the man's throat.

Another shadowy figure cried out and came running across the deck planks, cutlass in hand. Samona slung one leg over the bulwarks and cocked her pistol. "Hold up, you chuckle-headed fool," she cried. "Lay down that blade before I put a musketball in your brainpan." The man stopped in midstride, and Amer relieved him of the sword.

Even in the dark, she could see the flash of Amer's teeth as he smiled. "Why, you're a right conscious rascal, Sammie. Your plan worked like a trump!"

Samona put the gun carefully in her belt. "Caleb and your partners won't be coming back," she told the two pirates. "They made a proper good dinner for the goriest bunch of goblins I ever saw. Now, where's the captain?"

"Well?" said Amer, some days later, once they were inside their own cottage, leaving a grateful Captain Baldridge, King James, and crew in the harbor. Samona had seen to it she and Amer never had a moment alone on the ship. She needed the time to plan her speech.

She thought she saw humor in his eyes, and it made her feel optimistic. The words spilled out: the challenge with the button, the demon tree, the talk with the goblin mother. He hooted and laughed at that, declaring himself mightily intrigued by this new Talent. When she came to the part about the strange earth, and removed her scarf to hand it and its contents to him, Amer just stood with mouth agape. What she didn't tell him, until the end, was the reason for the treasure hunt.

"Amer," she said. "I had reason to worry that I might become a burden, so I wanted to add to our cache of funds— in case of emergency during my confinement."

"Your confinement?"

Samona put both hands on her belly. "By my guess, you'll be a father in a little over seven months. I—I hope it's happy news for you."

Amer put a hand to his head and went to sit at his table. "A baby. Our baby. Why, Samona, of course it's happy news. I'm just surprised is all. You go clean up and dress yourself properly. I'll try out this lovely Chaos! Why, the Philosopher's Stone is almost ours!"

Now I know, she thought. *Now I see which of my surprises he deems most important.* The knowledge was bitter as gall. But when she came back into the room, short damp hair in curls about her face, her favorite blue dress feeling oddly airy around her legs, Amer's mood was much less jubilant. "Why, what's wrong?" said Samona.

"It's not going to work," Amer said, prodding a glass athanor bubbling over a candle flame. He sighed and sank down in his chair, his eyes closed. "I'm no longer eligible for the Philosopher's Stone. Ah, well."

Despite her own pain, Samona wanted to comfort him. She sat on the arm of his chair. "You were so proud before of your attitude toward material wealth. What made you change?"

Amer put one arm around her waist. The other hand he put on her belly. "This."

Samona looked down into his face, barely daring to breathe. Did this mean? "My . . . our baby?"

"Your news has made me realize I was fooling myself all along. Pretending such a cool demeanor. You're the most important thing in my life, you and our new family. Which, after all, is as it should be. I want the best for you too much now to ever try for the Philosopher's Stone."

"Oh, Amer." The wound in her heart healed over, leaving a few tears to leak from her eyes. She hugged his neck, kissing the top of his head. Bartering her only asset for that special earth, and now . . . Samona almost laughed at the trick events had played on her. Still, here in Amer's arms, she felt secure enough. They would handle whatever happened.

She still basked in the glow of that feeling the next day when the knock came upon the door. She opened it to find two grand figures festooned with braid and ribbon and silver buttons.

"Captain Buttons—eh, Captain Baldridge! And King James! How nice you look! Please come in." She patted her hair, covered now with a stylish cap.

"Morning, good lady. I have business with your brother Samuel and your good husband. Are they at home?" The captain gave Samona a polite glance, but King James was staring at her, perplexed.

"Captain, it's me. I'm Samuel Goldman." Samona took off the cap. "My real name, sir, is Samona Crafter." She pulled a silver object from her apron pocket. "And here is something I'd forgotten to return. My apologies."

Captain Baldridge looked at the button, jaw agape. He looked at Amer standing behind Samona. Amer smiled and nodded. "Sammie!" cried the captain. "Capital! A woman as crew aboard my own ship. Well, well."

King James took Samona's hand in his, bowed, and kissed it. He came up from the bow, laughing. "Oh, Sammie. You a woman all along. And here I think I finally meet me a real gentleman!"

"Oh. Such a surprise, dear lady, I forgot my reason for coming," said the captain. He drew forth a bag heavy with clinking coins and handed it to Samona. "You may not know, Goody Crafter, but there was a reward for the capture of Peggity Hank Barlo's crew. Those two chaps we had clapped in irons were more than a little bitter about the turn of events, and, well, one thing leading to another, they gave over on the rest of Barlo's boys."

Samona looked inside and saw a flash of gold guineas. Her heart lurched. "Oh, Amer. It's a small fortune." Amer looked inside and gasped.

"I made good your request for the freedom of King James here," continued the captain. "Offered him passage to Jamaica on the *Chelsea Queen*. But the fellow had other ideas."

"It's James King," said the big man. "I'm a freeman now, no slave names for me." He squeezed Samona's hand in his huge one. "How can I leave when I have such good friends in Boston!"

Anno Domini 1685

THE SEAL
OF SOLOMON

by **Robert Sheckley**

Samona had been passing Edwin Lapthorn's house on
Bridlepath Lane and she'd heard soft, heartbreaking moans
coming from within. She knocked but no one answered.
She'd paused on the doorstep, uncertain what to do.

She and Amer had been married three years ago. When
their first child was due, they'd left Amer's beloved
mountainside home and moved to this town of Rock
Harbor, just to the south of Boston. Here there were
medical doctors for their baby girl, and Harvard College
nearby provided manuscripts for Amer's researches into the
properties of magic. The Crafters kept to themselves. The
last thing they wanted was any trouble with their neighbors
over witchcraft or alchemy. They needed a chance to rest
and take care of their new baby, untroubled by controversies.
They especially didn't want trouble with Edwin Lapthorn, a
jeweller who carried an unsavory reputation with him as a
skunk carries scent.

But there was a child crying in Lapthorn's house.

Samona rapped at the door again, louder. "Hello? Is there
anyone home?"

She knew little about Lapthorn, though there was much
gossip about him in Rock Harbor in that year of 1685.
People said Lapthorn had gotten into trouble in England.
Nobody seemed to know just what sort of trouble, but

something unsavory and perhaps uncanny was hinted at. He had managed to escape before the King's constables could arrest him, taking passage on the bark *Dora* out of Plymouth and coming to Boston. He lived quietly enough in nearby Rock Harbor, but there was that about him people didn't like. Perhaps it was his lean, lantern-jawed face, black eyebrows that met in the middle, bloodless lips set into a humorless grin.

Samona wanted nothing to do with the man. But there was a child crying in his house, and she thought it might be in serious trouble.

She had to go in! She straightened, a tall, beautiful young woman with long black hair, dark eyes, a haughty, arresting face, and a figure of such charm that even her modest costume could not entirely conceal. She tried the door and found it was unlocked. She entered the high old house.

She came out ten minutes later, shaken, and went directly home. After checking on her own child, Amy, aged fourteen months, sleeping quietly in her crib, Samona went to the drawing room and told Amer about her experience. Her husband listened, dark eyebrows drawing together in the scowl that appeared on his face when he was forced to listen to tales of man's inhumanity.

"I'll have a word with Master Lapthorn," he said. Putting on his overcoat and hat he went out. He sought out Edwin Lapthorn.

Lapthorn was just leaving Josiah's Publick House on State Street when Amer came up. The two men had a nodding acquaintance but had never talked together.

"Sir," Amer said, "a little while ago my wife had occasion to pass your house. She heard a child wailing. She took the liberty of entering—"

"Entered my *house*, sir? Just walked in?"

"That is correct, sir."

"Quite a sizable liberty, I'd call that," Lapthorn said. He was an immensely tall man, with a wiry mass of black hair pressed down by a tricorn hat. His face was weathered, reddened under the cheekbones from drink, and badly shaven.

He had a long upper lip, pulled awry by a puckered scar that ran down the side of his cheek, which gave him a permanent sneer.

"Your wife had no right to enter my premises, sir."

"Perhaps not, sir. But she found the child who lives with you was in trouble."

"Douglas in trouble? The child is perfectly able to look after himself."

"She found him screaming his head off and hanging by one foot from the top rung of the ladder to the root cellar."

"I had no idea he could even get the door open! Clever little fellow despite his idiocy! The experience did him no harm, obviously. Made of India rubber, that lad is."

"He's flesh and blood, sir," said Amer stiffly. "Like the rest of us. Your youngster deserves better looking-after."

"The idiot's not mine, you know," said Lapthorn. "Left to me by my former housekeeper when she died of a sudden fever. Out of the goodness of my heart I agreed to look out for him. He eats better than many in this town. But even if I starved him, sir, yes, and whipped him, too, what goes on under a man's roof is his own business and nothing to do with you. Your wife had no right."

"A child's safety was at stake," Amer said stubbornly.

"Even if that's true, it's none of your concern. Unless you choose to make it so."

The man's callousness, and his suddenly aggressive behavior astonished Amer. Lapthorn had his fists doubled; the scar on his cheek glowed. The situation was threatening to get out of hand. It was plain that Lapthorn was an ugly piece of work, and he was looking for trouble. Was it worth starting what might be a nasty situation for the sake of an idiot child who understood nothing?

"That's my last word on it," Lapthorn said. "And tell your wife to keep out of my house. If she comes in again uninvited, it may not be Douglas hanging by his foot from the root cellar."

Amer drew himself up abruptly. He was thin, dark haired, intense. The forward-leaning tension of his body conveyed menace. His eyes were blue and glittery. The hair of his head seemed to bristle. He said, his voice dropping half an octave, "Sir, do you threaten my wife?"

The two men stared at each other for several moments. Amer's neck began to swell with a rage he was having difficulty controlling. Then Lapthorn broke the tension, laughing and turning away.

" 'Twas but a pleasantry, sir. I would never offer violence to a lady. But I hope she will not essay my premises again, because a nasty shock might await her, and it would be none of my doing. There are defenses to my house, sir, which I had not set into place before this, but which I will do now. You are warned. Good day to you, sir."

And doffing his hat, Lapthorn strode away.

Amer returned home and told Samona of his conversation. Samona thought for a long time. Her eyes were pensive, and her gaze seemed far away. She poked at the fire negligently, barely noticing when the end of the branch she used as a poker caught fire. Then she flung it into the flames and said, "I wonder what he is trying to hide."

"His indifferent cruelty to Douglas, as I believe the child is called. What else could it be?"

"It wouldn't be that," Samona said.

"Why not?"

"It's too trivial. Nobody around here cares about cruelty to an idiot child. Except us."

"Come now, my dear. Some of the church folk around here would make it an issue if they knew."

"There's more going on here than that," Samona said. "I think our Master Lapthorn has other things on his mind. Something is going on in that house."

"It's none of our concern," Amer said. "Each man is free under the King's law."

For the moment, Samona had to be content with that.

In Lapthorn's house, the idiot Douglas sat on a little stool in the corner near the fire. He was big-headed and blank-expressioned with large, drooling mouth and small dull eyes. Douglas was a patient one, who could sit in a corner for hours, intently playing with a spider's web, winding and rewinding it, never breaking the skein.

"It's time," Lapthorn said to him.

A look of consternation crossed the idiot's face. You could have sworn he knew what Lapthorn meant. But he made no protest when Lapthorn led him to the special room, put him in his accustomed posture on the flagstones, drew the pentagram around him, and began to chant.

It seemed to take forever tonight. Then the candles flamed, though the air in the room was still.

It was the time Lapthorn had waited for, the great moment when the constellations had swung in their great circle to the correct astrological position. With Douglas in place on the flagstones, Lapthorn now made ready. The small altar in his back room, a room kept shuttered and locked to avoid any prying eyes, had long been prepared with the black candles and the specially treated mandrake root in its little pewter bowl. Lapthorn bowed down before the altar. He said, "I pronounce the words, O Shadrach, Asmodeus, and Belial, listen to me, give me this gift and I will repay you a thousandfold. And to bear witness to this, here is my blood."

So saying, Lapthorn pricked his thumb with the end of a stylus. A bubble of blood swelled and then flowed down the instrument's bronze side.

The candle guttered dangerously in its pewter holder. The window, with its parchment cover, creaked and strained at its latch as the wind pushed and tugged at it. The wind had long been his enemy.

"Come out," said Lapthorn, speaking directly to Douglas. A strangeness lit the idiot's face. His features twisted. His mouth opened. From it issued a fine mist. It hung in the air, picking up rays of light from the dying candlelight, then swirled around his face. When it had cleared, the idiot's face had changed.

"What is your name?" Lapthorn asked.

"I am Caspardutis," said a voice from the idiot's mouth. "I was known in ancient Egypt. The laboratories of the alchemists knew me. I have conversed with Paracelsus and the Great Albertus."

It was an elemental. These creatures had been known since earliest antiquity. They did not fit neatly into the theories of magic. They could not be said to serve either side.

"You have come in answer to my spell," Lapthorn said.

"That I have. But I beg you to release me."

"Not so fast, my fine ethereal friend! You know what I want."

"The same thing you wanted last time," the idiot said.

"And I will want it next time, too. What have you brought me?"

The idiot's hands opened, displaying a handful of precious stones: several uncut rubies, a big sapphire, a small but perfect emerald, and a few lesser stones.

"Are they good?" asked Caspardutis.

"They'll do," Lapthorn said. "Where did you get them?"

"I know a back entrance to the treasure of Ali Baba. But it is dangerous to go there."

"You must go back at once and bring me more! And more after that!"

"For how long, Master?"

"For as long as I say."

The idiot's head nodded. Then his eyes blinked and closed. His head drooped upon his chest. After a few moments, the head lifted again. The signs of intelligence were gone. It was Douglas again, until the next time he was inhabited by the spirit Lapthorn had captured.

Soon thereafter, Master Lapthorn opened his jewellery store in South Boston. It was an immediate success. People from as far away as Providence came to look at his fine rubies from Ceylon, his emeralds from Colombia, his pearls from the South Seas. To look and to buy. His sales were brisk, because, despite the growing difficulties between the Colonies and England, Boston was a prosperous small city and growing by leaps and bounds. There was money in the colony, and a great lack of goods to buy. Lapthorn's jewellery was like a reminder of the beauty and decadence of old Europe, from which many had come recently. Despite the Puritan indictment of luxury and extravagance, people found reasons why they simply had to have this brooch or that necklace, or that unique ring.

The man was a success. And even though Amer didn't like him, it was hard to begrudge him his good fortune. Amer didn't think of it again until the cow-killings began. Until children started to be lost in the deep woods, still haunted by recent memories of savage, pagan Indians. There was a bad fire that consumed half the town, and plague moved in to claim more lives.

Amer's relations were not good with the elders of the town. They had never liked him or approved of him. He was not a regular churchgoer, and he was rumored to use magic. The magicians and witches of the town didn't like him either, because he had spoken out boldly against the powers of darkness. But they had need of his services now. There seemed to be some sort of a spell over the town. Things were going badly for everyone except Edwin Lapthorn, who was prospering.

"It all has the look of an unholy pact with the Devil."

So Amer was told by Charles Swanson, a well-known local magician who had tried to combat Lapthorn with black magic. Swanson was crippled now. The magic backfired on him. The man Lapthorn obviously had a pact with the Devil. It would take another kind of magic to defeat him.

"You must do something," Swanson said.

"It is not my fight," Amer told him.

Next to visit was Obadiah Winter, the head of the local Congregationalist Church.

"We have heard, sir, that you are a considerable magician. We have need of your powers."

This conversation took place in Amer's sitting room, which was well lit by tallow tapers. Winter was a big, grim-faced man, a pious man without humor to him. He lost no time getting to the point.

"There is a matter my congregation would have me discuss with you, sir."

"Discuss away, sir."

"Do you know of this new fellow in town? This Lapthorn?"

"I have heard of him, though we have not met."

"Master Amer, let me speak to you openly. There has been nothing but disaster here in Rock Harbor ever since that man arrived."

"Coincidence," Amer said. "You can't blame a man for that."

"Won't you do anything, sir? We know you have powers."

"I'll think about it," Amer said.

"Superstitious fool," he remarked to Samona after Winter departed.

"In this case, he's right. You know that Lapthorn is causing all the current problems here."

Amer was sitting by the fire studying an old parchment he had bought in Amsterdam, a medieval manuscript which claimed to give the key to the hermetic science of alchemy.

"Causing what?" Amer said. He turned back to his manuscript. "You know, some of those old alchemists had some pretty good ideas. Let me read you this bit."

"Did you hear what I said?" Samona asked.

"I heard you, my dear, but I do not believe it."

"You do not believe the man Lapthorn has brought the bad luck with him?"

Amer scowled. He had wanted to spend the evening studying his Amsterdam manuscript. Now he saw that he was going to have to consider this matter of Lapthorn.

"My dear," he said, "it is coincidence, nothing more."

"I know what is coincidence," Samona said, "and I know what is caused by an evil presence. I took a look at Lapthorn the other day with the Second Sight."

"Did you indeed?" Amer was interested. He had spent many years working out the principles of magic, deriving them from those governing alchemy. Armed with that knowledge, he had been able to operate in both worlds, the natural and the supernatural. He always said that it was a difficult situation, because, although supernatural things did happen, it was mere vulgar superstition to attribute a supernatural cause to anything you didn't understand. Both magic and science existed, but all scientific tests had to be exhausted before it was correct to take recourse in magical explanations.

As a scientist, Amer was bothered by magic, because it presented him with situations that were not simply quantifiable, and with instances that were not repeatable. If they had been, they would have been scientific. Since they weren't, they had to be magical. Amer had a distaste for having his life ruled by irrational elements. He would have liked to reduce everything to science and reason. Life and circumstance had dictated otherwise.

He was also an honest man. He knew that Samona had a natural talent for magic, and a lot of it. She had some powers he did not possess. The Second Sight was one of them. It was typically, though not exclusively, the gift of a female witch. It gave her the power, when conditions were right, to see through the surface of things to the mystery that lay at their core. It presented the conclusion of things, but in a jangled and melted fashion, so that only afterwards did you know, could you interpret, what the Second Sight had shown you.

Not possessing the power himself, Amer was more than a little interested in Samona's accounts of its use.

"What did you see when you looked at him? And what were the circumstances?"

Samona's beautiful face was thoughtful. The firelight put a golden edge to her features. Outside, the wind moved, rustling branches and stirring leaves. There was a sound of crickets. It was a night in late summer.

"I was on my way to Charity Simpson's with the shawl I'd promised her. Lapthorn passed on the other side. It was a windy day and his cloak was flapping. I saw a face in his cloak."

"An act of the imagination!" Amer cried, disappointed.

"I think not. There was the feeling of uncanniness that so often accompanies a vision with the Second Sight. The feeling of a strange glamour. And the face in the cloak spoke to me."

"Are you saying that he spoke aloud?"

"I know not. Perhaps what he said was not audible to others. But he said to me, "Help! I need help!""

"Whose face was it?"

"I do not know."

"Was it the face of Douglas, the idiot?"

"It was not."

"Had you ever seen the face before?"

"Never."

"Is there anything you can tell me about it?"

"Only that it was not human."

Amer cleared his throat explosively, breaking the quiet that had fallen upon them. He got up from his chair and began pacing up and down the plank floor. His hands were clasped behind his back. His long dark hair, caught at the end in a black ribbon, had half escaped its confines and hung to one side of his face. His look was intent, annoyed.

"Samona, have you forgotten why we came here to Rock Harbor?"

"No, I have not forgotten."

"Then tell me."

"It was to live for a time away from magic and from those who knew of our powers."

"And why did we decide to do that?"

"Amer, please!"

"No, tell me, why."

Her voice dropped to a whisper. "We became tired of the loneliness and hiding from the fears of others."

"That is my understanding, too, my dear. We moved away and decided to live simply and sanely, and without witchcraft. Is that not correct?"

"That is correct."

"Why, then, are you using the Second Sight?"

"Amer! It did no harm to use it! No one could tell! I did it but to find out what manner of man he was."

"What do you mean, no one could tell?"

"You know as well as I do, only one with the power can detect another using the Second Sight. There are none in this town save us."

"And Lapthorn," Amer said.

"Lapthorn, a warlock? Are you sure?"

"Think about what you've told me about him."

Samona thought, then nodded. "Yes, he must be a warlock. His actions point to no other conclusion."

"And now," Amer said, "he knows that you are a witch, and probably believes that I am a warlock."

"I didn't think of that, Amer!"

"You're out of practice," Amer said. "That's probably why you were detected."

"But Lapthorn didn't see me! Only the face in the cloak!"

"And who will the face in the cloak tell it to? After all, it's Lapthorn's cloak."

"Yes, I suppose you're right," Samona said. "But it's no sin to use the Second Sight. Perhaps all this will come to nothing."

"Let's hope so," Amer said. "We didn't move to Rock Harbor to be drawn into a profitless battle of wizards."

During the next weeks, uncanny occurrences came to the little town of Rock Harbor. Weird noises were heard at night, such as the ominous twitterings of bats that had gathered in the woods near town in great numbers. They were joined by the eerie hooting of barnyard owls, and the cough and snarl of wolverine and wolf. Lapthorn's prosperity continued to increase, but the fortunes of the town began to run downhill. Flocks of small black flying insects began to proliferate. It was difficult to know if they were natural or not. But worst of all, little Amy fell sick of a fever. This was the matter that finally precipitated Amer to action.

Amer called up his own elemental. Through his alchemical researches he had long known that on the etherial plane, many strange beings exist. These were responsive to natural law, as expressed through alchemical manipulations. These beings were not really human, and their motivations were

strange and sometimes shocking. But they could be of
assistance to an alchemist who treated them with respect.

He burned the chemicals and repeated the incantations.
After a while, Robin Goodfellow, as Amer had come to
call him, appeared in the big glass retort. He was no more
than five inches high, and he had a heart-shaped pixie face
and long pointed ears.

"You always call me at the most inconvenient times,"
Robin said. He was almost incorporeal—a dancing flame
within the glass retort, a flame that changed color as he
expressed different emotions.

"I beg pardon," Amer said. "Perhaps another time?" He
already knew the trouble you could get into if you tried to
force an elemental to do what it didn't wish to do.

"No, it's all right," Robin said. "As it happens, I do have
some time on my hands. I had intended to attend Oberon's
fancy dress ball, which was to be held in Poictesme this
evening. But it has been cancelled due to sidereal effects
of a baleful nature, and so I am at your service."

Amer wanted to ask about Oberon and the fancy dress ball.
And where was this place called Poictesme? But he decided
he'd better stick to business. He explained about Lapthorn
and the mysterious happenings that had attended his coming
to Rock Harbor, and Samona's experience in the house.

"What do you want me to do?" Robin asked.

"It would please me very much if you went in there,
Robin, and tell me what you saw."

"Why not do it yourself?"

"That is more than a little difficult. Since Samona went
there unannounced, Lapthorn has set up his defenses."

"I will take a look," Robin said, "and we will see what
we will see."

That evening as Amer was going over papers in his study,
he noticed a green flame dancing in the big glass retort.

"Robin, is it you?"

"None other."

"And have you been to Lapthorn's house?"

"I have tried. But some sort of dire magic lingers around
the place. I sought to pass through a keyhole invisibly, but

something seized me by the hair and tried to pull me through. I got out fast, I can assure you."

"So I am no wiser than before," Amer said sadly.

"Not true. I can tell you that your suspicion of another elemental is confirmed. Even at that distance I could tell its presence."

"Is this spirit stronger than you? Is that what kept you out?"

"I wouldn't call it stronger," Robin said. "But there was much evil around that house, evil of the blackest kind."

"Is there no way to get inside?"

"There is for you," Robin said. "You have but to use the proper spell."

"And which spell might that be?"

Robin Goodfellow sat down on emptiness within the big glass globe of the retort. He was dressed in a tunic of russet brown, and wore a green shirt with wide sleeves and a green tunic. His heart-shaped face was nut-brown, and filled with many creases.

"Faith," he said crossly, "what does a spirit have to do to get some refreshment around here?"

"My apologies," Amer said. "I have victuals for you right here."

Amer put into the open-topped glass globe a little pitcher of milk and a plate of honey cakes that Samona had baked the previous night. Robin tested them and found them good. His appetite was soon satisfied, however, since elementals eat for the spirit of the thing, having no use for earthly provender. Finished, he wiped his mouth delicately on a tiny muslin handkerchief.

"My dear Amer," he said, "you have in your study the fourth book of the great Albertus Magnus?"

"Yes, I do," Amer said. "I've been studying it."

"Remember the formula that appears in Section Fourteen, which is entitled 'Getting Around Evil Influences'?"

"I remember it well. But it doesn't work. I have tried that incantation many a time, without result."

"Master Albert got it ever so slightly wrong," Robin said. "His third word begins with a *bet* in the language of the

Hebrews. Change that to a *shin* and see what happens."

"As easy as that?"

"Magic is very easy," Robin said, "when you know how."

After Robin had gone, Amer hastened to his copy of the Great Albert's book. He found the erroneous word and made the proper correction. He was ready now to enter Lapthorn's house. But there was still a problem. Lapthorn, perhaps sensing a contradictory magic that could work against him, scarcely moved from his home, except for rapid trips to buy provisions. His absences were unscheduled. Amer waited, two days, four days, a week. His opportunity still did not occur. He began to despair at getting into the house.

Samona and he were discussing it one evening. Amer was in a very bad mood, since this was cutting into his study time. And in the meantime, evils of various sorts continued to proliferate in the town. Strange sights were reported. There was panic among the citizens. Visitations of an uncanny and noxious nature were increasing—showers of toads, sudden eruptions of stinging worms, odd little red-furred bats that had never been seen before in the neighborhood. And there was no relief in sight.

"It's really annoying," Amer said. "The man doesn't even attend to his jewellery business any longer. It's as if he knows I'm planning a move against him, and is waiting to be ready for me. If only he'd leave the house for a decent length of time! Even an hour could be enough!"

"If an hour is all that you need," Samona said, "I think I could provide that for you."

"And how do you propose to do that?"

"Master Lapthorn has a considerable interest in me."

Amer raised both eyebrows. "I thought he was enraged at you for entering his house."

"He was. But that anger hides his deeper rage at my not returning his signs of interest in me."

"How do you know he is interested in you? Is that more witch's business?"

"It is woman's business," Samona said serenely. "Magic has nothing to do with it."

"I don't like it," Amer said. "Whatever you are proposing would put you at risk."

"I can take care of myself," Samona said. "As you well know."

"Samona! We had agreed that you were not to use any magic again!"

"I don't intend to," Samona replied demurely. "There are other ways of distracting men. Is Master Lapthorn at home now?"

"He has gone to the tavern, probably to bring home his customary tankards of ale."

"Then I could go out now and meet him on the street. Be you ready, Amer, for I will shortly give you the hour you need."

"What will you do?" Amer asked.

"Don't ask matters that will give you unnecessary pain. We must do this, Amer! Not just for the town; for our own lives, and Amy's!"

"Yes, so be it," Amer said sullenly.

Samona said, "Master Lapthorn! How providential that I run into you."

Lapthorn paused, two foaming pewter tankards of beer in his hands, a length of sausage under his arm. "Mistress Crafter! I would not have thought you glad to see me."

"Because you warned me to stay out of your house?"

"Why, yes," Lapthorn said. "Ladies do not take kindly to being given orders, even if they are for their own good."

"Some do and some do not, Master Lapthorn," Samona said, simpering, and so dense was Master Lapthorn, as she had suspected, that he did not take her conduct for fakery, but thought that some special essence of manhood in himself had called it forth.

"Master Lapthorn, I have heard you sailed from Plymouth in England."

"I have lived there," Lapthorn said cautiously.

"I have relatives from there," Samona said. "It would please me very much if you would walk me to the Buttery and tell me something of the appearance of that famous port."

"Nothing would please me better," Lapthorn said. "The harbor of Plymouth . . ." He began describing the place as they walked along.

As he approached the house, Amer felt a chill come over him. Waves of cold seemed to emanate from the doorway, and although there was no wind, Amer could feel the big old elm on his left peer at him as he came up the winding pathway that shielded the house from the main road. There was a hum and buzz of unseen things in the air.

A blazing log flew at him, although he could not see where it came from, or who threw it. He ducked just in time. Other blazing bits of wood came at him. Amer dodged them and hastily recited the version of Albertus Magnus' invocation which Robin Goodfellow had corrected for him, with the *shin* substituted for the *bet*. The shower of sparks died away. He tried the door. It opened to his touch.

The place was dark—it was just after sunset. The fading day cast oblong shapes of old gold through the windows. A low fire burned untended in the hearth. Somewhere a grandfather clock ticked with an ominous, syncopated sound. The place was as quiet as a mouse holding its breath. Amer walked in and glided ghostlike down a long hallway, with fading slabs of sunlight lighting his way. It occurred to him that the valley of the shadow of death probably began in sunlight.

And then he was faced with a door. He turned the knob. It was locked. Albertus' formula, repeated again, served to unlatch it. Or perhaps Lapthorn hadn't locked it properly in the first place. Amer knew you could never be too certain about what caused what. But then he was inside the room, and he saw, sitting on a chair before him, the idiot boy, Douglas.

"You're the boy, aren't you?" Amer said.

"Who the hell are you?" It was a surprisingly deep voice that came from the boy's mouth. A masculine voice, intelligent and of some years' experience.

"Who are you?" Amer asked.

"Caspardutis, so I am called in this cycle."

"You are an elemental?"

"That I am."

"Why do you occupy the body of this child?"

"Because I was lured here."

"Lured? How!"

The idiot turned his head slowly. His pale eyes regarded Amer with intelligent curiosity. Then he laughed.

"You do have a lot of nerve to invade Lapthorn's house this way. Or did you kill him beforehand?"

"With all your powers, wouldn't you know if I'd done that?"

"My powers are real enough," Caspardutis said, somewhat testily. "But I needn't waste them on a creature like Lapthorn."

"You call him a creature. Yet you serve him."

"Yes, I must. He enticed me with his spells. I was in no danger then, just curious to see what manner of man tried to attract the attention of an elemental, and to perhaps provide him with a mischief. Then, to my surprise, he flashed a symbol at me. It was a copy of the Seal of Solomon, not a very good likeness, really, and rather smudged—it was a rubbing, you see—but it was enough to trap me instantly. And so I must do his bidding for a time."

"How long a time?"

"We dwellers of the ether don't reckon by years. But we know when an account is settled."

"Your being here has attracted a lot of bad luck to this town."

Caspardutis shrugged. "There's nothing I can do about it."

"You could get out of here and not come back. Unless you enjoy playing fetch for Lapthorn."

"Me, enjoy it? Why, I'd rather rip the man's guts out, slowly, inch by inch. But as I told you, I'm bound to obey his orders."

"What has he asked you for?"

"Gems, precious stones. It's creating a lot of disturbance in some other realms, I can tell you, because I have to get those gems from somewhere. It's downright embarrassing, since I have to steal them, and stealing is no more approved among elementals than it is among men."

"Suppose I could find a way to set you free?"

"I'd take it most cheerfully. But you cannot."

"But if I could?"

"As I said, I'd take it."

"What is the first thing Lapthorn says when he summons you?"

" 'Come out, Caspardutis.' That is what he says. There's a great deal more to it than that, of course, spells and such, but that's what it always comes down to."

"And what do you do?"

"I drop whatever it is I'm doing and come into the pentagram where he has placed this child's body."

"Has anyone told you to come into the pentagram?"

"No. But it seems reasonable enough."

"But you are not specifically ordered to do so? Your going into the pentagram is your own assumption or interpretation of his command?"

"I suppose it is, if you look at the matter with a solicitor's eye."

"With what other sort of eye should one look at the details of a contract?"

"Well . . . All right, I take your point. But what does it matter if I appear within the pentagram or across the room or even in the stable?"

"None that I can see. You can respond to his summons by materializing as far away as you like, or as near."

"Near? What are you hinting at, Master Amer?"

"Yes, what indeed!" a voice thundered from the doorway.

"Now you're for it," Caspardutis said. "I'm getting out of here!"

The idiot's eyes went blank.

Lapthorn strode into the room, tall, scarecrow-thin, with dull black hair falling over his eyes. The scar on his cheek was livid with sudden anger.

"You'd come uninvited into my house, would you?"

"That is the case," Amer said.

"And you would learn my secrets, Master Crafter?"

"I have found out what I need to know. You have enslaved this child, Douglas, making him a conduit, a receptacle, for the elemental who calls himself Caspardutis. That, sir, is against the laws of God and man. Furthermore, you have enriched yourself at the expense of the citizens of Rock Harbor, since your diabolic work has attracted a host of evil spirits, and called forth a deal of bad luck upon the town. You are responsible for several deaths here, sir."

Lapthorn shrugged and grinned. "These petty people don't count, my dear Amer. Ordinary folk are always at risk when magic is afoot. You know this very well; you are a warlock yourself. We serve the same master."

"Untrue," Amer said. "I have never served Satan and never will. I am of the ancient and honorable guild of alchemists. We are investigators of hidden principles of the universe, not practitioners of black magic."

"Well, then," Lapthorn said, "so much the worse for you. If you won't serve black magic, sir, the Art will serve you, as it has already served your slut of a wife!"

"Samona? What have you done to her?"

"She tried to lure me away from my house, to give you time to enter and set up whatever feeble mischief you may have at your disposal. But I saw through your transparent scheme, and have dealt with her as a beautiful but treacherous trull should be dealt with."

Lapthorn chuckled and turned away. Amer felt a flood of rage rise in his heart. If this unkempt degenerate had touched a hair of Samona's head—At the thought, a blood-red mist rose before his eyes. An uncanny shriek like tearing brass came from his throat. He launched himself at Lapthorn like a mountain cougar—

And found himself a moment later flying through the air, to land in a heap in the far corner of the room.

Shakily he got to his feet. He was glad to note that he had broken no limbs in the violent fall. But he felt suddenly helpless; his psychic defenses were scattered by the intensity of the blow. And he remembered an adage that was as true for magic as it was for science: every action has an equal and opposite reaction.

He realized he'd been tricked. Lapthorn had sought successfully to provoke him, getting him to launch a blind and unplanned assault. Lapthorn's powers had enabled him to turn the force of the attack back on its perpetrator.

Now Amer's psychic force was spent. It would take him hours, days, to restore himself. Lapthorn, his enemy, wasn't going to give him enough time.

Then the front door creaked. Both men turned to look as it slowly swung open, letting in a sigh of evening breeze.

And Samona came in.

Cool and beautiful, neatly and modestly dressed, every hair in place, she advanced into the room.

"So, Master Lapthorn," she said sweetly, "you did not choose to wait for me while I got my shawl?"

"As soon as I was out of your presence," Lapthorn said, "I saw through your scheme and hurried home. And I found this." He gestured at Amer.

"You have been ungentle with him," Samona remarked, crossing the room to stand by her husband.

"I've only begun. When I'm finished I'll serve you, too, mistress of trickery."

Samona put her hand on Amer's shoulder. Amer could feel the pulse of vitality pass from her to him. He straightened, feeling strength return to him. But it was not enough.

Lapthorn surveyed the two, frowning. He drew back slightly.

"I could deal with you both myself. But why should I bother, when I command that which will harrow the flesh from your bones and carry your souls down to the special Hell that awaits those who try to thwart a magician? Caspardutis, come to me!"

The room was very quiet. There was no sound but the soft tick-tock of the grandfather clock. Douglas, the idiot boy, sat passive and dull-faced in his little chair. No trace of spirit animated his face or small body.

"Caspardutis! Do you hear me? I command you by Solomon's Seal to come to me this instant!"

Lapthorn stood in front of the pentagram, stretched to his full height, his hands upraised and head thrown back. There was a sound of crackling energies. The low-burning fire in the hearth flared up and cast blue and green flames. Lapthorn staggered for a moment, then regained his balance.

There was a strange look on his face, a look of alarm that swiftly changed to terror. "What have you done?" he cried. Then his hands clutched at his temples. "*Get out of there!*" he shrieked.

Samona turned to Amer. "My dear, what is happening?"

"Just watch, my love," Amer said, patting her hand.

Lapthorn clutched at his head and commenced to stagger around the room, bent almost double. He stumbled into a table, recoiled and knocked over a chair, almost tripped over it, recovered and began to turn in a frenzied hunched circle, like a rabid dog trying to devour its tail. His frantic circling brought him against a tall cupboard filled with china. He knocked it over, then fell to the floor where he lay amid the shards of porcelain, thrashing about like a beached trout, his hands tearing at his hair and his bootheels drumming frantically against the planks. Then his body gave one final spasm and lay still.

Samona asked, "Did you contrive to feed him poison, my love? For I know not else how you produced this reaction."

"Samona!" Amer cried. "Could you actually believe I'd poison a man in his own home?"

"I know you did *something*," Samona said.

"I did but acquaint Caspardutis, his captive elemental, with a possible loophole in the terms of his possession. It was not poison, or even witchcraft, or alchemy, either, but a lawyerly quibble that I suggested."

Lapthorn's body stirred. Presently he sat up.

"It was a good trick," he said. His voice was that of Caspardutis. "When I went away before, I considered your words. I saw there was indeed a lack of precision in the terms laying out how I was to present myself when Lapthorn called. But if you hadn't pointed it out to me, Master Amer,

I would still be running to the ends of the universe for his gemstones."

"I don't understand," Samona said. "How could it matter where you appeared when he called you?"

"Since the position was not specified," Caspardutis said, "I could appear anywhere at all—even in Lapthorn's own mind. That is what I did, and there was a struggle for possession of the body."

"Which you won," Samona said.

Caspardutis in Lapthorn's body bowed gracefully.

"And now what will you do?" Amer asked. "Will you continue to live on Earth as Lapthorn?"

"I shall not!" Caspardutis replied. "I have important business on the ethereal plane. I've been away from it too long as it is. I but pause to thank you, Amer, and now I'll discard this carcass and return to my true home."

"A moment!" Amer said. "When you depart, Lapthorn will return to himself and be able to call you forth again. Remember, he still commands you by the Seal of Solomon, if he can but regain himself."

"True," Caspardutis said. "Your grasp of the matter is incisive, sir! Again I am beholden to you. What a fine mind was lost in Hell when you failed to join the Devil's forces. But I see a solution. Farewell!"

Lapthorn's body gave one convulsive shudder and lay still. When Amer bent over him, he could feel no heartbeat.

"I had not expected that," he said. "Elementals don't often kill, no matter what the provocation."

"Nor has he this time," Samona said. "Look!"

In the corner, the idiot Douglas was stirring. His hands fluttered in front of his face like frightened pigeons. His mouth twisted as though he would speak but could not. His eyes were strained open, and the expression in them was baleful.

"It is Lapthorn inside there!" Samona cried.

"Yes, it is," Amer said. "He has been well and truly served by the magic he practiced. Equal and opposite reactions! As he served others, so is he served. He made the idiot a vehicle for a spirit, and now he must live within the idiot. And he's powerless. Caspardutis has sealed the idiot's lips and he cannot speak."

"But what are we going to do with him?" Samona asked.

"What do you mean, *do*?"

"I'm referring to the idiot child. No matter who lives inside him, he must be fed and clothed and sheltered. Who is to do that?"

Amer considered the question soberly. "My dear, that is for the town council and the witches' coven to decide. We have done enough. The rest is up to them. Come, it is time we went home."

"Yes," Samona said. "I will make us some dinner. It has been a hungry night's work."

"We will eat and pack," Amer said, "and prepare Amy for a journey."

"Where are we going?"

"Did you not hear me say before? Home! To our place on the mountainside! We've had enough of civilization for a while."

Anno Domini 1694

THE SEEING STONE

by Jody Lynn Nye

Jacob Crafter thought there was no greater penalty for being nine years old than having to face complex sums. The master of the schoolhouse had given him pages of mathematical problems to do before morning, and he couldn't! He couldn't! He stared at the numbers on the slate, trying to extract some sense from them, but they just blurred into insensibility before his eyes. There was a passage of Latin to learn, too. Jacob went back and forth distractedly between the Latin book and the slate until he felt like crying.

"I cannot learn this, Father," Jacob complained to Amer. "It goes past me as quickly as the wind." He whipped up the pages of his book with an impatient hand.

"It is nothing you do not know," Amer Crafter said, regarding calmly the small boy who looked so much like him. He smoothed the pages, and set his finger down beside a phrase. "Now, read this out to me."

Following his father's fingertip, Jacob read the passage aloud, and translated the words a sentence at a time.

"There," smiled Amer, patting Jacob's head. "You did it."

"But I couldn't before," Jacob said. "Why not?"

"I've been watching you to determine that very fact," Amer said. "You are not concentrating, son. You skip from fact to fact like a bee visiting flowers. Behave more as an ant does, carefully stowing food away in his nest one grain at a time."

Jacob stared at the page of Latin and shook his head despairingly. "But my thoughts skip so, I can't keep hold of one for more than a breath."

"You need to learn how to focus." Amer felt in his pocket and drew forth a pair of stones. "Look here, son. See what I found in my explorations today." Weighing them carefully with an eye, he handed Jacob one of them.

"Where did this come from?" the boy asked, studying the rock closely. It was about half the size of his hand. Part of it twinkled in the afternoon light coming in through the window, and part of it didn't.

"From the river's bed," Amer replied, taking it from him and turning it over to show him its features. "I have been studying its patterns. See how it is banded with color?"

"It is a wonder of God's work, Father, to paint such fine lines," Jacob assured him.

Amer smiled. "But it was not made all at once into a small, rounded stone, son. Haven't you observed the layers of color in the land? They were set down so, over many years, through the changes of weather and season, until each line above represented a time later than the one below it."

"To be sure, it is a wonder," said Jacob. "This one is edged with quartz, and here's its brother, broken from the same geode."

"Well observed, son." Amer was struck suddenly with an idea. "Here, Jacob, take it. Let this stone aid you in your lessons. When you need to concentrate, stare at this part, where the bands of color focus into a small spot. Do not let your eyes wander, and hold as still as you can, and your mind will unfold."

"Magic," the child breathed. He wandered away to sit in the window seat to study the new treasure cupped in both hands.

Amer let that distraction continue for a little while, and then put Jacob back to work on his school assignments. His daughter Amy came in with her lute, to practice scales and chords in the window seat. Samona and his younger son, Ahijah, joined them. Amy had improved markedly over the year she had been taking music instruction. Amer thought again about the treatise he was working on, which tied mathematics to music. He wondered if there was a possible connection to the laws of magic through music. It certainly seemed to have effects on man and animal which were difficult to explain.

He noticed abruptly that Jacob's attention had wandered again. The boy was supposed to be concentrating on the slate on which his sums were written. Instead, he was staring off into space and humming along with his sister's playing.

"Jacob!" he commanded. "Use your stone!"

"Yes, Father." The boy stared into the spot for a long time, and then resumed his lessons.

Samona stared from her son to her husband with a look of outrage. "Surely you are not giving that child a thing of magic?" she demanded. She watched Jacob turn occasionally from the slate to the stone and back again.

"No, I'd never do that, my dear," Amer assured her quickly. "It's only a simple river stone, but it may help him in his lessons."

Samona sighed. "Well, it would be magic if it can do that. I never knew such a cloud-minded boy could be born," she said.

"He has notable intelligence," his father responded complacently, "but he thinks of so many things at once, he'll never grow fruit from any of the seeds. To take the metaphor to its logical conclusion, he must plant and nurture each in turn, not broadcast them for the crows to eat. His creativity must be mastered by him, not the other way around."

An increase in concentration did help the boy to understand his studies. Jacob's improvement in mathematics was noted by the austere Rock Harbor schoolmaster over the next week.

"Well, young Master Crafter, it would seem that I've not had to apply the cane to your fingers so often this day. Why is that?"

"Because I have learned my sums, sir?" Jacob asked tentatively, glancing up at the teacher. Master Poggins terrified him. Behind his back, several of the other children giggled.

The teacher looked down at Jacob with a vulpine eye, and decided the boy had not been attempting to be facetious. The position of a schoolmaster was a tentative one, and he dared not let the brats take the upper hand, or he should lose his place as one unable to keep control in the classroom. As a result, Master Poggins was as stern as the back of a ship. "You have learned *these* sums. We will see if your improvement continues." He flicked his gaze around at the other students, who swiftly busied themselves at their own lessons lest they be caned for staring and inattentiveness. "The class is dismissed for the day."

"Goshen, you were lucky," said Octavius Winterbourne, as he and Jacob ran down the meadow together. Octavius was Jacob's best friend almost since the two of them could first toddle. Octavius had a quick mind for schoolwork, and the schoolmaster was already encouraging Master Winterbourne to allow his son to attend a University when he came of age. Poggins was not at all subtle in his musings about why his star pupil and Jacob Crafter, the class dunce, should be such inseparable friends.

"Father helped me," Jacob admitted to Octavius. "I'm learning to concentrate. It's hard work."

"Work! Don't say *work*. I've still got my chores to do," Octavius groaned.

"I'll help you," Jacob offered, "and then you'll be done twice as fast. We can go off and play in the park until supper time."

Octavius accepted the suggestion with alacrity. The boys chopped wood and pulled weeds for Goody Winterbourne, until she dismissed them with an apple apiece for thanks. Jacob thought his mother, with her wonderful black eyes and mass of black hair, was slimmer and prettier than Octavius', but Goody Winterbourne was kind to him, and he didn't mind helping out with chores if it earned his best friend an hour more of play.

"Octavius! Don't be late home for supper, or I'll skin you!" she called after them. Shouting with laughter, he and Jacob continued running.

The boys flung themselves onto the roots of a favorite oak tree and crunched the apples while Jacob displayed his treasure.

"See the way the colors are banded into circular ripples all surrounding one spot? It helps me to think hard when I look into the spot," Jacob said. Octavius examined the stone closely.

"It isn't a thing . . . against God, is it?" he asked cautiously.

"No, it's as God made it," Jacob said, taking the rock back and tossing it up and down in his hand. "Father found it in the riverbed."

"Well, you know, you hear rumors," Octavius admitted. "They say your father does black magic, and communes with devils." He looked around hastily to see if anyone had heard him.

Jacob looked scornful. He'd learned long ago not to try explaining alchemy to outsiders, lest they fail to understand that it was pure science. Octavius understood about the Crafters, but he had sworn a mighty oath with Jacob never to talk to anyone about them.

"Communes with devils!" Jacob scoffed. "My father wouldn't speak to a devil if he saw it on the street."

"Well, anything that can keep you from being rapped over the knuckles by Master Poggins is probably magic of some kind," Octavius reasoned mischievously. He jumped up. "Look at the sun! I've got to go. See you tomorrow!" he called, waving as he ran.

"Supper is ready," Samona said, coming into the study where Jacob and Amer were reading. "Please come and sit down before it gets cold."

"Do you hear that, Jacob?" Amer said jovially, rising. "It smells delicious," he told his wife appreciatively. "Though I would have gone on perfectly well eating my own cooking, I couldn't go back to such a state now."

"Thank you for the compliment," Samona said, nodding prettily. "Jacob?"

The boy still sat with his head bent over the book. "He's concentrating," Amer said, with a trace of amusement in his voice. "From the will-o'-the-wisp who couldn't light for more than a moment in one place—"

"Ahem!" exclaimed Willow, from her beaker on Amer's desk.

"I do beg your pardon, Willow," Amer said apologetically, then continued, "—he's become as concentrated a student as you could ever wish for. I think I've created a monster. When I said I wanted him to study until supper, I thought he'd realize when it was ready. He's so far away, I don't think he even smells it."

"Please bring him back," Samona said, alarmed. "He can't stay that way."

"He won't," Amer assured her. A tap might distract the boy too much, causing him to lose his grip on whatever he was reading so intently. Instead, Amer used a moment of mind-talk to break through. *Jacob*, he projected to the boy's mind. *Hear me. Dinner is ready*.

Jacob's head came up like a spring, and he dropped his pen. "I cannot only hear, Father, but see!" he exclaimed. "I see you! As though you and Mother were standing in front of me." He spun around, wide-eyed. "Yes, that's exactly how you looked. The stone made me see you!"

Amer blinked down at him. "It would seem that through the mere act of concentration, Jacob has bypassed the need for a far-sight potion. He's inherited both of our talents, Samona. I must study this further."

"Is his soul in danger?" Samona demanded, kneeling and wrapping her arms protectively around her son. Amer shook his head.

"Not at all, not at all. What he's gained is a natural skill, which may be of great use in his lifetime. I'd say he's paid for this knowledge with many years of being chided for inattentiveness." He patted Jacob on the head. "It isn't the lesson I hoped you'd learn this day, but well done, my boy. Now, come and eat."

• • •

The next afternoon, Jacob finished with his schoolwork so quickly that he was through long before his sister Amy had even finished unpacking the books from her satchel. Snatching up his rock, he dashed out, ignoring his mother's cry from the kitchen to come and carry wood. She was baking, and if he stopped to help her, he'd be doing nothing else all day. Amy could carry wood, for a change.

Jacob wandered down the streets, occasionally looking deep into his stone's heart, and smiling. It was honey season, and the nectar which Father had extracted from the hives in the forest was draining into crocks in the storeroom. The family tradition was to use up all the last year's remaining store before the next year's was touched.

With the leftover honey, Mother was making a cake for Sunday. Jacob could see with his far-sight that she had had enough batter left over to make cakelets. As they came out of the oven, steam rose in a faint white cloud, so real in his mind he could almost smell it. He counted the patties as they came off the pan. There were ten, eleven, twelve! Enough for two each for the family, if you didn't count baby Margarethe, who was still suckling, and that left two over besides.

As he turned the corner into the street where Octavius lived, Jacob watched the image of his mother pile the small cakes on a platter. Well, she couldn't be leaving them out. There wouldn't be any left for him if Amy saw them first. No, Mother was putting the honey cakes away, but not in the big wooden breadbox. The wall opened up above the box, and the platter slid inside without leaving a trace. So that was the hiding place whence good things came. There had been a cake on his last birthday whose existence he hadn't so much as imagined until it appeared. Probably it had been kept in there. Well, now. Twelve honey cakes divided by five Crafters went twice, with two odd ones left over. Perhaps he should abstract those two and eat them later with Octavius. He grinned. It was a naughty plan, but so long as Mother still believed her secret was secure, he wouldn't be suspected when the loss was discovered.

"Honey cakes!" he breathed.

So intent was he on his spying that he never saw the foot that tripped him, nor the hands that shoved him to the street. He landed on his face, and the stone flew out of his hands.

Standing over him were five boys, all bigger than he was. At their head was Laban Thomas, the biggest bully in school. He was nearly of apprentice age, so he wouldn't be in Rock Harbor school much longer, but while he was there he ran things. Jacob picked himself up from the cobblestones and glared. Small as he was, he refused to knuckle under to bullies. His father wouldn't, and he would rather be damned and eaten by demons before *he* would.

"Yah, you don't look where you're going," Laban sneered. "I thought warlocks' children flew through the air. They don't crawl in the dust."

"My father's not a warlock," Jacob said, stoutly holding his ground, even though the five boys towered over him. "He's an alchemist and a good Christian."

"That's just another name for it," one of the other boys taunted him. "You're going to burn when you die." He shoved Jacob into one of the others. "You'll burn!"

"You'll burn!" echoed the next one. They kept on pushing him and chanting until Jacob ducked under their arms and ran away, with the echo of their voices in his ears. The stone lay forgotten on the cobbles behind him.

Laban laughed as Jacob hurtled down the street. "What a rabbit," he said, scornfully.

"Is his father really a warlock?" one of the boys asked.

"Well, they came from Salem. Practically everyone there was burned or hanged for witchcraft," Laban said vaguely. "Stands to reason they're witches, too."

The other boy stooped to pick up the stone Jacob had dropped, and turned it speculatively in his hand. "He was smiling down at this rock when he came up the street. Doesn't look like there's anything special about it."

"Nah," Laban agreed. "He said 'honey cakes' to it. Was he asking a devil to turn it into honey cakes for him? Or summoning honey cakes with it?"

Laban took the stone to his father, who was the church sexton. "It's a witching thing," the boy said. "Jacob Crafter was talking to it. It's an evil amulet! The Crafters are magicians!"

John Thomas took the stone from his son and studied it. It had been a difficult thing, raising the boy by himself since his mother had died, and not another female relative alive to take the boy in charge. "I feel no taint of hellfire over this thing. If it's evil, it is a subtle spell. How did you obtain it?" He eyed his son suspiciously.

Laban felt it was better to equivocate. "From Jacob Crafter."

"And did he give it you? Did he?" Thomas, a big man strong enough to turn a shovel in the graveyard even in the depths of winter, loomed over his son.

The boy shrank away from him. "No, sir."

Thomas grabbed one of Laban's shoulders and shook him. "Then you have stolen it. Evil must not be compounded by evil, on your soul be it. If there's anything to it. I will go and talk to Goodman Crafter tonight."

"We'll have something to go with the apples today," Jacob promised, as the boys left the Winterbourne house. "My mother made honey cakes."

Octavius' eyes lit up. "And she'll give us some?"

"Well," Jacob said, with a grain of truth, "she didn't say I may not have any."

He left Octavius sitting on the roots of the oak tree, and ran back to the house. Samona was behind the cottage with Jacob's older sister, Amy, hanging up clothes. He crept inside, and went to the place near the stove where he'd seen Samona hiding the small cakes. It was a nearly invisible square in the wallpaper, just above the place where Father had installed a breadbox to keep the daily baking fresh. It was a good hiding place, for the wall was only a hand-span thick. No one would think to seek anything there.

"Open," he bid the square, as he had seen his mother do, in the stone. The panel opened to reveal a deep cabinet fitted with two shelves. Jacob recognized the style of storage his father made to contain some of his more delicate and dangerous philosophical apparatus. The inside of the chamber was in a different dimension from the room where the door to it lay. Jacob guessed that the magical link led to one of the sealed wooden boxes that lined the cellar. He took two of the sticky cakes from the plate on the top shelf, carefully rearranging the rest so it looked like none were missing. With his treasures in hand, he ran out to rejoin Octavius in the woods. His mouth was already watering.

Master Thomas came to the house after dinner that night. He seemed uneasy when he greeted Amer, looking surreptitiously at his hand after Amer had grasped it. Samona seated the two men cosily near the fire. Amy, Jacob, and Ahijah sat on the floor not far away. Jacob glanced up once from their game, and recognized Goodman Thomas, but didn't seem interested in their conversation.

"I have a serious matter to discuss with you, Crafter," he said at once.

Amer steeled himself. It had been some time since he had faced an accusation of witchcraft, but he recognized the solemn expression on Thomas' face as one his Salem neighbors wore when delivering tidings of that sort. "And what is that, Goodman Thomas?"

Thomas himself was not that comfortable voicing an accusation of such magnitude. "You're a good churchgoer and I've always thought you a God-fearing man, Crafter. My boy brought me a tale today, said your son was talking to this here stone." Thomas produced a bundle of kerchiefs from deep in his pocket. He undid several layers of cloth, finally exposing the small rock. "Laban said your boy was talking to it, like it was a very soul. Now, what I want to know is, does this have anything to do with black magic?"

"Do you mean, did my son expect the stone to answer him back?" Amer asked, smiling at Goodman Thomas. It was clear the sexton didn't want his fears confirmed, and in this case it was easy to dispel them. "Not at all. The stone is only a stone. A pretty one, wouldn't you say? If your son has taken a fancy to it, he may have it if my son says he may." He drew Jacob near, and asked his leave.

"Of course, Father," the boy said, only a little reluctantly, looking at the stone in the other man's hand.

Thomas shook his head. "Nay, if it is a thing of magic, I want it not." He turned up the bundle of kerchiefs and deposited its contents in Jacob's hands.

"It is but a stone, I assure you," Amer said. "Well, if he doesn't want it, and Jacob's given up his claim, we will throw it away. Surely I would never do that with an item of enchantment, would I?"

"You imperil your soul. It isn't funny," Thomas said, with real distress. "There are those who wouldn't question a boy twice to learn the truth. Do not talk of such things!"

"Then let us talk of more pleasant things, Goodman," Samona said, entering with a platter on which were piled small, fragrant cakes. As soon as the treat appeared, Jacob's big sister and small brother clamored for some. "May I offer you something from today's bake?" Samona said cordially to Thomas. The neighbor didn't need very much persuading.

"Ah," he said, relieved to have the uncomfortable subject shelved. "Thank you very much, Goody Crafter. You have a true skill for baking." He took the topmost cake, which Jacob remembered longingly was the largest one left.

"Take two," Samona urged the neighbor, clearly much pleased. "They're small."

With ill-disguised eagerness, Goodman Thomas took another cake, and accepted a glass of Amer's homemade cowslip wine. Amer took two cakes from the proffered plate and poured himself some wine as well. He stirred up the fire so it danced brightly.

"Boys can be cruel to one another," Thomas admitted, and took a bite of cake. "Laban'll be by to apologize to Jacob in the morning, or I'll know why. These are the best I've ever tasted, Goody Crafter."

"Thank you, sir," Samona said, and then turned indulgently to her clamoring children. "Peep, peep, peep! You all might be a nestful of little birds." She passed the plate to her three children. Each child greedily snatched two cakes apiece. Jacob noticed how Samona regarded the platter as it was returned to her empty. She looked first disappointed, and then upset. She appeared to do some mental calculation. Jacob quickly ducked his head and swallowed the last mouthful of honey-flavored crumbs, which suddenly tasted dry and sandy. During the rest of Goodman Thomas' visit, he tried guiltily to appear inconspicuous.

He mustn't have been doing a good job, for as soon as the neighbor left, both parents appeared before him and escorted him across the hall and into Amer's study. Amy eyed them curiously as the door swung shut.

His father boosted him up on the laboratory table and met him eye to eye. Jacob was very uncomfortable, between the glare and the cold seat, but he didn't squirm.

"Jacob, did you know something about the dessert your mother just served?" Amer asked in a mild voice. Jacob recognized his father at his most dangerous.

"I knew she was baking today," Jacob admitted, very cautiously. His parents exchanged glances, and he knew he was in deep trouble.

"That's a most evasive answer," Amer said, his brows lowered together. "Did you take any cakes before they were served to you just now?"

Jacob could barely force his voice past his teeth. "Yes, sir," he mumbled.

Samona let out a wordless exclamation. "But how did you know where they were? I hid them as soon as they were cooled."

"I saw you in the stone," Jacob blurted out. "I was watching you when I went down to see Octavius."

"Ah," said Amer, his face expressionless. "I think I see. Jacob, do you remember my teaching you the laws that govern Nature as well as magic?"

Puzzled, the boy replied, "I believe I do, Father. There is the Law of Contagion, in which a thing which touches another thing continues to react upon it from a distance."

Amer nodded. "How about the Law of Equivalence? For every action, there is an equal reaction?"

Jacob felt his cheeks go red. "Yes, sir," he replied in a very small voice. Amer took his arm and nodded pleasantly to Mother.

"Excuse me, Samona. An equal and opposite reaction awaits a cake-snatcher." The two of them marched down the steps and outside, the boy with his head hanging, toward the woodshed.

"It isn't so much your act of stealing the cakes I mind," Amer said as the two of them walked in the woods after Jacob had suffered his switching. "It's the betrayal of trust. Your mother trusted you not to get into things she had put aside for the pleasure of all of us. Or to pry into a secret she was keeping. There is a heavy responsibility in the use of magic, which you have to learn. We do not sell our souls through a contract with the Devil, nor abuse the talents we have been given. You do not deserve your skills if you don't use them wisely."

"I am sorry, Father," Jacob said remorsefully. "I'll never do it again. Shall I help her to make new cakes?"

"I think she would appreciate the offer, after you apologize. Because of your greed, she was unable to enjoy the cakes with us."

"I won't eat any on Sunday, sir," Jacob promised. "Mother shall have all of my share."

"That will be punishment enough," Amer acknowledged. "Well, I've given my word to throw away your study stone. You need a new one. Would you like its twin?"

Jacob considered it. "No, sir. I'd rather not remember it, because a bully took it away from me. I'd recall that instead of my lessons."

"Very wise," Amer said approvingly.

In the dwindling twilight, they browsed through stones tumbled by the side of the river. Jacob chose a new one that was plainer than the first, but it had a depression worn in it by the pebbles of the stream. "I don't need to see the indentation, Father," he explained. "I can feel it with my thumb and know where it is. That way I can have the stone in school with me, and Master Poggins will not worry me about it."

*   *   *

"Octavius and I have been playing a game with my study stone," Jacob announced to his mother a few days later. "When I touch it, I can tell if he's thinking of me or not."

Samona was unsure whether it was a good idea for anyone else to know about their magic, but it was also bad for the children to grow up never trusting another soul. She reasoned that if anyone could be trusted with their secret, it might as well be Jacob's best friend. "And is he now?"

Jacob reached for the study stone, which he now kept hidden in his pocket. "Yes," he said, brightening. "He wishes to play with me. He's thinking of the oak tree."

"Finish your chores, and then you may go play," Samona told him.

Now that a link had been established, the boys made the best use of it. But no matter how they tried, the link only worked one way, from Octavius to Jacob.

"I don't understand it," Octavius admitted. "I concentrate and stare at the stone until I think my eyes are going to pop out, and I still can't hear you. It must be something special to your family."

"Must be," Jacob said, but added loyally, " 'cause if it had to do with being smart, you'd be able to do it better than me."

The system followed their natural inclinations anyway. Jacob was more content to follow his friend's lead. He learned to distinguish when the faint mind-voice wanted him to come to the woods or to the Winterbourne house. Gradually, in an admirable scientific manner, the two boys maximized the extent of the skill. Octavius' summons seemed to work best when coupled with some strong emotion, like excitement. When he was very happy, it was easy for Jacob to know that his friend was trying to attract his attention.

"May I go out with Jacob this morning?" Octavius asked his mother, on a fine day when there were to be no lessons.

"Heavens, no, it's market day," his mother exclaimed, tying on her bonnet and collecting her basket. "I need you to watch the supper."

Octavius accompanied her to the door and opened it for her. "May I go when you come back?"

"Yes, of course. But don't let the supper burn, or I'll skin you alive!" she said, emphatically. "Read your lessons, or the Bible, and keep an eye on that joint!"

Goody Winterbourne let herself out at the gate, and turned into the lane. Octavius waved farewell, and went inside.

Laban Thomas and his cronies were waiting in the nearby lane for Octavius to come out of the house. Laban had suffered a tremendous beating at his father's hands for stealing the Crafter boy's stone and trying to get him in trouble with the elders.

"I'll get even with him," he said through his teeth.

"Then why are we waiting for Winterbourne?" one of the bully boys asked. "Why don't we go up and throw Crafter into the river?"

"No!" Laban said, turning white. "They're witchfolk. They'll curse you if you lay a hand on them. We can make Crafter sorry by making trouble for his best friend. Come on, the goody's gone." He made a vicious grin. "She left him alone to mind the cooking. Look." He held up a bucket of wet straw. "We'll stuff the chimney full of this, and give him a face full of smoke."

"We'll get in trouble if anyone sees us."

"No one will see," Laban sneered. "We'll go back and pull it out later. That way, no one will know what happened. I just want him to get a faceful of smoke."

Octavius sat beside the fire, keeping one eye on the meat, and the other on the book he was reading. It was nice and warm inside, but he would rather have been out in the crisp fall air with Jacob. The warm, fragrant fire made him feel comfortably drowsy, and soon the book slipped out of his grasp. He never noticed when the bushed of wet grass slid down the chimney and dropped the well-larded roast into the fire.

Smoke filled the room as the fire hissed its protest. An ember jumped away from the coals and landed on the rag rug in front of Octavius' chair. Flames began to lick away at the tight braids. Octavius forced his eyes open. Immediately, they watered as the smoke flooded the sensitive tissues. He scrambled up from the chair, and kicked at the burning rug. It was burning too fast. Waving the smoke out of his face, he tried to find his way to the door, or the window, or whatever way out. His eyes were burning.

Octavius took in a lungful of air to call for help, but the full force of the wet smoke choked off his breath. He sagged to the floor. He woke up to cough and cry out again, then fell, overcome by the smoke. He was only a short way from the kitchen door.

Jacob sat dejectedly reading Shakespeare's sonnets in the parlor, waiting for Octavius to signal him to meet. Samona had gone off to the market. The children had assumed that since it was market day, they might have a day away from lessons, but Amer, left in charge, had declared that it was a good time for extracurricular education. Hopefully, Jacob had thought it might be lessons in magic. Instead, it was moldy old poetry. He and Amy shared the huge book between them.

He was finding it hard to keep his mind on the fourteen-line stanzas, and had to apply his hand frequently to the smooth stone, now on the window seat beside him.

" 'Shall I compare thee to a summer's day?' " Amy read, and sighed deeply. "That's so romantic."

Utterly bored, Jacob reached for the study stone, and put his thumb in the depression. Suddenly, he had the strongest intuition that Octavius needed him. The emotion was strong, all right, but that emotion was fear! Alarmed, Jacob sprang off the window seat, dumping the book onto Amy's lap. He snatched up the stone, and hurried out.

"What are you doing?" Amy demanded. "Father!"

Jacob left the room at a run without saying a word. Amy, aggrieved, put the book down and ran to Amer's laboratory.

"Father, the stone has ceased to work," Amy complained. "He just ran off. He paid no attention to me at all."

Amer was grateful that his experiment was one in stable compounds, and not volatile chemicals. He put it aside at once and stripped off his lab smock. "I'll find him, Amy. You go back and read."

Amer set out in pursuit of Jacob, guided by the touch of his son's mind. By the feel of his thoughts, the boy was agitated. He wondered what was wrong.

As Jacob ran through the town, the feeling that worried him was growing stronger, but he could no longer feel Octavius' mind-voice. He clutched the stone, and rubbed his thumb furiously in the small depression. A distant feeling tickled at the inside of his nostrils, hot and close, though the air was crisp and clean. Fire!

"Fire!" Jacob cried as he ran toward the Winterbourne house. As he got closer, he could see that there *was* smoke coming from under the door and out an upper window. "Help! Fire!"

The entire neighborhood of houses were wooden-framed. The cry was not one to be ignored. "Fire!" was echoed up and down the street. Anyone who could carry a bucket or broom rushed toward the Winterbourne house.

"It's just a cooking fire," Laban Thomas shouted over the crowd.

"It's not!" Jacob protested. "The house is on fire!"

Men and boys started filling buckets from the pump at the end of the street as two big men forced open the Winterbourne's front door. Smoke poured out, followed by the tongues of flames as the fire, suddenly freshened by more oxygen, burst into new life.

"Hurry up with those buckets there!" one of the men called to those at the pump.

Drenching themselves with water, the men started dousing the walls and the floor inside, anything that had not yet caught fire.

"It's in the cooking area, all right," one of the men shouted from inside.

"Octavius is in there!" Jacob called, pushing forward. "Get him out, please!"

The man looked back at him pityingly, and shoved him back. "It's a sheet of flame, lad. Stay back!"

They didn't believe him. Jacob, panicked to think that his friend might burn to death before anyone found him, raced around the back of the house, and threw open the kitchen door. The fireplace and everything in front of it was ablaze with a smell like burning flesh, and Goody Winterbourne's favorite chair was flaming like a torch. Some of the floorboards had taken fire, but others were smoking under a layer of a thick, dark mass.

Jacob had to find Octavius. The feel of the stone guided him through the thick smoke to where his friend lay on the floor. He could hear yelling and splashing coming from the front of the house, where the volunteer fire brigade had formed its bucket chain. Jacob called to them, but the roar of the fire overpowered his voice.

It was hard to see, but it looked as if a tall man in a cloak had gained entrance to the kitchen, and was bending over a small heap on the floor. It must have been a trick of the light, because when Jacob raced up no one was standing there, although the heap on the ground was Octavius. Coughing, he knelt beside his friend and tried to wake him up. The boy only stirred and muttered.

With a heave, Jacob picked up his friend and started to carry him back toward the door. As Jacob looked back into the smoke, he got a brief, almost illusionary, glimpse of a skull with glowing eyes, nodding approvingly at him in the same way Amer did when he did something well. Not stopping to think further about it, he bustled Octavius out into the air and dumped him on the grass.

Members of the fire brigade clustered around the two soot-smudged boys. Jacob was praised for his heroism, but he ignored everyone's attempts to pull him away until Octavius opened his eyes.

"You heard me," he whispered, and Jacob nodded.

"Now, don't speak," Amer said, rushing up to the boys and kneeling down beside them. "Just breathe in and out until your lungs are clear. That's good," he said, nodding, as Octavius drew in long breaths of air.

"Will the house burn down?" Jacob asked fearfully, looking up at Octavius' house.

Amer shook his head. "I don't think so. They've nearly got it under control. You alerted them in time to prevent severe damage."

Jacob let out a heartfelt sigh of relief. Goody Winterbourne, riding pillion behind a neighbor, began shrieking when she saw the smoke pouring out of her doors and windows. Amer met her at the gate and led her to where her son was resting in the care of neighbor goodwives. He assured her that the fire was out, and that the damage was minor. All the other neighbors immediately began to help clean up the damage and clear away traces of the fire.

Laban Thomas tried to sneak away in the confusion, but his fellows, alarmed by the tragedy they had precipitated, confessed, and named him as a conspirator. As soon as their attention was not entirely centered on the Winterbourne house, men-at-arms took the four boys into custody.

"Restitution to the Winterbournes will have to start with replacement of their dinner," Sexton Thomas informed his son as the boy was marched away.

"Your sister was concerned when you ran away, my lad," Amer admonished Jacob as they walked home later.

"I am sorry, Father, but I had to go," Jacob explained. "I did not mean to leave my books, but the compulsion was so strong. I could not concentrate on my studies when I felt there was something ill befalling my friend."

"I am not taking you to task," Amer assured him, wiping a smoke smudge off the boy's nose with a pocket cloth. "All is well as far as I am concerned, my young son. I think for once you may be praised for a lesson very well learned indeed."

Anno Domini 1712

EDUCATION
by Anna O'Connell
and Doug Houseman

Margarethe sat on the floor and watched her father grind things into powder.

"Daddy, why are you doing that?" she asked.

"Because it needs to be done," he answered.

"Daddy, why does it need to be done?" she inquired further.

"I need it to do my work," he grumped.

"Daddy, why do you need it to do your work?" she asked.

"Margarethe, go ask your mother."

"Why, Daddy?"

"Because I told you to."

"Why are you telling me to?"

"Just go, no more questions."

"But Daddy, why?"

"GO!"

Margarethe toddled away slowly, glancing at her father every now and again over her shoulder. She had just learned to walk without a wall to hold on to.

"She'll be the end of me yet with all those questions."

Willow appeared and answered him. "There is a good college near Boston. Perhaps she should go, once she's old enough." At Amer's insistence the being had improved her language skills for the children's sake.

"She is a girl, and girls don't go to college."

"This one needs to. Besides, after sixteen more years of this, you'll need the rest."

"Willow, you may be right."

"Margarethe is listening through the walls again," Willow reported.

"Well, we can't have that. She isn't old enough to understand."

"She is a very smart little girl, though," Willow replied.

"Yes, but at six you can wager she does not know when to be quiet. She could tell the whole village about what I am doing. Or worse, try some of it herself."

"So when are you going to teach her?" Willow asked.

"When she is old enough."

"And when will that be?"

"When she can be trusted not to talk outside the family about the craft."

"Have you ever known Margarethe to tell anyone anything? All she ever does is ask questions. With her it's always 'How?' or 'Why?' or 'Who said so?'"

"You have a point, Willow. But she's still too young."

"But . . ."

"No *but*'s, no *and*'s, and no *if*'s, it's final."

"Tomorrow is my wedding day, Cynthia," Margarethe scolded, "I have so much to do."

"But Margi, I want to hear about the city," Cynthia wailed.

"All right, Cynthie, but I am going to only list the main points. I have work to do. My dress needs another fitting, and the food needs to be checked and . . . oh, there is simply too much to do!"

The six-year-old buried her face in the pillow and wailed, "Please, Margi, please tell me about the city."

"Oh, all right. But you must help me with the rest of the preparations."

"I will. I promise," Cynthia replied.

• • •

A little more than three years ago, Father took me into Cambridge to find a job where I could get more learning. We stayed at a rooming house while we searched for a position that would let me be near Harvard while earning my keep. Father heard about a Dr. MacLean of the Arts Department, specializing in mathematics. The Professor had lost his wife in childbirth and was looking for a nanny. So Father went around to Harvard and was able to get an appointment to see the Professor. Father talked to Professor MacLean and what they said, I will never know. Father refused to tell me any of the details. The only thing he said was that I was not to let Professor MacLean know that I could read or write.

Now, I was proud of my ability to read and write, and I had thought that Father was, too. I was very angry that he wanted me to keep it a secret from a prospective employer. Two days later Father took me to meet the Professor. I was immediately introduced to the children, and then told to await the Professor's convenience in the parlor. It was then that I realized that I had already been hired. Father had made all of the arrangements for the job, and I would have no say in the matter at all. Father tipped his hat and left, with a kiss on my hand as his only parting comment. As Father left, I noticed a smile on his face unlike any I had ever seen before. I still do not understand why he smiled like that.

The Professor summoned me to his study, and proceeded to let me know what my job was to be.

"You have met Sean and Katherine," he began pompously. "It will be your job to look after them. You are responsible for dressing them properly and teaching them manners. You are not to let anyone read to Katherine, nor are you to let anyone teach her her letters," he continued without pause.

"Yes, sir," I replied.

"By Cromwell, you will not let that child learn to read or write or argue with a man! She will learn to be a proper woman, unlike her mother. She will cook and sew and have children.

"You are not to take tea with the other servants or the faculty wives," he continued without acknowledging me.

"You will assist the housekeeper during the children's naps. You will have them dressed and ready to greet guests on Saturday and Sunday afternoons. You will bring them on my command and display them for the guests."

"Yes, sir."

"You will keep the children out of the parlor, my office, and the library. Their clothes and toys will be kept in their rooms, and those rooms are to be kept tidy. The children will take exercise on the green only under your supervision. I hold you responsible for their effect on my reputation. Do you understand?" He didn't wait for an answer. "You will keep them out of the sight of my students, and any other adult that enters this house, except when I call for them. When I do call for them I want them brought immediately.

"Starting Monday week, you are responsible for seeing that Sean is in his seat at the dame's school each morning, and you are to accompany him home each afternoon."

He droned on. "Sean is a trifle headstrong, and has not been watched over for the past three months. You may stay at the school for short periods of time when you take him to school. But you must not have Katherine in the school building during class time. I dismissed the last nanny for arguing with me about Katherine's future. Women have only one proper future, marriage."

His lecture continued.

"Your room is at the top of the stairs to the left, third door. Dismissed." He turned away and started to fill his pipe.

"Yes, sir," I muttered, dropping a curtsey. But he had already forgotten that I existed.

Throughout that entire, amazing speech, I had grown angrier and angrier. How could anyone leave two children with a man like this? Sean was almost five. He looked innocent as a cherub and had run totally wild for the three months since the last nanny had been dismissed. Kate was a two-year-old with flaming red hair and a temper to match. She simply did not know the meaning of "no." How could Father have thrown me into such a situation with no warning? I stormed out of the room the instant the Professor dismissed me. I was so angry that I took a wrong turning at the top of the stairs and ran right into a strange room.

But what a room! All the walls were lined with books. There were more than a hundred. I stopped and counted, and as I counted, I calmed down. Father had promised me an opportunity for learning. There were three hundred and seventeen books in that room. Most seemed to be in English. Some were in Latin and some were in languages that I didn't recognize. I was exalted and furious at the same time. Stunned at the learning contained in a single chamber, I found my way to my room, to think. I sat for a long time. Finally, I opened my bag, and there was a letter written in Father's hand.

> *My Dearest Margarethe,*
> *I know you are angry with me right now. This is the best I could do. You will get a pound a month and your room and board. Willow and I had a long talk about this and decided you would learn to love it. The good doctor demanded a girl who was ignorant. His wife had too much education to suit him and an Irish temper as well. Your days should be mostly your own, as the children are too young for school and the Professor stays in his office at the College all day long. He hates his children, but knows he needs to appear to be a good father to keep his standing in the community. The Professor holds lectures in his library three nights each week. The library adjoins your room, and I know you are good at listening through walls. Please be good to him and enjoy the library. Take care of the children, and the Professor will take care of you.*
> *Your Loving Father,*
> *Amer*

Cold fury ran through my veins. I didn't know what to think, what to do. How could Father leave me to deal with a man who hated his children, listening to lectures on mathematics all night? And a spoiled two-year-old to deal with. I remembered what you were like at two,

Cynthie. How could he? Then I took another look at the letter. In spidery silver letters, I saw:

> *Margarethe,*
> *Your father loves you and this is truly the best he could do. You will learn more than you think possible from living in this house. It will work out for the best. Trust us.*

I have no idea how it got there. I would swear the second note wasn't there when I had first read the letter. In fact, I could swear the letter had not been in my bag when I closed it to leave the rooming house.

Cynthie, I can't tell you what I felt then. I sat in a daze for a while until I heard Kate crying. She wailed as you used to do when you were little. It seemed to go on forever. Finally I knew I had to do something. I went down the hall to her room, only to find her sitting on the floor with a cut finger. All that noise for a little cut on her finger! I wanted to grab her and shake her, but I didn't. Instead, I picked her up and held her. She cried more softly for a couple of minutes, then fell asleep in my arms. Her finger was no longer bleeding, so I took her to her bed and laid her down. That poor child needed me.

I felt so trapped. Children who needed me, a father who seemed to have abandoned me, and an employer who did not want his own children, except insofar as they would enhance his status. The lectures would be primarily a nuisance. The library, if I could find a way to use it without betraying myself, would be my only salvation. By the time I fell asleep I was terribly confused.

Morning came early. Kate woke crying. Little did I know that crying was the only way she knew to communicate with the rest of the world. The Professor shouted at her to be quiet. I rose and pulled on my robe. I went down the hall and lifted Kate from the bed to my shoulder. Poor child, no one had loved her since she was born. It was then I knew that I had to stay, if only for Kate.

I carried her down the back stairs to the kitchen and started to find her some bread and butter to keep her quiet while I got her dressed. Just then, Mistress Brown, the housekeeper, came in from her own house down the street.

"And just who do you think you are, missy, prancing in here with that brat and messing up my clean kitchen? Do you think I have nothing better to do than clean up after the children and you as well? There will be porridge for the brats once I've attended to the Professor's breakfast. Now get out, before I take the broom to you."

Astonished, I stood there open-mouthed, staring at her. Was I to have this same disastrous effect on everyone I met in Cambridge? After a few seconds, Kate's sniffles reminded me of what I had come for.

"I've come for a piece of bread for Miss Kate. She's hungry now, and too little to understand that she has to wait for her porridge. There will be nothing to clean up after, if you will excuse me." I seized the heel of the loaf, and retreated with Kate back up the stairs. Once she had gulped a few mouthfuls of bread, she quieted enough that I could dress her for the day. Then, I went to call Sean. As he was being very quiet, I had hoped he was still sleeping.

He was not. And every piece of clothing he possessed was on the floor. I told him to dress, and he gave me a blank stare. I started picking up clothes and proceeded to stuff him into them. I didn't do a very good job that first day. I had him in proper trousers and a shirt, but the socks were mismatched, and he had a house slipper on the left foot and a shoe on the right. It took me more than twenty minutes to dress him and get back to Kate. By that time, Kate, too, had managed to strew her nightclothes and quilts all over the room. I soon learned that I had to keep both children under my watchful eye every moment they were awake.

Two very frustrating hours later, both rooms were in some sort of order, and I took the children down to the kitchen for breakfast. They were both terribly hungry and a bit unruly after the unaccustomed discipline of "make your bed before breakfast." Kate was snuffling continually. Sean just kicked at everything, including my leg. I was black and blue for weeks.

Breakfast was another exercise in patience. More oatmeal ended up on the floor than inside the children. It seems that Sean ate his oatmeal with molasses. Kate, on the other hand, would not touch molasses. She had to have butter on hers. But no bowls were broken, and we all eventually had something to eat.

It was a sunny day, so I took the children into the yard to play. I kept them there until lunch time, then took them back to the yard. I told stories to Kate, and Sean ran around picking up sticks and throwing them at things, dogs, and people. He hit a woman as she walked by, and I knew I was going to have to punish him. I hoped I would handle this correctly. The Professor would be furious if I was either too strict or too lax.

"You must not throw sticks or stones at people!" I scolded, as I gave him three good swats on the bottom with my hand. He sank to the ground and wept. He cried and cried. It seemed, as the moments wore on that he was crying harder and harder. I began to be afraid that I had hurt him, though I certainly didn't think I had spanked him that hard. When I knelt down beside him and touched his shoulder, he flung himself against me and held on as if for dear life. He kept crying and whispering, "Mama, Mama come home."

I hugged him hard, and smoothed his hair. He cried some more, eventually seeming to grow calmer, although the tears still ran down his face. I settled back on my heels, rocking and soothing Sean as best I knew. After a few moments, Kate, also crying, crawled over to us and into my lap.

The Professor came home for supper, and found us that way. Sean was asleep against my arm and Kate in my lap. The Professor let out an oath.

"What in the name of Cromwell the Protector are you doing?"

In my concern to comfort the children, I had somehow failed to notice that the patch of ground we rested on was more mud than grass. We were a mess. There was nothing I could say that wouldn't make matters worse, so I bit back my explanations. I woke Sean, lifted Kate, and proceeded to the house with all the dignity I could muster. I knew that supper with the Professor would be awkward because of the state he had found us in. I hoped that neither child had a cold. The housekeeper snickered nastily as we went past her and up the back stairs. Within the hour, I had the children fed, clean, and in bed and myself in a state more suitable for meeting my doom.

The Professor was chewing on his fingernail when I knocked on the door to his study. He bade me enter. On his slate was a number problem, such as Father does. I knew how to work the problem, and could see that the Professor had made a mistake early on. I did not have a chance to construct a discreet way of telling him about the minor error before he launched into a tirade.

"How could you be so stupid, girl, as to take the children out rolling in the mud at your very first opportunity? What did you think you were doing? Heaven knows, practically everyone in town must have seen you out there, wallowing like pigs! But of course, you didn't think, did you? You're a woman, and women can't think."

He went on and on in a similar vein, calling me names and asking questions which he gave me no opportunity to answer. I fear it could have been much worse. Awakened by her father's shouting, Kate started to cry. I knew exactly how she felt, but was determined not to break down in front of this cold, cruel man.

"Excuse me, sir. Your daughter is crying." I turned and vanished up the stairs before he could deny my permission to leave. Kate soon quieted, and I crept silently into my room.

That night, I was an uninvited guest at my first lecture on modern mathematics. The Professor put long and strange names on things that Father had already taught me. It would take some time to learn the vocabulary, since I couldn't see the figures the Professor drew to illustrate his lecture. Kate interfered with the lecture a total of three times, and Sean once. At this rate, it would take me years to learn about mathematics, let alone the rest of the arts. Obviously, I would have to find a few books on the subject and study, or I would never catch up with the students.

Later that night, I sneaked into the Professor's library and borrowed my first book. It was a text by that Sir Isaac Newton whom I had heard Father mention. I also fixed the error in the Professor's problem so that he would be able to finish it. Since it was a mistake in sign, I didn't think he would catch me at it. I vowed to learn to imitate his writing, so that I could make changes in future problems. It wouldn't be so bad, playing dumb, if I could correct the Professor's mistakes without his ever noticing he had made them!

The remainder of the week went by in much quieter, but equally frustrating, fashion. The children and I developed a routine, the housekeeper and I negotiated an uneasy truce, and we all tried to stay out of the Professor's way. I would read for at least three hours every night once I was sure the Professor was asleep.

Saturday came, and I was again invited into the Professor's study. He asked if I had seen one of his students depart with a book while he was at his office. I replied that I had not. He then wanted to know if I had seen the housekeeper with one of his books. I again replied that I had not and held my breath. I expected him to ask next if *I* had taken a book. To my intense relief and frustration, he then commented, "I know you couldn't have taken that book. You're too stupid to even understand what it's for." Oh, I was so angry! Next time I would introduce sign errors in his problems, rather than fix them!

The incident taught me something about Professor Mac-Lean's routine. It seems that he counted all the books most Friday evenings, after the lecture was over. He would then select a book to keep at his bedside during the coming week. It was his custom to read for an hour or two each evening before falling asleep. In the future, I learned to return whatever book I was reading to its place on the shelf on Friday during the Professor's absence, and borrow it again on Saturday when I helped the housekeeper dust the library. One Saturday, when I reached for the volume I had been reading, it wasn't there. I suffered agonies for several hours until I was able to sneak into the Professor's bedroom and found it on his table.

The first day that Sean went to the dame's school was hilarious. That morning he first refused to rise, so I dragged him out of the bed by his feet. He started to cry and flail at me. I dropped him the several inches to the cold floor and reminded him that it was his first day of school. He jumped up, forgetting his indignation, and proceeded to dig clothes from his trunk and scatter them around the room faster than crows scatter from a gunshot. He found his favorite shirt, one that I had darned for him the week before, and hurriedly pulled it on.

"Let's go. I'm ready for school," he announced in a rush.

"Trousers, Sean?" I asked.

"What about my trousers?"

"You are not wearing any."

He frowned, then started to laugh. He ran to me and hugged me, then backed away with a red face. Still laughing, he announced, "Yes, I'll need trousers. Thank you, Ma'am, for reminding me."

The rest of the dressing and breakfasting routine was hurried, as Sean wanted to get to school and Kate did not want to be dressed. She kept pulling her dress off. Finally I slapped her hand in frustration. She cried and reached for Sean.

"Katie," he told her, "you'll have to look to Ma'am now. She is your keeper now, not me. I'm a big boy now." She cried harder and tried to crawl into Sean's lap, getting oatmeal on his shirt.

"Kate! Look what you have done. You dirtied my best shirt. Now I'll have to wear my Sunday shirt to school."

Kate cried harder and crawled into my lap, leaving a trail of oatmeal up my dress. I sent Sean up to get his Sunday shirt on, and took Kate like a sack of grain under my arm and went straight for my room. I would have to wash her and change my dress before I could take Sean to school.

When we were finally all dressed, we left for the school. Sean kept running ahead, and I kept reminding him that gentlemen did not abandon their duties as escorts to the ladies of the household. He would return to walk with us, but a few minutes later he was off again. The fifteen-minute walk to school seemed to take an hour. I sat in the hallway with Kate for the first half-hour. Once I was sure Sean was settled and would do as the schoolmistress instructed, I took Kate to the green.

"Where Sean?" Kate asked for the tenth time.

"He is in school, Kate. He will be home tonight," I replied again.

"Why school?" she asked.

"Your father ordered it," I replied, feeling fustrated.

"When Sean?" she asked.

"When school is over today. Go play, Kate," I ordered.

"Sean, Sean, Seeaann!" She wailed and began to cry again. I hugged her to me and let her cry. It had been this way all day.

When school was over for the day and Sean met us on the green, Kate had a smile for her beloved big brother that was brighter than the sun.

Sean adjusted to the school quickly, and did well at his lessons. He even shared them with Kate and me. He knew that his father did not want Kate to have even the rudimentary education that was common for girls from well-to-do families, but Sean loved his sister and wanted her to share in everything that he did. In fact, both of the fights he got into that year were over his being a "woman's man," which he was called because he spent so much time with his sister and very little time with the other boys. Both times he was wearing his Sunday best. Both times, the garments were utterly destroyed. Not even my augmented mending skills could salvage those clothes. Each incident brought a predictable tirade from his father.

In the second fall of my stay with the Professor, we lost our housekeeper to marriage. This meant a disruption in the routine of the house. The Professor took his time about finding a new housekeeper. I had to watch Kate all day, see Sean off to school, run tea to the library at night, cook for all of us, and clean. It was exhausting. The Professor told me over and over again that it could not be that hard. After all, I had but two children to look after, and the house. He, on the other hand, managed quite easily to teach three classes and look after a total of forty students. MEN!

It was during that time that I first met Robert. I was tired, and the tray was so heavy as I struggled up the stairs. There were eight for the lecture that evening, the usual six and a pair of brothers that I had not met before. They were from Virginia, I had heard the others among the Professor's students groan when he announced that these two were to join the group. I walked into the room and nearly tripped over the outstretched legs of one of the brothers. The second jumped to his feet, and seized my tray. We were both off balance and the contents of the tea tray went everywhere. The pot landed on the Professor's desk. I knew what was coming next.

"You clumsy child, can you not do the job for which I pay you?" he railed at me.

The one who had grabbed my tray came to my defense.

"Sir, it was entirely my fault. I will take the blame for this unfortunate accident. And how dare you talk to a lady in such fashion?" he shouted at the startled Professor.

"Young man, you will wait in the hall. Margarethe, you are to clean up this mess and apologize to each of these gentlemen. If there is a broken cup in the ruins, you will purchase a replacement from you own funds."

Just then I turned to see the other brother crush a tea cup under his boot and smile.

"Gentlemen," the Professor announced, "let us retire to the parlor. We obviously will be unable to continue the lecture in the midst of this ruin. Margarethe can bring us our refreshment there." The next comment was icily addressed to me. "Margarethe, we will finish our discussion in the morning."

I worked like a fool for the next hour, cleaning up, refilling the pot, getting a new cup down from the cupboard, and taking the tray into the parlor. I escaped without having to say a word to anyone.

The next day the Professor was true to his word. I cried for an hour after our "discussion," during which I had said not a word. I was in ruins when there was a knock at the front door. It was one of the Virginia brothers, but I didn't stay to see which. I ran up the stairs. I am sure he saw me, but I did not answer the door. He was still standing on the porch when I went out the back way to fetch Sean from school.

Each day for the rest of the week, he would come to the door and knock. I would refuse to answer. I knew it would not be too long before this comedy drew the attention of the gossips in the town. Something had to be done. On Friday, I answered his knock, intending to send him firmly away.

"Good morning, my dear lady. Thank you for answering the door. May I come in?" tumbled from his mouth.

"Good day, sir. You are welcome, and no," I responded.

There was a good thirty seconds of silence as he fit my answers to his questions. They were obviously not the answers he had expected.

"Dear lady, may I have the pleasure of your company at the next dance?"

"No, sir, I do not dance."

"Then, may I please escort you during a walk on the green some evening."

"No, sir, I do not walk."

"But, dear lady, you have two legs and they appeared at the lecture on Tuesday to be in good working order. Why is it that you do not walk?" he asked, raising an eyebrow as he did so. I chuckled. This could not be the brother that had caused the problem. It was, perhaps, time to change tactics.

"With whom am I speaking, sir?" I said, imitating his drawl.

"Why, I am Squire Robert Allen Singer of the Virginia Singers. My family has a large plantation in Virginia. We are the largest growers of fine tobacco in all of the Colonies. Even the King uses our tobacco," he replied. "May I have the pleasure of your company after church this Sunday?" he continued as if in a single breath.

"No, Mr. Singer, I am sorry, but I have two small children whom I must mind during the service. Good day, sir." I closed the door on him, almost shutting his fingers in the door. The nerve of him. The King uses his tobacco, indeed! Everyone knows the King will have nothing but Jamaican tobacco.

Every day for the next several weeks, Squire Robert, as he passed the house, doffed his hat and bowed. Word of this worked its way back to the Professor, and he confronted me one Sunday after church.

"That young man was making sheep's eyes at you all through the service," the Professor declared. "Don't let any ideas about how you will run off and marry him enter your head. Not that it isn't the proper role for a woman. But your first duty is to me. And your getting married would leave me in an awkward position just now, with no housekeeper and two small children."

"Sir, I assure you that I have no intention of marriage. I am totally uninterested in seeing anything further of Squire Singer."

"Margarethe, I assure you that he has every intention of marrying you. He has already had the enormous effrontery to tell me so. And, so long as you do not inconvenience me with an abrupt departure, I have no objection," the Professor announced. "You will, after all, need to marry in order to have children. That is a woman's calling. There is no other reason for women to exist."

I was furious. I wanted to cry. I wanted to scream at him. Instead, when he turned his back to fill his briar, I curtseyed and replied, "Yes, sir," and departed the room quickly.

The routine became almost bearable when the Professor announced that he had hired a new housekeeper. Betsy was two years my junior and rather slow. We got on as sisters, though. She took over almost all the housework and would even watch Kate for me while I took Sean off to school. She, unlike the old housekeeper, was to live in the house with us.

I now had a roommate, and found that I could no longer read at night without awakening Betsy. Kate solved my problem by becoming very sick for several weeks. We almost lost that little girl. At the doctor's suggestion, I moved into her room at night. I gave her the medicine the doctor had brought, I bathed her in cool water when she grew too feverish. For almost a month, I scarcely slept. But, once Kate was able to sleep quietly, I managed to read two whole books from the Professor's library in only one week. After that, I moved into Kate's room permanently. That solved the problem of being able to read at night.

The Professor was willing to let Betsy watch the children two evenings a week while I went to prayer services. Robert was often there, though I never spoke with him alone, or accepted his perennial offer to escort me back to the Professor's door. Since the Professor seldom returned before the dinner hour, I could slip away mid-afternoon for a walk in the nearby woods, or to sit along the river and think. Twice, Mother came in the shape of a bird, and spoke with me for a few minutes. Those were some of the happiest times during the whole of my stay in Cambridge. In return for the evenings of child-minding, Betsy would take two mornings a week to go to the village green and to the market.

That winter, building on the letters that Sean had taught to Kate, I started teaching Betsy how to read. Little did the Professor know he had two literate females under his roof. He would have fired both Betsy and me if he knew.

Robert's brother called one day to pay the Professor for his classes. He handed me an envelope with one torn corner. I told him that I could not take the payment for the Professor. He insisted. I asked him his name.

"Can't you read, girl? It's written clear as day on the envelope," he said in a sarcastic tone.

"Professor MacLean prefers that the women of his household do not read," I replied. It was true enough to ease my conscience without betraying my secret.

"I am James Cameron Singer of Virginia!" he exclaimed. "The finest family in all of Virginia. You will take this envelope and give it to Professor MacLean. See to it, my girl."

"I, sir, am not your girl and you will not tell me my

business," I replied, getting angry.

"You will take this envelope or I will tell the good Professor that you have been spending your evenings with my brother, instead of at the prayer service."

"Sir, you would not."

"Yes I would! Gladly!" he replied as he pushed the envelope into my hands.

I shuddered and shut the door in his face.

When I handed the envelope over that evening, the Professor opened it and glared.

"The amount enclosed is short by two pounds, Margarethe. Since you tore the corner of the envelope, your wages will be docked to make up the deficiency," he proclaimed. I knew argument would only enrage the Professor, and so I nodded and left the room. Somehow, Mr. James Cameron Singer was going to hear from me!

He tried twice more to leave me torn envelopes. Being wise now to the trick, I refused each time. When I was not there to warn her, Betsy accepted the second and was docked two pounds, six. Sean was the one burned the third time. He lost two pounds. We all wanted a piece of Mr. James Singer!

Just before last Christmas, I noticed that more books than usual were missing from the Professor's library. I counted and found sixteen books not in their places on the shelves. One was in Betsy's room and one in mine. Fourteen books missing. When the Christmas recess came, the Professor would audit his library, and there would be the very devil to pay.

During the next lecture, I watched carefully through the vent in the library wall. I thought I saw one of Robert's friends slip a book under his waistcoat while the Professor was writing on the blackboard. I nearly denounced him to the Professor at once, but then realized that I could be in more trouble than the thief. I was torn, with no idea what to do. That evening was the last lecture before the College was dismissed for Christmas holidays.

It was the day after Christmas, and the students had not yet returned from their holidays at home, when Sean caused the problem. In the middle of the night, I looked up from my book, and realized that I smelled smoke. I ran from Kate's room with Kate bundled in my arms. The door to Sean's room was covered in flames. I could hear him crying inside the room. I was uncertain what to do next. Kate was crying, and everyone else seemed to be asleep. I did not know if the Professor was home or not. I ran to my old room to wake Betsy. I handed Kate to her, and shouted for her to run out of the house.

I went across the hall to the Professor's room and called for him. He was not there. His window was open, and I could see a track in the fresh snow on the roof of the porch. The smoke was getting thick and the flames were very hot. I wanted to follow the Professor out the window, but Sean was my responsibility.

I ran along the hall until I was opposite Sean's door. It was now open so I gathered my nightclothes closely around me and dashed through the flames that filled the doorway. Once through, I could see the remains of a pipe, matches, and tobacco pouch lying on the floor. Through the window I could see the snow filling the sky, large white flakes melting in the flames. The bed, and the edges of the room were hidden in the smoke and flames. Sean was there, apparently unconscious, in the arms of a skeletal figure. I recognized him from Mother's story of how she had finally convinced our father to marry her. It was Death who was holding Sean.

"Good evening, sir," I addressed him politely, as I reached out and firmly seized Sean's ankle. It was the most accessible part of his anatomy, cradled as he was in Death's arms. "How considerate of you to tend to my charge in the midst of his unauthorized experiments with tobacco. But, since I am now at hand, I'll relieve you of any further duty towards the lad."

"What's this?" cried Death, peering at me intently. "Another fool eager to die for tobacco?"

"Why, no sir. I despise the stuff myself. The smoke makes one cough, and one's clothes smell terrible. I'm just trying to do my job. But I always understood you to prefer wormwood to tobacco."

With that, Death leaned forward to peer at me even more searchingly.

"I thought you looked familiar. You must be related to that alchemist with the excellent trick of transporting spirits. Amer—yes, that was his name."

"Amer is my father," I replied. "And Samona, the witch whose life you spared that evening, was my mother." As I talked, I slid my other hand up between Death and Sean, lifting the boy up and against my bosom as one does with a sleeping baby. Now I was holding Sean, but Death was still between me and the window through which I could fling him to safety.

"And here are you, quite a grown-up lady! What is your name, my dear?" asked Death.

"Margarethe Crafter," I replied, pacing back and forth while bouncing Sean as if he were still only two and being a bit fractious. "Why do you ask, sir?"

"I always like to keep track of the family doings of my friends. And how is your father these days?" was Death's suave response.

"I'm afraid I do not know. I came to Cambridge to study mathematics, because with mathematics you can describe any thing or place or event in this universe or several others. But the only position I could find was with Professor MacLean, who will tolerate no woman with intellectual pretensions. Since my ability to read is a secret from him, I have not received nor written any letters for over two years. But, If I may say so, I am very pleased that you need to ask, sir. That means you have had no call to visit any of my family while I have been in Cambridge." As I spoke, I continued to pace, edging closer and closer to the window. Sean's room overlooked the front of the house. If I could roll him out of my arms onto the roof of the porch, he would slide down into the snowbank below, and thus escape Death.

"You are every bit as clever as your father. A most excellent young woman indeed. But you are distracting me from my duty. The boy you are holding must come away with me. Tobacco is a killer, you know."

"I had not known, but if it is, as you say, a killer, then I should think you would prefer that it be less widely used." One more round of pacing, and I would be close enough to fling Sean out of the window.

"Eh, why do you say so?" Death looked puzzled.

"Because of the workload for you, sir. If the craze for tobacco spreads throughout the world, how will you ever keep up with all the people you have to summon to their doom? It must be terrible to have to travel so widely and work so hard." With the last sentence, I flung open the shutters and rolled Sean out into the snow and safety. I quickly turned, expecting Death to seize me, since I had deprived him of his intended victim. But he was still looking puzzled and bemused.

"An absolute wonder. Here's a slip of a girl who doesn't swoon at the sight of me, from a family who all insist on learning about the universe for themselves. She comes to the city to study mathematics, even when she must pretend to be stupid to obtain the opportunity. And study she does, so diligently she refuses all suitors, but she snatches a child from my very arms. And she's concerned about my workload. Whatever am I to make of these Crafters?" And with that, Death disappeared.

The next thing I knew, I awoke in a strange bed, covered from toe to nose in stinking bandages. In the next room, one of the faculty wives was prattling on about spirits and ghosts. I wasn't sure what she was talking about, but I heard "Salem," and "witches," and I was very frightened.

After listening carefully for a few more minutes, I heard enough to realize she was talking about the story Sean had told after they pulled him from the snowbank. Sean had claimed that a snow ghost had come for him during the fire, had snatched him away from the black ghost, and blown him out the window and into the snow. Another woman objected that Sean must have seen me, all aflame in my white dressing gown, and thought that I was a ghost. A third said that of course there were no such things as ghosts, that it was just a little boy's tale.

Since it seemed that I was not a suspect, I kept my eyes closed and drifted back to sleep. The next time I woke up, it was dark. My first thought was that it was all over, that I had died. Then I moved, and realized Death would not cause so much pain. I started to cry, and a candle bounced into the room. It was followed by Betsy. She stroked my head and calmed me down. She told me that the children were both all right, and that the Professor was arranging for a place to stay. She also said that there was a gentleman to see me, who was claiming to be a friend of my family. Curious to see who might make such a claim, I asked her to help me sit up, then to let him in.

"Good day, my lady. I am Mr. Abdul, a poor apothecary who has corresponded with your father for the last ten years," he introduced himself. "Your father had asked that I look in on you from time to time. Because I was not aware of your posting, I did not realize until today where you were. I am so sorry that the fire occurred. I hope that you will be well."

"Sir, the doctor thinks that she will live," Betsy told him.

"Water," I croaked, my throat sore and dry. Betsy was reaching for the water glass when Mr. Abdul stopped her.

"I have something here that is better for her than water. I was taught how to make it in London, and I have seen its effect on several patients there. Please. If you would allow me."

"Yes, sir," Betsy replied, stepping out of his way. Mr. Abdul, a short bull of a man, reached into his satchel and extracted a vial.

"Here, try this."

He held the vial to my lips. At first I thought it was water. Then the taste penetrated. It was awful. I wanted to vomit.

"It has a strong flavor, but you will become accustomed to it as you take more of the medicine."

For a second, I thought that it was poison, and started to scream. He put a finger to my lips and whispered, "Samona said to tell you that it was all right."

I lay back quietly on the bed. If Mother had told him that it was all right, and he knew her given name, then it must really be all right.

"Betsy, can you find me some food?" It was the last thing on my mind, but it would get her out of the room for a few minutes.

"Yes, Margarethe. Will you be all right with this gentle-man, or should I send one of the daughters of this nice family up to sit with you?" Betsy asked, hopeful that I would want a chaperone.

"I think it will be all right, Betsy. After all, he is an apothecary." It hurt to talk that much, but it worked. She curtseyed and exited the room.

"Sir, who are you, and how do you know my mother?"

"I was a friend of your father's in Europe. When he emigrated, we continued to write letters. He has supplied me with many ingredients for the elixirs in my shop, and I have sent him a few rare items that he required to continue his research. He asked me to look in on you when I moved to Cambridge. Since you and your Professor MacLean are so reclusive, I did not have a previous excuse to call upon you without causing gossip. When I heard about the fire, I came as soon as I had finished compounding this elixir. Your charming mother, Samona, visited me last night and asked me to help you. She fetched Willow, who has volunteered to stay in Cambridge until you are well. I have her in my satchel. I told her that I would let her out when the two of you were in the same room. She wants very much to see you," he said quietly. At this point I knew he was either a true friend of my father or one of the coven. But if he had Willow and was willing to release her in the same room, I knew he could only be a friend.

"When can I see Willow, sir?" I asked.

"How about now?" he said, producing another bottle from his case and pulling the cork. "Now, Willow, here is your mistress. But you may only stay out a minute."

The shining light that was Willow poured from the bottle and into my lap. I was so happy to see her, I could have wept. I think I did, but there were no tears. I was that dry.

"Margi, are you all right?" Willow asked immediately.

"Yes, Willow, I'm going to be fine. It's so good to see you. But you have to go soon, or Betsy will be frightened."

"Yes, Margi, I just wanted to see you." She started back into the bottle. "Bye, Margi. I will talk to you again in a week or so." Her shining presence now filled the bottle and not the room.

"Thank you for bringing Willow, sir," I said dreamily.

"You are very welcome, miss. Sleep now, and take more of the elixir when you next wake up." Mr. Abdul's hypnotic voice was quietly commanding. I do not remember him leaving.

When I next woke up, I reached for the bottle of potion and pulled the glass stopper out. I dribbled a little bit on my tongue and laid my head back on the pillow. There was a dull ache all over my body. There was a bell on the table, too. As I tried to put the bottle back on the table, my arm caught the bell and knocked it to the floor. Betsy appeared a few moments later with a tray of food. After the potion from the bottle, I was sure I could not stand to eat. But Betsy persuaded me to try a little, and I found my stomach subsiding. I was surprised to find I was actually quite hungry.

As I ate, Betsy told me the news. More than two weeks had passed since the fire. The bedroom wing of the house had been completely destroyed, but most of the downstairs and the library had been saved by a heavy snow storm. Professor MacLean was in the process of assessing the damage. He had wanted to discharge me, since I couldn't take care of the children, as badly burned as I was. Kate had cried for two days without ceasing, until her father relented. Sean was back in school now, but everyone was watching him closely, since it appeared that he had set the fire.

I was puzzled. I had slept for the better part of two weeks? Yes, and after my brief interview with Mr. Abdul, I had slept like the dead for a full five days. Betsy warned me that she would have to change my bandages that afternoon, and that it would hurt. So I promised her not to hate her for tending to my wounds. She left me alone to rest until she could prepare the tray for the lint and linens.

Later in the day, one of the medical-faculty members and Betsy returned to redo the bandages. I was pulled into a sitting position and thought that I was going to scream, the pain was so awful. Betsy, under the watchful eye of the doctor, proceeded to remove the bandages from my hands and arms. The doctor let out a startled yelp when he saw my skin. I thought that perhaps I had gangrene, and would lose a finger or hand. I started to cry, becoming hysterical. Without my hands, I couldn't work. Then the doctor's words came through. "How could she have healed so quickly?"

Heal? Quickly? Losing two weeks seemed an awfully long time to me. Then I remembered the potion. I also realized that I was growing sleepy again. Well, maybe Father had known something all along when he talked about the healing magic.

I really missed the chance to read during the next few weeks while I finished healing, but the faculty wives often met for tea in the house where I was staying. They provided a good deal of education on topics that would never be taught in the College. I learned about how to persuade a husband that my ideas were really his, also which students were paying extra to stay in classes that they could not otherwise have attended, and who was walking out with whom and other gossipy topics of the town. I came to be accepted by most of the faculty wives. This made my life somewhat easier if dull, as it gave me women friends to discuss things with. I even persuaded two of the wives to approach the Professor about the idea of my learning to read during my convalescence. Unsurprisingly he did not like the idea, so they abandoned it. Little did the Professor know that I could read and write English, French, and Latin. I had even begun to puzzle out Greek before the fire.

Two weeks after the College had reconvened, I returned to my job with Dr. MacLean. My notes had been hidden in the chimney of the old house. I was sure they were lost, until Sean tapped at my door one evening.

"These are yours, Ma'am. I know that you can read, better even than I can. And, unless you give me all the candies and cakes I want, I'm going to tell my father."

"That trick will only work once, Sean," was my immediate response. "And once you use it, I won't be here to walk you to school, or sew your shirts, or to make the cakes you like. If you are to tell your father that I can read, you should make sure it's over something more important than sweets." He puzzled this over for a few moments.

"I won't tell. I'd rather have you than anyone but my mother." He hesitated before continuing, "But, you will make those good little cakes with the raisins? Please? We didn't get any at Christmas, because you were ill."

"Sometime soon," I laughingly promised. "Now, give me my papers, and off to bed with you. And don't forget to wash your feet."

When classes resumed, the Professor called each student to the house individually and asked them about the missing books. So far, all had denied taking the books or seeing anyone else take them. I dreaded the day when James Singer was to appear and be questioned. Little did I know, that both of the Singers were to visit on the first occasion that I left the house after the fire, to attend an evening prayer meeting. When I returned that night, the Professor was waiting for me at the door. I knew immediately that I had a serious problem.

"You deceitful bitch," he roared. "I have been harboring a snake in the very bosom of my family. You lying, thieving, clumsy cow. I found one of the missing books, and notes from your reading, hidden among your things. You have deceived me all along. You steal my books, you teach my daughter to read against my orders, you make me a laughingstock in front of my students. You will pay for this, Margarethe. As God is my witness, you will pay for your ingratitude."

"Ingratitude?" I exclaimed. "When have I ever had anything to be grateful to you for? Since the first hour I arrived, I've had nothing from you but abuse and ill-treatment. You call me 'stupid' every time you speak to me, but I was smart enough to learn everything you had to teach and more."

This was too much for Professor MacLean. "Be silent!" he bellowed.

I surprised both of us by obeying.

"You have until Friday to leave my house and this city,

or I will report this theft to the magistrate and have you whipped and thrown in gaol. I should be able to arrange for a new housekeeper by that time. Until then, you are not to speak to the children. You have infected them quite enough with your rebelliousness. You will remain in your room whenever you are not required in the kitchen."

I finally realized what had to have happened. In the next two days, with Sean's help, I was able to confirm it. James Singer had been stealing the books and the tuition money in order to pay some tavern debts. To protect himself from discovery, James had broken in, hidden one of the missing books in my drawer, added my notebook, and departed. He went around to the front door and joined his brother Robert, whom he had forced to be his lookout. They were announced, and James proceeded to tell the Professor that I was selling the books. He knew which book merchant had the Professor's books. He would be happy to retrieve them if Professor MacLean would provide a list of titles. The Professor had then confronted Sean, Betsy, and Kate one at a time, and drawn out the whole story of my being able to read. Betsy was dismissed, and fled immediately in the face of the Professor's rage. I had been permitted to stay on for several days only so the Professor could eat.

The next day, it was Robert Singer who returned with the books and a bill from the merchant. I offered him a cup of tea, carefully adding to it a measure of the truth potion that Sean had fetched from Mr. Abdul that very afternoon. When the required ten minutes had passed, I dragged him into the parlor and confronted him in front of the Professor. I asked him all the questions that would lead to my acquittal. Little did I realize that I was still doomed.

"Squire Singer, did not your brother and his friends steal all of the books?" I asked.

"Yes, ma'am. James and two of his friends took the books." He replied woodenly.

"Why did they take the books?" I asked.

"They wanted the money the books would bring in town."

"Did you help them?"

"I stood lookout when my brother put the book in your room. I did not want to do it, but he insisted. He said he would make it even worse for you if I didn't. I love you and I could not let that happen."

"You—you love me?" I stammered.

"Yes, I love you, I have since I first laid eyes on you," he replied.

I was stunned, and didn't know what to say.

"How long have you known she could read?" the Professor asked.

"Since the second time I saw her in church and noticed her turning her Bible right side up, when Sean knocked it from the pew."

"Why did you not tell me? You know of my orders."

"Sir, I could not let the lady be thrown out."

"Did James short the Professor his tuition?" I asked hastily, recovering from Robert's proclamation of love.

"Yes, he was greedy. He wanted more than Father would send him for a stipend," Robert replied.

"Why did he need the money?" I asked.

"So he could impress his friends."

"Thank you, Robert, that is enough," the Professor interrupted. "Margarethe, you are dismissed. You have lied to me since the beginning. You are deceitful. Leave my presence immediately!"

"Why did you let James hide that book?" I asked, not finished with this yet.

"I wanted him, and our family name, clear of any taint."

"What about me? You claim to love me. Why did you let him do this to me?" I asked, my eyes tearing over.

"I thought the Professor would turn you out, that then I could get you to marry me."

"I will never marry you, now or ever! How could you!"

"I love you."

"MEN! I will never understand men." I stormed from the room, I did not bother with the proper by-your-leave, or even curtsey. I was livid.

I fled the house and ended the flight at Mr. Abdul's. He let me in, and both he and Willow listened without comment as I related the whole terrible tale. When he prepared a cup of tea for me, I watched carefully so I knew it was just tea. We talked that whole night through. In the small hours of the morning, we developed a plan. I would become Mr. Abdul's housekeeper, at least until spring, when the roads were fit to travel home. I could continue my studies by borrowing books from my new friends and their husbands. I could also learn more of the Craft, and of medicine, from Mr. Abdul. And until spring, I could keep seeing both Kate and Sean from time to time on the green.

I moved the next day. Mr. Abdul hired a wagon and driver to help me. All my possessions were out of the Professor's house before he was fully awake. I still remember his yelp when he took his first sip of coffee that morning.

I settled in at the apothecary's house, and life almost returned to normal. But after only a week, my nemesis confronted me in the market. Mr. Singer begged, nay demanded, the pleasure of my company at the dance that Friday. I refused in the strongest possible terms and fled, leaving my market basket behind. That was a mistake. He had one of the other housekeepers point out the house where I was staying. For the next two weeks it was like being in prison. Here was Mr. Singer camped on the doorstep. Mr. Abdul ran him off two or three times a day. Finally, the poor, patient apothecary demanded that I confront the man. I did so in the parlor of Mr. Abdul's home while that gentleman remained as chaperone at the back of the room.

"Mr. Singer. How could you imagine that lying about a woman to her employer, telling her secrets, and allowing your brother to steal from her are ways to endear yourself to anyone with an ounce of intelligence or self-respect?"

"Mistress Crafter, please forgive me. I am most humbly sorry."

"You don't seem to realize how deeply your attentions insult me. You may have been attracted to me, but it was because you thought I was naive and uneducated. You were attracted to the person I was pretending to be in order to further my studies. You seemed surprised that I don't care two pence for your large plantation and your fine tobacco. Why, it's tobacco that caused the fire that almost killed Sean and myself."

"Please, dear lady, I promise to spend my entire life attempting to expiate my sin. Accept my most humble apology, I beg you."

"You pester me in the market, making a spectacle of us both. You camp at my doorstep, inconveniencing my friend and employer. What can I do to convince you to go away and leave me in peace?"

"Please, please, Mistress Crafter. I will obey your wishes completely as soon as you tell me that I am forgiven for the grievous wrong I have, in my ignorance, done you. But, if there is an ounce of kindness or mercy within you, you will allow me to make some attempt at reparation before you cast me out into the wilderness." With this, he threw himself face down on the carpet, at my feet.

This was too much. My indignation was transformed to laughter by the sight of this excess of repentance. I could not quite restrain my chuckles.

"All right. I accept your apology for the incident about the books. I believe you did not mean to be insulting in your offer of marriage. Now, will you please leave me in peace?"

He rose to one knee, and reached out to seize my hand.

"Dear lady, your graciousness has made my life worth living again. I exist only to serve you. Please honor me by becoming my wife."

"Never, if such brief and fraudulent acquaintance is your notion of a proper courtship. You scarcely know more than my name and my looks."

"Then teach me how I should court you, my fairest one. I will obey in every detail."

"You must begin by standing up, and releasing my hand," I began. He did so.

"Now, then. You must never cause me to come to harm, or to lose the respect of the community," I continued. He returned to his seat and pulled his mortarboard from his head.

"You will greet me politely, as you would a lady of your

own rank," I went on. He reached for his stick of lead and a sheet of foolscap.

"Would you be so kind as to repeat that last?" he asked in all seriousness.

"I said that you must treat me with proper respect, not bring harm to me or soil my reputation, and . . ." He was bent to his task, taking notes. I did not know whether to laugh or to cry.

"You will not create scenes in the market, you will offer to carry my market basket home. You will call on me only during those hours when a chaperone is present. You will, if I give permission, escort me to and from church. . . ." I watched his hand crabbing quickly across the page.

"Please, kind lady, slow down. I cannot write so quickly as you speak."

"What are you doing? Taking notes for a book?"

"Please do not make fun of me. I only wish to honor your requests."

"Kindly dispense with the 'dear lady' and treat me as your equal. With respect, mind you, but as an equal. No husband of mine will kneel at my feet nor tower over me."

"Yes, dear lady. I mean, Mistress Crafter." I could see the flush forming on his face.

"You will respect my answers to your invitations, especially if I tell you 'no.' I do not wish to dance. You will wear ordinary clothing to walk out on the green, not your student gown.

"You will call not more than once a week. I will decide if the time is proper to go for a stroll or to sit in the parlor and chat. You will inquire as to my preference in all entertainments and refreshments." He reached for another sheet of foolscap.

"You will attend all of your classes. You are to devote sufficient time to your studies so that you have a future." He continued to write in large letters; I knew this lecture would be more expensive than any Dr. MacLean might give.

"When we meet, we shall discuss intellectual matters, or the business of the town. And you, Squire, are not to ask me to marry you again." He looked up hopefully, having come to the bottom of both his page and his stick of lead.

"I will obey your wishes, sweet lady." He struck himself on the forehead with his writing hand and started again. "I hope to have the pleasure of calling on you in the very near future, Mistress Crafter."

He looked positively absurd with the large smear of lead on his forehead and nose and on his hand.

"By your leave," he asked.

"Have a good evening, sir." I replied, opening the door for him.

The instant the door shut behind him, we burst into gales of laughter. Both I and Mr. Abdul laughed so hard at the spectacle that our ribs hurt for the rest of the week.

Mr. Singer then began to court me exactly in the manner I had described. He did it so well I had a hard time continuing to refuse his invitations. He kept at it until spring.

My studies were going well, and Mr. Abdul seemed content with my housekeeping, so I resolved to spend another year in Cambridge. At least I could now send and receive letters. Robert kept at it all summer, and my resistance weakened a bit. I permitted him to walk me home from church on Sundays, and from some of the prayer meetings. He kept the courting up through the fall and winter. On New Year's Eve, under the clear bright stars, he asked me again to marry him.

"Whatever took you so long?" was my response. He silently slipped this ring on my finger and gently squeezed my hand.

"If you will set a date for the wedding, I will write to my family in Virginia to make the arrangements," he said. "We can get married in the manor house. It's very beautiful in the spring, with all the magnolias."

"I think I would prefer to marry at my parents' homestead," I replied. "You haven't met any of my family at all, you know. We could leave in May, marry in June, and visit with each family for two weeks over the summer. Doesn't that sound more reasonable? Besides, isn't your brother James the overseer at the plantation now? I really would prefer we didn't spend our wedding night under his roof, after that nonsense about the tuition money." Robert had no argument with that, so it was settled.

Two weeks ago, once the roads were passable, Father drove down to get me, and here I am. And the wedding is tomorrow, if I get this dress hemmed in time.

"So what will happen after the wedding?" Cynthie coaxed.

"He has received a letter of acceptance from Oxford," Margarethe replied. "We are leaving for England on the first of August."

"How long will you be gone?" Cynthie questioned.

"Oh, a year or two I think, maybe a little longer," was Margarethe's patient reply.

"Why are you going," Cynthie continued.

"Stop it! I have to get this dress hemmed," Margarethe snapped.

"But why should I stop?"

"Because you're going downstairs to help Mother with the pies. Now shoo, before I take a broom to you."

She chuckled as she left. Margarethe thought wistfully of Sean and Kate, and then of the children she and Robert hoped to have. This was only a taste of her future. "Better get to work," she murmured to herself.

Anno Domini 1721

A LITTLE LEARNING

by Esther Friesner

The Widow Mansfield glided into her prize boarders' room with the silent grace of a well-trimmed merchant ship running fair before the wind. Both the young gentlemen were out—of that she was certain, having seen them head off early in the direction of the New Haven town green as the October morning mists were lifting. "Young" she called them, yet guessing by his looks, she suspected that she and Ahijah Crafter were nearly of an age. That other one, though . . .

She put away all thoughts of that second, more uncanny-looking boarder who shared Ahijah's room. Widows were reputed to be overly prone to weird fancies, if they did not steer their vagrant musings into more productive channels.

"There, now, Dorcas," she exhorted herself. "To work, to work! 'Ware idleness. It is the very breeding-ground of all manner of devils." Her pretty dimples showed as she smiled at her own mock severity. "Hark to the woman! Next you'll be donning breeches and studying for the ministry at Master Crafter's side." Laughing, she closed the chamber door behind her.

Having heard no sound from the room above, and not having seen either of the young men return while she was hanging the wash outside earlier, she had decided to take advantage of their absence to do a little tidying. Scholars were notoriously lax in such matters. Their hair might look

135

like a squirrel's nest and their rooms like the aftermath of
all Ten Plagues, but so long as they coaxed their precious
Greek and Latin discourses into apple-pie order, they saw
nothing amiss in the world.

Perhaps it was better so, the Widow Mansfield reflected.
Had her own dear Thomas been a member of this newly
founded Collegiate School, rather than a scamperer after
barter and trade, his bones would not now be lying on the
bottom of the Atlantic Ocean. No, he would be content to
do all his adventuring and wrangling with the comfortable,
harmless contents of old books, and she would not be condemned to a cold bed so young.

Thoughts of her longstanding sorrow and nightly depri-
vation filled the Widow Mansfield's clear blue eyes with
tears. Briskly she dashed them away. It was not her way to
wallow in self-pity, particularly when it would do no good.
Better to turn her energies to the task at hand. A thorough
turning-out and cleaning-up to occupy mind and body, that
was what she needed. She straightened her slender shoulders
and grasped her besom more firmly, ready to do battle to the
death against mouse-smut, dust, muck, and cobweb.

In the shadowy chamber, wood and ropes creaked.

What was it that she had said of idleness, scarce moments
before? A breeding-ground of devils? She had spoken without knowledge, yet in this moment no student of the Collegiate School was receiving a more thorough education
than Dorcas Mansfield.

Scarce sunlight made the dust motes dance above the
narrow bed reserved for her two boarders' use, but oh!
more solid shapes than dust motes were doing far more
than dancing there. She felt the bodice of her gown grow
tight as she stood staring. Her breath slipped in and out
between painfully tight lips, making a small, whimpering
sound. Cast aside on the floor beside the bed was the
roughspun, sober garb of a poor student, but overlaying it
were the softer folds of a fine lady's gown. The rope-slung
bed frame squeaked and complained at such vigorous use.
The bedclothes twisted and shifted, yet never quite enough
to let the Widow Mansfield know which one of her lodgers

was *not* attending to his studies this morning.

She had to know. Female curiosity was all the reason she gave herself, yet why then did she feel as if a block of granite rested on her chest? Nigh unbearable pain choked her as she forced her throat to utter: "Ahijah?"

Oh, how weak, how pathetic it sounded! The name emerged from her lips no louder than a sigh; still, it was enough. The shapes beneath the bedclothes froze. A girlish voice smothered a giggle. By degrees the thin quilt was pulled down so that the Widow Mansfield might see a clump of tousled black hair (*But both of them are dark-haired men,* she thought), a brow ivory-pale from long study (*Either one may own such, Lord of mercy, either one. . . .*), and eyes—

Certainly not Ahijah's eyes, for which deliverance her heart rejoiced.

Certainly not the eyes of any human thing, for which she felt an icy terror close about her soul.

Yellow, they were. Slit-pupilled. Knowing. Sly. Eyes that met hers, only to slip nimbly down to the swelling of her bosom and pierce it, dragging out every guilty secret of a too-young widow's lonely dreams, laying them before her in the sunlight, shameful, shameless, bare. Every one.

The creature among the bedclothes smirked and brushed back stray locks of ebon hair. Small and white, yet smooth and sturdy-seeming, two infant horns winked out from among the black curls.

The Widow Mansfield's screams were heard all the way to the New Haven green and partway across the harbor.

"No, please, I pray, don't trouble yourselves any further. I am all right."

"Are you certain, Dorcas?" The Widow Mansfield's brother Napthali knelt beside the bed, sweat carving rivulets of clean skin down his face.

From the other side of the bed, a quirky, nervous voice cut in awkwardly before the lady might reply. "She fainted. I found her so when I came into my room. It was the heat. Heat does funny things, you know."

Napthali Weaver glowered at the dark-haired young man who hovered far too close to Dorcas for any right-minded brother's liking. "Heat? This late in October?" His stubby nose distended in a scornful snort. "A simple man I be, and unlettered, but all it takes is a stroll out of doors to tell the weather."

"Napthali, please." Dorcas turned the brightness of her morning-glory eyes to her brother. "Ahijah is quite right." Her gaze warmed and sweetened as it drifted back to the fidgety young man. "Cool it may be out-of-doors, but some of these rooms can hold the heat almost unnaturally well."

"Rooms ain't the only things with suchlike properties," Napthali growled to himself.

"It would be possible, Mistress Mansfield, for me to adapt some certain few features of this house to provide better ventilation." The young man seized upon the widow's last remark with the eagerness of a terrier pup assaulting its first rat. "Nor would you need to sacrifice warmth in winter. The designs I have considered are entirely flexible to the season. If you and your good brother, Master Weaver, would give me leave—"

"No," said Napthali. His froglike mouth shut with an audible snap. His expression seemed to say that the only leave he would gladly give this overzealous, intrusive person was free and willing leave to return to the Massachusetts wilderness that had misbegotten him.

It was unfortunate that in all his years of education at the Collegiate School—to say nothing of his less orthodox, more private studies—Ahijah Crafter had never been taught that there comes a time when the wise man holds his tongue.

"But Master Weaver, the benefits to your house would be extraordinary, the cost minimal. You would not labor alone. My tutor tells me that I am making excellent progress. I could easily afford to give over some of my usual study time and help you. I hope you will not think me immodest, but I do have more than a little skill with carpentry tools. If you're willing to wait, I have a series of sketches in my room which I will—"

"Progress, you say?" Napthali interrupted.

Ahijah's black eyes sparkled with almost pathetic joy. It was the first time the beauteous Dorcas' beastly brother had ever addressed a question to him that showed some human interest in the young scholar's work. *A garden enclosed is his sister, my bride*. The scandalously thrilling words of the Song of Songs were not supposed to occupy a future minister's thoughts so often, nor so inaccurately quoted. On the other hand, neither were a future minister's thoughts supposed to stray so often to the bewitching face and entrancing person of his landlady. Time not wasted daydreaming about Dorcas Mansfield was squandered fantasizing about the best way to gain the support and favor of the lady's brother. You had to start somewhere.

"Progress?" Ahijah parroted. "Oh, yes, wonderful progress. My Greek and Latin were a trifle laggard, but now they are both coming on much better than I ever—"

"Good. The sooner you progress, the sooner you'll have your degree, and the sooner you'll be gone from New Haven."

"*Napthali!*"

Dorcas' loud reproof had no effect on her brother. "Don't you be taking on that way with me, Dorcas. I know what I said and I meant it, every tittle. Why in the name of all holy you had to take in these scribble-scrabblers, anyway, is beyond my knowledge. Not as if there's any decent money in it."

"Money is it, Napthali Weaver? Shall we speak of *money*, you and I?" Dorcas thrust herself up in the bed, eyes ablaze. Her brother cringed, aware he'd trespassed on dangerous ground. The earth was the Lord's but this brave house, and the fullness thereof, was Dorcas', her dead husband's legacy. Napthali had talked his way beneath this roof ostensibly to lend strength, respectability, and succor to his helpless, widowed sister. In truth, he and she and half of New Haven knew that Dorcas Mansfield was about as weak and helpless as a bull with nettles tied under its tail.

"I only—" he began.

Dorcas was not interested in hearing his excuses. "These *scribble-scrabblers*, as your ignorance calls them, are the

future hope of the Church, brother mine. How would *you*
preserve the pure religion if not through well-educated
ministers? Ignorance may be a comfortable thing, but so
is lying down to sleep in a snowbank. Comfort costs too
much, if we're speaking of financial matters."

"I don't much care." Napthali was sullen before his
sister's hot defense of the scholars. "You see this boarding
business as some sort of holy mission, hey? I've a clearer
eye. *And* nose. What's all them stinks as sometimes twist
out from beneath that one's door, then? More holiness?"
Again that snort which made squat Napthali resemble the
tribe of pigs he pastured. "If I had it my way, I'd ship
the lot of 'em back to Saybrook, else upriver to Hartford.
Let *those* towns cope with the college men, and welcome.
Little good will ever come to New Haven from such bookish
do-nothings."

Ahijah was abashed. Purely from reflex, his long, thin
hands folded themselves into an attitude of prayer he did
not feel. Staring down at them, so as not to have to meet
Napthali's hostile eyes or Dorcas' kindly ones, he said, "You
may yet have your wish, Master Weaver."

"Ha! Likely, that." Napthali's caustic laughter ate to the
marrow of Ahijah's bones. "You lot of ink-lickers are like
fleas: once you've found warm lodging and good feed,
there's no rooting you out." As if to emphasize his firsthand
knowledge of the subject, he scratched himself vigorously.
"If I'm to see your learned backsides soon, then whyfor'd
that school of yours r'ar up that great, ugly building hard
by the green, then? Housing for every moldery clutch of
useless jabber ever put down on paper, that's what! Books
and books, and the squint-eyed moles who read 'em, all
to have a finer roof over their heads than many an honest,
hard-working man of the colony!"

"Really, Napthali." For one who had fainted from the
heat, Dorcas' reply was astonishingly frosty. "Your ignorance doesn't need to be paraded like a prize sheep; we're
all well acquainted with it. The Collegiate School will bring
only benefit to the town that sponsors it. Why, just see what
life Harvard's infused up Massachusetts way! If the school

were a bad thing, would so many towns be fighting for the honor of claiming it?"

Fighting, indeed. The lady seems to have some Talent of her own, Little Brother, if only for stating the obvious before it becomes so.

Ahijah's pale face lost several more layers of healthy tint as the gibing words knifed directly into his mind. His goggling eyes shot from Dorcas to Napthali, yet their expressions had not changed. He never had been able to get over the mistaken feeling that everyone near him could hear that silent speaker's words as clearly as he did.

"Ahi—Master Crafter? Are you well?"

A sudden warm pressure on his clammy hand broke him free of the webwork of intrusive words and snide laughter in his brain. Ahijah saw the Widow Mansfield gazing up at him with genuine concern.

"I—A touch of the heat, Mistress Mansfield. You will excuse me."

As he staggered from the lady's chamber, his ordinary ear heard Napthali resume his diatribe against the milk-blooded tribe of scholars. At the same time he heard, with that inner ear he wished he'd never discovered, a too-familiar voice crowing: *'A touch of the heat, Mistress Mansfield?' An, yes. Now tell her whence that heat rises, lad, and I'll be pleased to call you a man.*

"A curse on you, Juvenal. Be still!" Ahijah snarled under his breath.

More laughter echoed through his brain. *Speak to me so, do you, Little Brother? Aren't you afraid that some- one will overhear, and think you mad? Madmen speak to themselves all the time. So do poets. Not exactly the reputation to do a future minister good, being named poet to his face.*

Ahijah made the shelter of his chamber and threw himself full-length across the bed. "I said be *quiet!*"

Quiet? So I am. I promise you, by the blood binding us, no one here suspects I am carrying on a conversation with you. It's bad manners to talk while drinking. Foam comes out your nose.

Instantly alert, Ahijah demanded of the wall, "What? Drinking? Where are you?"

A mental chuckle answered him. *Ah, Socrates! Here's a pretty paradox. He bids me be quiet, then orders me to give him information. How like our initial meeting, this is. The first thing you did was scream for me to begone, the next moment you were pleading with me to aid you with your Greek.* The chuckle became a cackle, and a pinpoint of light twinkled inside Ahijah's skull. It irised out to let him see a common taproom, a comely wench simpering at the sender of the vision, and a familiar pair of boots propped up on a table. *Now you see where I am as well as I do. Care to join us?*

The peace-starved part of Ahijah's soul which had driven him to seek an education so far from his Harvard-bred siblings had had enough. Rolling from the bed, the young man strode across the room to an old square-built wooden case of his own design. He had always been fascinated with problems of space and shape. As a boy, he had taken the measure of every ox-cart he could find, and concluded that the wise merchant could carry more freight if the average cart was loaded with goods packed in uniform cases of these specific dimensions. He had given teeth to his theory by building one such case with his own hands.

His father, Amer, had been kind if not lavish in his praise. His mother, Samona, had said that it was all very nice, and the case would be just the thing to pack his linens in when he went off to school.

The case did not now hold linens. It was lined with several layers of straw, out of whose fragrant depths Ahijah now drew a book, a bowl, and a little clay figurine. He opened the book casually and propped it up behind the bowl, into which he placed the figurine. It was not a very good representation of a man, having as it did rather bandy, overly hairy legs that ended not in five-toed feet but neatly split hooves. The pert tail did not help the resemblance either. The horns, however, were a masterstroke, precise miniatures of a young goat's curving buds, painstakingly carved from wood by a hand that understood carpentry much better than clay.

"Now," said Ahijah to the little statue, "if you are not back here by the time I count three, I am going to fetch a cupful of whatever I can find and dump it over your head."

Whatever you can find? Dear Little Brother, if you but try the rear of the topmost shelf in our delicious landlady's pantry, you'll encounter a bottle of geneva spirits Master Weaver's been hiding for 'medicinal use only,' and much obliged I'll be to you.

"I doubt that."

Hmm?

"I'm not looking for my cupful up in Mistress Mansfield's pantry, but under Master Weaver's bed. Though what I turn up may have been geneva spirits, once upon a time. Care to find out? One . . . two . . ."

The sunlight flickered, as a dark shape passed between Ahijah and the light. "Really, Little Brother, your manner of command has become positively crude!" Swaggering on sturdy boots—incongruous footgear when worn with a student's threadbare suit—Ahijah's roommate had returned. The figurine, on the other hand, was gone.

"Crude? You're one to talk, Juvenal!" Ahijah laced into the truant with enough fire to make even Master Weaver reconsider his slurs against scholars' natural spunk. "What were you about this morning, frightening poor Mistress Mansfield senseless with your—your—?"

"Tut, Little Brother, a man who can't call a spade a spade has never learned to delve. If you can't say it, why not *think* it at me? You've the power."

Ahijah's mouth tightened. "Not that again."

"Why *not* that again? By my horns, I swear you've more fear of honest mind-speech than of your Hell, yet it's the strongest touch of Talent you'll ever own." Juvenal dropped onto the lone stool in the room and pulled off his boots. Stray sunbeams gleamed on his hooves, and he stretched and flexed his legs. *Ahhhh.*

Ahijah shuddered as the satyr's pleasure raced through his mind, suffusing his flesh with alien warmth. It wasn't the mind-speech he feared so much as the subsidiary Talent it brought of making him share sensations as well as thoughts.

"Get thee behind me . . ." he muttered.

"So I am behind you. And evermore shall be." Juvenal winked, and his dark, human eyes were transformed into two burning yellow sparks of mischief, each bisected by a black slit that seemed to crackle with its own secret fire.

Ahijah's fists came down hard on the tabletop. The book toppled over and sent the bowl skittering. "Do not taunt me!" His shout dislodged a sprinkling of dust from the newly whitewashed ceiling.

Rapid footsteps clattered up the stair. "Master Crafter, what is wrong? Did you call for something?" The Widow Mansfield's voice betrayed her anxiety.

Yet another reason for you to drop your silly prejudices and attempt a skill you already possess. The satyr's thoughts were more smug than his looks, which was saying a great deal. *Then you could shout at me to your heart's content without setting a whole innocent household on its ear.*

Quiet, you!

Ahijah's hand flew to his mouth, as if to stifle an oath. But not a word had passed his lips, to be called back again. Juvenal laughed, this time aloud.

"You'd best answer her, Little Brother," he directed, smirking.

Ahijah scowled at the satyr, but heeded him. "It's nothing, Mistress Mansfield," he said in more measured tones, speaking through the crack in the door. "I—I stubbed my toe against the stool."

"Oh." She sounded disappointed. "Well . . . I suppose I shall be back to my work, then." He heard the patter of her light foot upon the stair, then silence.

Glowering, he rounded on the satyr. "I've had enough of your escapades, Juvenal. From the moment we met, you've been an embarrassment and an encumbrance. I gave you your freedom long since. Why linger?"

"What?" The satyr feigned a hurt look. "Depart when a year's further study brings me my Yale degree? I had so looked forward to graduating with you, Little Brother, although I feel it fair to warn you that only *one* of us will be taking the highest honors in Greek."

"Greek," Ahijah growled. "I curse the tongue."

"Why? Because you couldn't master it without me?" Juvenal's slanted eyebrows rose in one of his more provoking expressions. "*I* bless it. If not for your backwardness with Greek, you'd never have grown desperate enough to try summoning help." He leaned forward far enough to pluck the little book from its place behind the bowl. "Poor as you were in the language, you couldn't know you'd opened this to a passage dealing with the ancient and noble tribe of satyrs. I am grateful. Without your ignorance, where would I be? Still kicking my heels in some Arcadian backwater."

"Where you belong!" Ahijah snatched the volume from the satyr's hands and tossed it onto the bed. "And where you'll find yourself once I find the means to send you packing."

"Of course you will," said Juvenal, in a tone that added an unsaid *when pigs fly.*

Ahijah started to reply, but either thought better of it or found he lacked sufficient verbal ammunition to put the uppity creature in its proper place. After four false starts and a sputter, he ended by exclaiming, "Oh, pox take you and your Greek honors! Stay, then. And when all's done, what will *you* do with a Yale degree?"

Juvenal chuckled. "Plague Harvard men. Just as you intend to do with regard to your Boston-taught brethren. You care nothing for the ministry. You'd rather be up to your elbows in cedar shavings. If you have to prove yourself to your family, there are cheaper I-told-you-so's to be had than a college diploma."

"How do you know—?"

The satyr shrugged. "Your mind's an open book to me. As is the mind of any mortal to one with the Talent to read." He gave Ahijah his most vexing grin. "I can teach you more valuable lessons than mastering Greek verb forms. What coin would you pay to learn whether a certain lady— I mention no names, mind!—holds you as dear as you do her?"

The blood drained from Ahijah's cheeks, only to rush back into them on a tide of outrage. "You pry so into my mind, uninvited. Into *hers?* You *are* the Devil!"

"A satyr, a satyr, please. And a Yale man. You can call me no worse than that."

"Well, soon enough I'll only be able to call you a satyr, plain," Ahijah spat.

"What? How's that?" Juvenal was genuinely taken aback.

"Wouldn't you like to know?" It was Ahijah's turn to taunt.

Yes, I would. And I will.

The satyr was in earnest, all humor gone. His words lanced into Ahijah's mind. Wince and draw away as the young man would, the satyr was still an inescapable mental presence. In a moment, the room where they sat vanished and Ahijah walked in a gray place where pure thoughts shimmered and sparkled like fiery gems. Here a musing less brilliant than the rest lay dull and lightless at his feet, and there the ember of an inspiration glowed with fire not yet blown to full flame. He looked around, ravished by the riches of his own mind surrounding him.

Bah! This is nothing. You ought to see what my *mind looks like since I commenced my education.*

The satyr's face loomed high above the mountains of jewelled thought and gilded memory. Long, spectral fingers appeared to probe the piles of thought, freely rifling them for the information Juvenal desired.

NO!

Ahijah reacted automatically to the threat of invasion. The one word of denial was more than a thought; it was a battle-call. The heat of it caused the nearest heap of glittering thought to run into a molten stream. A wisp of suggestion from Ahijah, and the liquid gold rose up in a wave that dashed itself against his body, leaving him armored head to foot in the bravely gleaming metal.

How did I—? He turned his mailed fist slowly before his eyes, rapt by the newly tapped power of his Talent. Wonder swiftly gave way to joy. *It does not matter* how *I did this. I did it, and that is all that counts!*

A new unvoiced command, and a sword sprang white-hot from his hand. The satyr's ghostly face lost all its casual confidence as Ahijah's sword gestured and the thick, unyielding walls of a fortress rose up to enclose the trove of his thoughts. Clear as glass the walls were, but both attacker and defender knew them to be impregnable. Shielded, armed, and ringed by a mental stronghold of his own making, Ahijah watched the satyr batter uselessly against the walls.

Through his own peals of laughter came the single, exultant thought: *Victory!* He brandished his sword high.

A pounding on a more earthly door broke through his celebration, shaking down the walls, shattering the armor, making the golden sword melt away like an August icicle.

"Master Crafter! Master Crafter! Please, I must talk to you!"

Ahijah gasped and staggered, overwhelmed by the battle he had just fought and won. The satyr sprawled on the stool, a hand to his chest, new respect dawning in his yellow eyes as he stared at the young man. "You are . . . a quick study, Little Brother," he rasped.

Again the pounding, and the Widow Mansfield's voice shook them both to the bone. "Master Crafter, pray open!"

Juvenal blinked his eyes human again and struggled into his boots while Ahijah warded the door. When all was safe, he opened it. "Yes, Mistress Mansfield?"

She burst into the room and grasped his hands, unaware at first that anyone was there to witness the gesture. "Oh, Master Crafter, such news I have just heard! Mistress Miller was passing by and told me, but you know what an unreliable gossip she is. I said to myself that you would be the one to tell me whether what she said is true—Pray God it is not! I heard—"

"That the books are lost."

WHAT?

The satyr's mental roar was red pain in Ahijah's skull, an agony so unexpected that he was unaware of the moment when the Widow Mansfield dropped his hands and gasped, "Oh! Master Sylvan. I had no idea you were—that is, I didn't see you return."

"I have often been told that I am remarkably light on my feet," Juvenal said. For all his bitter wit, he looked grim. "What rumor is this of lost books, Mistress?"

"Let her be, Juvenal." Ahijah closed his eyes wearily. "I was about to tell you myself. Some of our more mystically inclined classmates would say that this is but the latest sign of Divine disapproval for the Collegiate School."

"Stuff!" The satyr snorted in a peculiarly equine way that made Dorcas regard him askance. "There once were troubles for us, to be sure. Little money, and few books, and no true fixed abode for school or scholars, but that's past. Haven't we that fine new lodging near the green? Did not Elihu Yale himself, over in London town, make us a grand bequest fat enough to earn him the memorializing of his name in our own beloved school?"

"What school, if there be no books to learn from? And the books of Yale College are still in Saybrook."

"And then? I think our masters have at least the brains to order the library sent here, to its permanent abode."

"It is not that simple, Master Sylvan." Sorrow only made Dorcas Mansfield's face all the more adorable, to Ahijah's eyes. "The Saybrook folk resent the loss of the school to New Haven. They have sent word, I hear, that they refuse to surrender the library."

"A finer library than even Harvard boasts," Ahijah supplied glumly. "Solicited book by book in England and shipped here by good Master Dummer. Boyle's work! Newton's! More than these, many contributed by the very hands which wrote them, and all in the grasp of Saybrook town." His shoulders slumped. "They might as well be on the moon."

"Is that all?" Juvenal pounded Ahijah on the back. "Well, what won't be sent must needs be brought!"

"I know. Such a plan is already underway. This very night, in fact, we leave for Saybrook to fetch back the books. But it will be a perilous journey. We have our enemies. There are more than the Saybrook folk who'd like to see the Collegiate School rooted out of New Haven, building or no building."

"*We* leave?" The words were uttered simultaneously by Juvenal and Dorcas, but the satyr's lively interest in the plan alarmed Ahijah so much that he missed the equally avid look on the young widow's face.

"*We*, meaning myself and a few others. Only enough to manage the loading of the books and the driving of the ox-carts and *no more*," he said firmly. "Too many hands to this rudder will alarm the Saybrook folk, or push them into taking some rash action against the books themselves."

"Ahijah, no." Dorcas was honestly affrighted. "They would not—they *could* not harm the books!"

Of course not. Ahijah felt Juvenal's smirk in his mind. *Like those 'fine champions of education back home in Massachusetts. Why would anyone imagine that people capable of hanging the innocent for witchcraft would* ever *do something as naughty as burning a book?*

"Pox take it, the bridge is gone!" Philip Lawes leaned against the off-ox's yoke and rubbed sweat from his forehead.

A clean kerchief, sweetly scented with lavender, was at his elbow and a treble voice piped in his ear, "Are you certain, Lawes? Mightn't we have missed the proper ford in the dark?"

Philip frowned and used the kerchief as gingerly as though it were made of living snakeskin. What was it about this fellow-traveler of his—what *was* his name?— Thomas Mansfield? So small, so slight, and with a voice to mark him as a more proper inmate of the nursery than the Collegiate School. All Philip knew was that Thomas made him nervous.

His nerves were frayed enough without having had the ill luck to draw this odd bird as his helper in the great enterprise. Although each turn of the ox-cart's wheels brought them closer to New Haven, he was growing steadily more tense. It had been a bad time in Saybrook, with the townsfolk not even bothering to conceal their hostility to the removal of the books. Several of the ox-carts had been attacked and broken. Only through a miracle had the books themselves been preserved.

Miracle, and the work of Ahijah Crafter. Philip blotted away the last of his sweat and patted the sturdy, square crates which had been Master Crafter's unexpected contribution to the expedition. True, some might question the dedication of a scholar whose spare time was turned to carpentry when it might better be reserved for the further study of Holy Writ. Still, there was no denying that Master Crafter's boxes were a godsend. Not only did they protect the books, their unique design allowed the two undamaged ox-carts to efficiently carry the full contents of the Yale library out of Saybrook.

Now, if only Crafter himself were here to cobble together a bridge of boxes!

"I haven't mistaken the ford, Mansfield," Philip replied. "Come nearer the bank and you'll see the wreckage of the bridge itself. They're confirmed in their enmity to us, these Saybrook folk."

Cautiously Philip's companion picked a way down to the waterside and peered at the ruin. "What are we to do now? Turn back and seek another road?"

Lawes sighed. "That, or wait for the other cart to join us here and see what they advise." A second sigh turned into a yawn. "It wouldn't be amiss to seize some sleep while we wait. I'll spread a blanket for us over the crates."

"I'm not weary." The response came rather hastily. "Perhaps I should keep watch while you rest."

"Have it your way." Lawes shrugged and made his hard pallet atop the perfectly level platform the boxes made inside the ox-cart. Soon his snores rumbled through the night.

Effectively alone, "Thomas Mansfield" gathered the collar of her dead husband's coat more closely around her neck and peered into the darkness. Where was the other cart? Where, above all, was Ahijah?

"Better if he'd gone a different way," she murmured, rubbing her hands together for warmth. "If he should see me dressed like this—!" In the beginning, when she had joined the Saybrook venture, there had been carts and men enough for her to be lost in the crowd. Since the bad doings at Saybrook, there were considerably fewer carts, and as for the men, those who hadn't turned white-livered and run at sight of the axes had been dismissed as superfluous after the two remaining carts were loaded. When she tried to slip away with the scholars who would return to New Haven afoot, that strange Master Sylvan had blocked her path and told her that "Thomas Mansfield" was wanted to help Lawes with his cart.

Dorcas still trembled when she recalled Master Sylvan's mocking eyes. He had looked right at her, yet gave no sign that he recognized her. Was Master Sylvan so shortsighted, or was her disguise that good? Would Ahijah too be unable to penetrate it? She had her doubts.

She wondered whether he would be horrified, or merely scandalized if she were discovered before him. A little smile touched her lips. *On the other hand, it might be good for you, Master Crafter, to see me as more than a source of hot meals and clean linens. Learn, Ahijah, that you are not the only one with a love of learning.*

Her smile vanished. The angry faces of the Saybrook folk rose up in memory, making her shiver with more than cold. No love of learning had made them fight to keep the library, but a tradesman's keen eye for what future profit the Collegiate School might bring their town. She could still hear the hungry sound of axes biting the ox-carts to flinders, the terrified bellowing of the beasts, the shouts as the men of law were summoned to drive back the crowd and let the students depart in peace.

Here in the wilderness between Saybrook and New Haven there were no men of law. In the three-days' journey, much could happen. Dorcas Mansfield pulled her Thomas' hat more snugly down to shade her face and tried not to see enemies in every shadow.

That was a mistake.

Just one more round of the game? Please, Little Brother? The satyr drummed his hooves against the side of the lumbering cart and juggled a set of wooden dice from hand to hand. *You're* so *good at it,* he wheedled.

Ahijah trudged on beside the oxen. *How you ever convinced me to play this "game" of yours . . . There's something wicked about it, I'm bound.*

Juvenal affected an offended look. *Wicked?* Ego? *It's only an innocent way to pass a tedious journey, and to sharpen your Talent in the bargain. Look, this time I'll make it easy for you. Try to reach out and tell me what the tavern-owner's thinking right now, back in Saybrook.*

I will not. It's a violation of privacy.

You violated merrily away, since we left Saybrook, so long as you were winning. Be a good sport, now.

Instead of pestering me, Juvenal, see to it that you keep an eye open for any other travellers. I don't want us surprised with you looking like that.

This time there was nothing affected about the satyr's offended look. Laying one hand to his hairy breast he demanded, *What's wrong with the way I look?*

Nothing, to my eyes. But the first unsuspecting farmer or tradesman we encounter will imagine he's seen the Devil himself coming for him on an ox-cart.

No one's abroad at this hour, I've my cape close at hand, and I'm more comfortable travelling naked. Pettishly the satyr added, *No sense being bored and itchy, both. And I am fearsomely bored.*

That isn't my problem. Amuse yourself.

Very well, I will. Juvenal tilted his horned head back and began to serenade the darkened treetops: "One hundred amphorae of Falernian wine on the wall, one hundred amphorae of Falernian wine . . ."

He had only gotten the tally down to ninety-one when Ahijah pulled up short, eyes staring into the night. The oxen rumbled to an easy halt, but the satyr hadn't been paying attention and tumbled from the cart. His furious thoughts assaulted Ahijah, demanding an explanation.

Hush. Ahijah's reply carried a metallic tang of urgency. *There is trouble with the other cart up ahead.*

Trouble? Are the books—?

More than the books are in danger. I heard a cry for help. We're needed now, and we must move swiftly. We'll have to leave the cart.

We can't! The library—

All the vigor of Ahijah's newly accepted Talent poured into Juvenal's mind as the young man compelled the satyr to share his vision:

Axeblades caught a dappled glimmer of moonlight in the forest. Five grim men moved with deliberate intent toward the riverbank, where a cart waited to cross a bridge no longer there. The student asleep atop the stacked crates in the cart awoke and shouted, only to have his objections cut off by a neatly thrown rock the size of an apple. Blood, black by night, spread across his forehead as he fell. His smaller companion knelt beside him.

"You've killed him!"

The voice was no longer disguised. Startled, the five men paused. One among them took a tentative step forward.

"You?" His expression held mixed recognition and something colder, more unhealthy.

Then the vision tore away as Ahijah and Juvenal raced through the forest. The satyr soon outdistanced the man. The woods were his element, his ancient home.

Juvenal! Wait for me! Ahijah panted for breath, but words uttered in mind-speech did not depend on anything so fragile as the capacity of human lungs. The satyr could not claim he did not hear.

I'm sorry, Little Brother, I can't. You saw who that is they've brought to bay by the riverside. If I wait for you, it will be too late for her.

They won't harm her! How could they? If you saw her, you had to see who that man is with them. He's not one of the Saybrook lot.

It might be better for Mistress Mansfield if he were.

What? But he's her brother Napthali!

And Atreus was Thyestes' brother! Which didn't stop him from chopping up Thyestes' children and serving them to their father over some family spat. I must run on. You crash so through the brush that they'll hear you long before you're there, and my lord Pan works terrible tricks on men surprised by night, who fear discovery. We don't want them pushed into an act they'll regret, to say nothing of Mistress Mansfield. Farewell! A flash of hooves, and Juvenal was out of sight.

Ahijah pressed on, part of his brain cursing the satyr, the other monitoring the scene beside the river.

Only a little watching, and Ahijah bitterly admitted that Juvenal had been right in his assessment of mortal family relations:

"Napthali! What are you doing here?"

Another of the men started and turned to Master Weaver. *"The wench knows you? How is this?"*

Napthali was sweating. *"Impossible, friend Seymour. I never saw her in my life."*

Master Seymour dealt Napthali's arm a sturdy blow. *"Fool! We agreed to keep our names hidden. Now the slut knows who I am."*

Strangely enough, Napthali smiled and adjusted his grip on the axe he carried. *"Knowledge cuts with two edges. Who'll take the word of some college brat's whore? My life was snug before they brought their cursed school to New Haven. Oh, not so snug as it would be were I master of my own house, rather than dependent on my dear,* dear *sister's spotty charity. Still, if you fear the slut's testimony, I've a way to buy her silence."*

Master Weaver strode forward, full of purpose. His four comrades exchanged doubtful looks, and Master Seymour reached out to lay a staying hand on Napthali's shoulder. *"Let the wench be. It's only the books we're after."*

Napthali roughly cast off Master Seymour's hand. *"If we let her go, we'll get more than books for our trouble."*

"Wait! I have some little coin. Give it to her—"

"—and have her take your coin and still hale you before the justice? Women are vindictive beasts. That's her lover as your rock's laid low, Master Townsend! Will you trust her silence? And you, Master Hubbard, Master Skinner?"

"You idiot!" Seymour bellowed. *"Now she knows us all!"*

Napthali smiled. *"For now. Brothers, your cause is mine—to get the Collegiate School out of New Haven. You just leave me to handle this my way."*

Master Seymour tried again to hold Napthali back. This time a wedge of sharpened metal answered. Master Seymour's scream rang clear in Ahijah's ear as he lost all contact with his mental vision. He needed it no longer. He was there.

Breathing hard, he leaned against a pine tree. The scene before him was twin to what his mind had seen, only from a different vantage. *I must have been viewing it through Dorcas' eyes. After all, it was her cry for help alerted me.* He saw her, still crouched near Lawes's body, and without really thinking about it, his mind launched a heartening sending to hers. *Dorcas, dread not! Help is here!* Then he *did* think, and looked to his weaponless hands. *Help . . . he* mused. *But how?*

How else, Little Brother, but with what the gods have given us! There was a deliberately loud rustling from the bushes beyond where the five men stood. Even Napthali stopped short at the sound. Another strong shaking of leaf and branch, and Juvenal burst forth among them, goat-footed, horned, and fiery-eyed. He pranced forward, tail flicking madly, and cut a courtly bow before the stunned Napthali.

"Well done, thou good and faithful servant!" he cried.

The results were *almost* as might be anticipated.

Three of the sturdy Saybrook men exclaimed as one, "The Devil!" and bolted for the woodland. Master Seymour stood amazed, holding his bleeding arm. Napthali had dealt him a shallow cut, but the shock of it combined with Juvenal's sudden appearance was not conducive to giving a man's feet wings. Frozen, he watched Juvenal at his fiendish leaps and capers, and began to pray.

Unfortunately, Napthali neither ran nor froze. Juvenal skittered closer. "Kneel, man, before thy hellspawned lord!" he commanded, striking a grand pose.

Napthali blinked. "Hellspawned, my arse," he said. Doubling his free hand into a fist, he bashed Juvenal across the point of his chin. The satyr sprawled.

Master Seymour fell to his knees. "Praise God, he has overcome Satan himself!"

"Stuff," said Napthali. "That's just one of them Yale men as boards with my fool sister. I've seen that face across the table enough times, sopping up an honest man's victuals, to know him when I see him."

"But—but his hooves! His horns!"

Napthali spat scornfully. "You a college-bred man, Seymour? Or ever seen one naked?"

Master Seymour allowed that he lacked either experience.

"Well, all them trappings—horns and fur and hooves and all—they're likely just more affectations as they pick up in school. You know, like Latin."

"Even so?"

"Harvard men's got bunny tails in their britches," Napthali assured him. He took his axe in both hands and looked at Dorcas. "The sooner New Haven's cleansed of them, the better."

"No, Napthali." Ahijah stepped out of the woods. "I will not let you harm your own sister."

"Your sister, Master Weaver?" Master Seymour goggled. "Not the widow? But what is she doing here, dressed so?"

"Shut up, you!" Napthali snarled, shaking the axe at him. "I say that wench is no sister of mine, and if you think of saying otherwise, this can silence more than one wagging tongue." He gazed coldly at Ahijah. "Yours first."

"You may try," Ahijah replied. "And I will try to stop you." He thrust out his hand, though it held nothing more formidable than the little Greek text which had originally been the summoning of Juvenal. It was all he had that even vaguely resembled a weapon. If he were to deal with Napthali, he didn't want to go about it empty-handed.

"What, waving a sermon volume at me, Master Crafter? For what good it'll do you." Napthali laughed hoarsely. "I thought you'd be along. Travel in gaggles, you bookmen do, like geese. Well, I know how to handle geese." He raised his axe and came for Ahijah.

Ahijah watched him come, heard Dorcas' prayers, heard her sobbing and calling out his name. His mind raced as outer time slowed. *Juvenal said we can only use what the gods—I mean, God has given us,* he thought. *But what have I got? Mind-speech? That's no weapon, and all I recall of Father's teachings is the Law of Similarity. Like calls to like, but how can that save us from a greedy madman with an axe? Ah Lord, I wish I'd paid heed to more of Father's lessons! Like calls . . . like calls . . .*

His fingers clutched the little Greek text so tightly that the thin leather binding slipped from his hand. He fumbled to catch it before it fell, and found himself staring at a moonlit page. The letters danced, his eye followed. *Like calls to like.* He recalled his scholastic desperation that had driven him to that first, tentative summoning. *But then I had the herbs, the bowl Father gave me . . . How can I accomplish anything without them? These are only words.*

Only words. Just as the books now helpless in their boxes were only words. Yet how many souls stood ready to die defending them! Juvenal, who for all his cynicism had insisted on coming to the library's rescue. Dorcas, who might have stayed safe at home, yet who had come into the wilderness to protect the future of the College. And what did a college produce? Only words.

All the power of his mind drained down into the open page. The words called to him. Their magic drew him deeper in until he was there, mind-led, dashing across an ivory plain, sounding the alarm. *To arms, to arms! Your brethren are in danger!* To each letter he passed, he sent an ice-clear vision of the college books sliding from their ravaged crates into a watery grave.

Behind him, he heard a chittering, as if a cavern full of monstrous bats had been roused from sleep. He turned, and saw the letters swelling, bristling, the black of ink deepening to the fiercer black of rage. He gasped in wonder as the word *harpyiai*—harpies—sprouted wings and talons, soared into the sky. *Kentauros*—centaur—grew sleek and swift, took spear in hand and galloped after. At his summons, the Cretan minotaur and the Nemean lion broke roaring from the page's prison. Like called to like, letters called forth the dreadful, marvellous beings they symbolized, and all answered to the will of one brave human mind.

This time Napthali did not stop to ask whether this new crop of monsters held Harvard or Yale degrees. Giving the squawk of a hawk-snared chicken, he flung down his axe and ran for his life. Master Seymour clutched his bleeding arm and sprinted away in his own direction. In his wild scramble, he tripped over the just-rousing Juvenal.

The satyr saw what was happening and shook cobwebs of disbelief from his head. *This won't do. Ahijah. Ahijah!*

Hmmm? The response came from very far away. Juvenal clicked his tongue and trotted over to where the young man still stood entranced, gazing into his book. Briskly the satyr took it from him and slammed the cover shut. From the forest the sounds of many monsters roaring, shrieking, bawling, and generally mucking about, ceased abruptly.

Discreetly veiled in a greatcoat borrowed from Mistress Mansfield, Juvenal came around the corner of the cart to announce, "Lawes will be fine. I've bound his wound and he's sleeping naturally. We can recover the other cart and drive on to New Haven as soon as it gets li—"

They did not hear him. Miffed, the satyr leaned against the near ox's flank and eavesdropped openly.

"I thought my heart would burst when I heard your cry for help," Ahijah was saying. He gently touched her face.

Dorcas did not object, although she did say, "I didn't. I was too frightened to call aloud, for fear of what they'd do."

"You didn't? I swear I heard—"

"—but it was kind of you to risk discovery by shouting for me not to fear. 'Dorcas, dread not! Help is here,' you shouted to me. With one so brave to save me, I knew all would be well." She snuggled deeper into his arms.

Ahijah's embrace tightened, his eyes were fixed on her, but his startled thoughts flew to Juvenal. *Did you hear?*

I heard, the satyr replied, very grave. *Just as you heard a cry from her that never was. Just as she heard—*

A cry . . . Ahijah recalled "hearing" Dorcas sob. His fingers searched for sign of tears on her cheeks and found none. She sighed, content. Bewildered, he looked to the satyr, who shrugged.

I suppose this means you must wed her, if only to further the cause of scientific investigation into the phenomenon of mind-speech, Little Brother.

Ahijah brightened. *Why, of course! Surely I must!*

"Must what, dear?" Dorcas purred sleepily in his arms.

It may mean the end of my studies—they don't permit married men at Yale—but I can open a carpentry shop, earn a decent living, pursue my studies independently, you can remain at the Collegiate School to take your diploma, no shame in honest work— Ahijah's thoughts bubbled on, sparkling with the unmixed sunshine of a happy future.

"Ssshhh, love. You chatter so, you'll bring a plague of squirrels down on us." Dorcas reached up and, in the interests of preserving them from the predations of vicious, night-roaming squirrels, sweetly silenced the flow of words she thought came from Ahijah's lips.

She'll learn, thought Juvenal. *And so will he. The gods know, Aphrodite keeps a livelier school than any human tutor.* So he left the pair undisturbed to follow their own particular path of education, for God, for country, and for Yale.

Anno Domini 1735

A SPELL FOR BRASS BUTTONS

by Ru Emerson

Lucinda Amelia Crafter Greene stood against the ship's rail, eyes fixed eagerly on what could be seen of the shore—in truth little, between the very early hour, fog, and the smoke which her father had cautioned would be a part of everyday life for the next three years. He had not properly warned her of the odor carried by that smoke and fog, nor of the noise, already near deafening. On sober reflection, Lucinda doubted words could have conveyed the sense of either sound *or* smell.

All the same: London! From the day her parents had spoken of the opportunity to enlarge Father's connections and to buy into a Dutch shipping company, she had envisioned this moment, and it was no less exciting than she had dreamed it. The shallow-drafted carrier that had brought them from Greenwich when the tide turned sought the docks, a wind sprang up with the first hint of sun—a broad smirch of orangy-yellow within the gray—and suddenly, there was the Saint Paul's Cathedral looming vast and enormous above Tower Bridge with its ramshackle motley of houses. And there, the Tower . . .

There was a long delay, while the ship was made fast to the docks, and then Customs men swarmed the decks. Finally they were able to bring Lucinda's poor, pale mother ashore. Arabella laughed faintly; Lucinda was more than half-supporting her as they waited for Andrew to hire a coach. "Your father told me I should not care for sea travel, and he was right! I shall feel the land swaying beneath my feet for days!" She sighed faintly and leaned into her daughter's arm. "Now, do remember, Lucy! Your aunt Bettany has offered to bring you out, since you are here and of an age. You must pay very close heed to all she tells you; your father will not always be in London to pass judgment on the young gentlemen you will meet, and I am no judge of city fellows." She glanced around cautiously, lowered her voice and spoke rapidly. "But *you* must use all the wit and skill I have passed you, remembering that Aunt Bettany, has expressed a strong desire against use of any of my family's talents in her household!" Lucinda nodded dutifully, and hoped her face did not show boredom. She had heard this lecture *so* very often!

I know very well how to deal with young men! Boston is not London, but London lads will surely wrap about a finger as easily as any. Particularly when the finger belonged to a young woman blessed with her mother's intelligence and dark-haired, gray-eyed beauty, as well as her father's wit. Wit was as prized in London, they said, as beauty or form.

Arabella had been unable to work any Crafter skill since the ship left Boston Harbor—whether due to sea sickness or because of the water itself—and the wisp whom Lucinda's grandfather Amer had called Willow had been silent and unseen since they'd stepped onto the ship.

Lucinda had not been able to utilize her power, either, but she had not particularly cared to try aboard ship, with no one about save common seamen and two gentlemen her father's age. *She* could not use it to heal an unhappy stomach, since she'd never felt the least interest in her mother's herb gardens. And Arabella's alchemic studies bored her. If she had not discovered a year or so earlier that the family talents were useful in reading—and controlling—the few beaux her parents permitted her she would doubtless have eschewed them entirely.

Andrew Greene came back with two skinny boys and a square-shouldered man to transfer cases to the carriage.

Lucinda remembered very little of that ride to her Aunt Bettany Greene's town house, save a confusion of people, smoke, noise, and the nearly overwhelming stench of the mud thrown up by carriage wheels.

Aunt Bet lived on a street only slightly quieter, in a two-storied, comfortable new house. There were separate apartments for her parents, and a room for Lucinda nearly as large as the entire second floor of their Boston house. Aunt Bet herself welcomed them, though she was still in dark, practical night robes, a frilly white cap covering her gray curls. She was actually Andrew's aunt, and must, Lucinda thought, have been at least fifty, for her face had set into lines that gave her a formidable appearance on the rare occasion she wasn't smiling or laughing. All the same, that so elderly a dame must accompany her to parties and dinners! She tried to dismiss such a thought as unworthy and ungrateful, for after all, without the elderly dame, there would *be* no parties and dinners. And surely Aunt Bet would not accompany her everywhere once she was introduced into the level of society where she would be circulating! Certainly not all chaperones would be so ancient, and so many years past their own season.

The level of society Lucinda would circulate in would of course not be Royal, or even noble. All the same, Bettany Greene must be wealthy, for there were two menservants to carry baggage from the carriage and there seemed to be young servant girls everywhere: dusting, sweeping, even one to unpack Lucinda's few bags. Aunt Bet followed them all up the broad staircase and came into the room after her great-niece. "There! I thought you should have a room away from the ones I gave your parents. A young gel should have a little privacy! This looks out over the street. Mind the curtains when you look out; there are *always* folk about. If you are not overtired from the ship, this afternoon we will visit my seamstress and begin a wardrobe for you, child. That's a sweet gown but at least a year out of style here and the color doesn't suit you. I know, I know, practical and dark for travel. All the same! I've planned a tea here, tomorrow afternoon, so you may

meet some of the young ladies in your circle. There is a
dance two nights after; we shall go through your gowns
to see if perhaps you might attend that. You surely cannot
go to your first London dance in an outmoded garment!"
Her aunt glanced over her shoulder, took a step closer to
Lucinda, and lowered her voice. "Mind now! Your mother
wrote you were a practical and sensible lass; I can see your
father in you, so p'raps you've a share of his brains. Not
all the young blades in London are suitable company for a
proper young gel; mind you have nothing to do with any
I warn against!" She eyed Lucinda anxiously until the girl
nodded, then smiled and backed away. "That's good, then.
We understand each other. You rest if you like; little Amy
will bring you tea and toast in a while." And with that, she
was gone, door closed behind her. Lucinda smiled sourly
and made a face at the inside of the door. *As if I would ever
take up with an unsuitable man!* she thought rather smugly.
*Does she think I'll run off with a servant, or someone like
that brute on the docks? Or a rake? I should know what
to do with such a man!* she thought, and turned away to
remove the heavy brown dress. Aunt Bet was right about
the gown, whatever else she did not understand: the brown
dampened the deep red highlights in her hair, dulled her
eyes, and made a botch of her complexion.

Poor old Aunt Bet, she reflected as she tightened the belt
of her wrap and stretched out on top of the bed. She'd been up
since well before dawn, and her eyes burned from the London
air. Perhaps a few moments to close them . . . *What would
Aunt Bet know about the wild lads?* They weren't talked
about in polite society—the hard-drinking, hard-gambling
men with their private clubs—and never around unmarried
young ladies. *Aunt Bet wouldn't know one if he—well, she
wouldn't.*

London! She found it hard to believe, still, that she was
here. Andrew Greene was a kind and reasonably indulgent
papa, but he had wanted his daughter to marry and remain
in Boston. He'd even chosen a husband for her, in the
old-fashioned manner: the eldest son of a business asso-
ciate, a boy she could scarcely bear to look at. But her

mother had argued for her—vigorously for Arabella, who ordinarily took the course of least resistance. "The girl is too young to be a wife at seventeen, and London will be a good experience for her." Andrew had been overwhelmed, and finally agreed.

"Oh, yes, Mother," Lucinda whispered to her new, and very private, ceiling. "I do intend that it shall be an experience."

The afternoon was a whirlwind: Arabella still slept, and Andrew had gone in search of business associates he ordinarily dealt with by letter. Aunt Bet went through Lucinda's clothing, *tched* over everything, directed her to dress in the dark blue as "the least outdated thing you own," and carried her off bodily to the shops. There had been a seamstress and a French modiste who had both measured her and consulted with Bettany as though her great-niece were a wax figure. There had been other shops then: for the newest shades of silk and taffeta, for several pairs of gloves, for hats and fittings for shoes that could withstand the London streets.

The seamstress came to the house later the same afternoon with fabrics, lace, and sketches; she left over an hour later with Lucinda's dark blue, promising to return it in two days at the latest, altered enough that it could be worn to a dance without embarassing the wearer.

Bettany's tea the next afternoon was a great success: somehow the maids had steamed the worst creases from her nutmeg-brown afternoon gown, and with the accessories her aunt had purchased for her, it somehow looked not so out of fashion. Bettany's own maid had dressed her hair in tight curls and covered it with a tiny white lace cap.

I still look like a country cousin, Lucinda thought anxiously, *but not awful*. She went down to tea with knots in her stomach. Young men were one thing, but it was other girls one spent the most time with. Their reaction to her would be most important.

Arabella, in deep-green silk, her dark hair glossy but her face still too thin and so pale, stayed throughout the meal;

Andrew stopped by for a very few moments, just long enough to look over her new friends, Lucinda supposed. Fortunately, he was more open-minded than many a Bostonian; mere lightheartedness would not offend him. He seemed to find the half dozen or so young ladies acceptable, for after three sips of an excellent tea, he put the thin porcelain cup aside and left.

It would be several days before Lucinda could remember the names of all the girls and connect them to individual faces. Particularly since she'd had to swear so often not to attempt magic in London, let alone in this house. *And I won't—well, unless I wish to enhance an attraction,* Lucinda promised herself. *That* was something her mother had not taught her; she'd worked it out on her own. A sensible girl would keep such a skill to herself anyway.

Blond, stout Jemima wore pale pink with a little too much lace and a neckline a trifle too deep for a day gown, but she was the most amusing of the group. Lise, too, was golden-haired but slender, exquisitely gowned in a darker shade of pink in the latest French cut. She spoke with just a touch of a French accent. There were two girls named Ann, both dark and ordinary enough they might have been sisters; Katherine, whose very red hair would not stay up where it belonged; restless Carlyle, who more often paced than sat, even when taking tea. They were enthusiastic in their welcome of Bettany's great-niece and after a while Arabella withdrew to talk to the older women while the girls talked and giggled together.

"Surely it's an improvement on Puritan Boston, Lucy, but I must warn you the season is a dull one, compared to past ones," Katherine began. Jemima snorted.

"That's always said. Women like my eldest sister have such wild tales of their own seasons, but I'd wager those same stories have come down every year, and they were never true to begin!"

"But a dull season is better for all of us," one of them—an Ann?—put in timidly. "Because the chaperones pay less attention, and put fewer restrictions on us."

"*You* say that because you were permitted to go to Vauxhall twice the past fortnight," one of the other dark-haired girls told her in mock severity. "Lucy, dear, we'll have such fun, particularly since it's Mistress Bettany who's sponsoring you. Nothing gets by her, of course. You'll need to do exactly as she says. All the same, *she* hasn't forgotten what it's like to be a girl in London." She turned to her friends. "Whom shall we find to introduce to Lucy? She must have an escort to the Hanstead Ball in two weeks, don't you agree?"

It hadn't been at all what she'd expected—or feared: the young ladies weren't snobbish at all; no one made fun of her gown or her much-too-long hair. And their enthusiasm was catching. By the end of the casual little meal, Lucinda felt like she'd known them all forever. They were all bent over the tea table while Carlyle related a horrible embarrassment that had happened to someone they all knew and loathed— and who'd richly deserved snubbing—when the parlor door opened and one of Aunt Bet's servants came in, followed by a gloriously golden young man.

Richard Coucey was the perfect end to a lovely afternoon. Lucinda was vaguely aware of the girls around her sitting a little straighter, of eager smiles and a hushed giggle or two as the young man bent low over Bettany's outstretched hand. He was laughing quietly as he straightened. "Now, Miss Bet, please don't be cross. I should have awaited an invitation—"

"When have you ever?" Bettany replied severely, but her eyes were warm and a smile was tugging at her mouth. She patted his hand. "Impatient boy, you always were that." She introduced him to Arabella, and Lucinda thought her mother looked a little wary—as though so much physical prettiness and charm must mask *some* flaw—and then called her niece over. "Dear Richard calls me Aunt when he chooses. His father spent most of *his* childhood in our country house. I've known both Richard and his sister since they were babes. You'll like Elizabeth," she added. Richard Coucey extended both hands, captured one of hers, and gave her a smile that sent the blood to her cheeks. "I spoke of you to

Richard," Aunt Bet continued, "and he's wanted ever since to meet you, Lucinda dear."

He was so very good-looking, she thought giddily. The current style suited the very slender such as he: the long, straight waistcoats, knee-breeches, the frocked coats. The deep sky blue of his frockcoat matched his eyes, as he surely knew. But standing so close to him now, Lucinda could not be so cool and analytical. His hair was pale gold; it lay in crisp curls across his forehead and over his ears. His mouth was a generous bow that looked as though it knew best how to smile, and something in his eyes promised mischief. But the long-fingered, narrow hands were unexpectedly strong. "So pleased," she managed, and *was* pleased she didn't stammer.

"And I am delighted," he returned with another of those radiant smiles. His teeth were small for a man's, very even and unmarked. "Perhaps your aunt will vouch for me to your parents, and allow me to escort you about the City tomorrow. I have a small open carriage, quite suitable for showing the sights to a young lady. And, of course, her chaperone, if Miss Bet wishes to accompany us." He turned to glance inquiringly at Bettany. Lucinda, to her annoyance, found herself waiting with held breath for her aunt's reply, and her mother's.

"Well—" The older woman glanced at Arabella, who nodded. "If I didn't know you so well, young Richard, I *would* call it impertinent. A short drive about London, in an open carriage—it won't reflect on the gel's repute. You must swear to have her back by one o'clock, mind! We have an appointment with the modiste not long after, and she must be presentable for the Connelaigh dance. Of course, if Lucinda does not wish to go—"

"Oh," Lucinda replied as Richard raised his eyebrows and turned back to await her reply, "I should be quite glad to." *What very thick lashes he has*, she thought as he pressed her fingers again and took his leave, and this time she could feel her face turning red. Fortunately, he was already gone. The girls teased her for the better part of an hour over the conquest she had made.

As they were leaving, though, Carlyle remained a little behind and took her aside, glancing cautiously around to make certain they had a space to themselves before whispering against her new friend's ear. "Aunt Bet won't have heard anything—she has a particular fondness for the Coucey family and particularly Richard—well, who wouldn't, just looking at him? All the same, he has a certain repute: not enough to keep most of the London mothers from trying to snare him for their daughters, I assure you! Just— oh, he and his friends ride and gamble; he's dueled, up in Cambridge where his father owns a summer property. And he's fond of the ladies but has never taken deeply to one. He has no repute as a rake, of course, for no mother would want him then, looks and money or no," Carlyle assured her. "All the same, he's not entirely a safe young man. You mustn't let him too near your heart, Lucy! He's broken plenty of those the past three seasons! Just a warning, do you see?"

"I see. Thank you." Lucinda smiled and followed Carlyle from the room. "He certainly is a fair pretty creature; but I have at least two years in London. I want to see some of it, to enjoy parties and dances. I cannot if I attach myself at once to one man, can I?"

"Besides, think how people would talk," Carlyle said, and her mouth quirked. "That you accepted the first man who presented himself—as though afraid no other would. How dreadful for a girl's reputation. And how very dull!" They both laughed, and Carlyle left with the rest.

The hall was very quiet, and a servant was lighting lamps; despite the early hour, it was nearly dark outside from all the smoke. Lucinda heard her aunt and her mother on the landing above; she gathered up her skirts and followed.

They were in her parents' apartment; the door was not quite closed. Lucinda would have passed by had she not heard her own name. She paused, then stopped altogether. Wrong to eavesdrop, of course. All the same . . .

Arabella was speaking in that flat, emotionless tone that meant her mind was set. "I cannot put a name to my dislike for the lad, mistress Bettany. If I could—but it's my daughter he's made a set at."

"So he has," Aunt Bet replied coolly. She was clearly affronted. "Richard Coucey is an excellent catch, and he's made no such set at any gel this season. Your Lucinda took his eye. He's of good family and well-to-do—"

"So why has he made this set at my Lucy? I know my daughter is worthy of the finest gentleman, but I find your Richard Coucey's sudden attachment unsettling. But in any event, Lucy is too young to wed," Arabella said flatly.

"No gel is too young, and *I* was wed at seventeen. Though I agree, there is no reason to settle on one man at the beginning of the London season. I have known Richard since his poor mama, rest her soul, bore him. There's no temper in him, no mean spirit; he has funds of his own and his father owns considerable property in the north. Oh, he drinks and gambles in the company of his friends—what young man doesn't?"

"Ask *that* of a Massachusetts colonist raised around Puritans," Arabella said dryly.

"Oh, well. If they're all like your Increase Mather, who once came here to impress society with his wit and talent, and proved himself merely dull, narrow, and unappetizing—! Richard has a club, but all young men do. They drink and talk of business and other things most women find boring. Like all gentlemen, Richard keeps his club life separate from his dealings with young ladies, and *those* are impeccable, or I should have heard, believe me!"

"I don't doubt you. It's just—" Arabella's voice trailed off. Lucinda pressed against the wall, anxiety tightening her stomach. If her mother forbade her this lovely young man—!

"It's not that—Andrew called it a talent—of yours, is it?" Bettany demanded sharply. "Some family sorcery? I did warn you, Arabella, I'm an open-minded woman, but I'll have none of that in my house!"

"You wrote to say so, and I agreed, if you recall," Lucinda's mother replied coolly. "If Andrew told you about my family, he'll have told you I'm no witch; I've made no pact with the Devil. I seldom use magic, anyway, but I haven't been able to since we left Boston." She sighed. "I do not know, and so I see I must give over to you, Bettany. He is a rarely handsome and well-mannered lad. No mother could fault him."

"Perhaps it's knowing the gel's moving into another part of her life, where a mother becomes less important than a husband," Bettany said. Arabella snorted.

"I knew that day would come. John, my son, is already on his own."

"A son at Harvard College is not the same as a daughter taking her season in London. Consider this, then: Richard will prove a good escort until she is introduced to other young men. With Richard dancing attendance on her, believe me, she won't lack for such young men."

Lucinda, her ears extremely warm, moved on down the hall to her own room and shut the door behind her. "But I don't want other young men," she whispered. She could feel her heart thumping against the nutmeg bodice—an extremely unfamiliar sensation in one ordinarily so cool and collected where young men were concerned. "I want none but Richard Coucey." Lucinda sat on one of the small satin-cushioned chairs to think. She would see to it that Richard did dance attendance on her; and then, whoever else might choose to seek her attentions, he'd not get them.

The weeks flew, and she found it difficult to separate events one from another. There were fittings, new gowns and two pairs of square-heeled dancing shoes, soft slippers. Her aunt arranged to have her hair cut and curled in the new style, and got her more lace caps and two of the wide, pleated sack gowns. There were teas, an endless number of mothers and chaperones to meet and try to keep straight, and more girls, though she found herself settled into friendship with the ones she'd first met at tea in her aunt's parlor. There were dinners, and dances she attended with her mother or her aunt, or in the company of the girls and their chaperones.

And there was Richard Coucey, everywhere she went. Somehow she never seemed able to wield the tricks she knew to capture his attention and bind him strictly to her, but it hadn't proved necessary. Richard took her about London, showed her the sights, the gardens; he escorted her to a water carnival, with ships and boats plying the Thames and Master Handel himself conducting his *Water Music*; he took her to plays and concerts, he danced as many dances with her as the girls and their chaperones would permit.

She no longer even tried to pretend to herself or to him that she so much as looked at other young men. "My darling Cinda," he said, "you cannot think how pleased I am to hear that."

Her father spent little time in London, and now he was in Holland, bargaining with the Dutch East India Company, seeing about certain products he wanted to ship into Boston. Arabella visited members of her own family—distant connections of Lucinda's grandfather Amer—and through them had managed an introduction to a private scientific association attached to the Royal Society, one of the rare ones that accepted women. She was frequently away from home, and though she attended dances and teas with her daughter, she seemed willing to leave society and its finer points to Bettany. "You won't mind, Lucy darling?" she asked rather anxiously at one point. "A girl should be permitted such frothy activity and conversation, but it bores me dreadfully, and there is so much I can learn here! Besides"—Arabella smiled—"I doubt you see much but Richard, do you?"

Well, that much was true: Lucinda often found the conversations boring, but Richard made up for all.

Her father returned from Holland and almost at once went away again, this time to Italy, where he would remain for most of the fall.

The weather had stayed warm, unusually so they told her. Lucinda was dressed for an open carriage ride, Richard was to escort her to a party where it was rumored Royalty might actually make a brief appearance. She'd spent hours readying herself, and now waited anxiously in the lower hall, unable to stand her room any longer. Richard had said that when Andrew came home he would seek her hand, but he'd asked that meanwhile she say nothing to Arabella. "Your mother does not quite like me, sweet Cinda, and

I cannot think why." The clock in the hallway struck the hour; he was late, adding to her anxiety. Lucinda walked down to the door, back up toward the parlor, and stopped abruptly. Her mother had apparently come home early from her scientific-society meeting; she and Aunt Bet were in there arguing furiously.

"I discovered only today that someone has been giving me a dose to dull my power! I am amazed, Bettany, that you should stoop to such a thing!"

"I've done nothing of the sort!" the older woman replied shrilly, but Arabella overrode her.

"Not only that, but I've learned a thing or two of your precious Richard Coucey! Have you heard of the Hellfire Club?"

"Bah!" Bettany replied angrily. "That was twenty years ago; it's long disbanded."

"Is it? There are such clubs all about London, young men drinking and pursuing loose women, pretending to conduct Black Masses—"

"How *dare* you suggest that Richard—!"

"It is worse than that, Bettany. There is a club called the Devil's Advocates—you'll have heard of it."

"Aye, a gambling club; they say it was involved in scandal in Cambridge."

"A girl, an innkeeper's daughter, fell from a window and died. During a Black Mass that was no pretense."

"Oho!" Bettany crowed. "And you will connect Richard Coucey with such an unsavory thing?"

"I need not; he has done it himself. Bettany, there is no question now of his having any association with my daughter. I will not allow Lucinda to see him again."

They continued to go at it; Bettany now shouting an angry defense of her young protégé. Lucinda heard nothing else, however; she gathered her skirts close and hurried to the front door, worked the heavy bolt, and ran down the steps to the street. Her heart was laboring, her breath coming short; fortunately for her peace of mind, a familiar carriage was just coming down the street. She drew her hem up and ran to meet it.

• • •

At her urgent request, Richard drove as rapidly away from the house as traffic would permit. He listened gravely to her story, patted her hand, and shook his head when she'd done. "Poor dearest Cinda, I see old malicious gossip has surfaced and must be dealt with." He held her fingers to his lips. "Sit back, close your eyes a moment. You're distraught, and it will do no good for you to arrive so upset. I shall drive along the Strand, shall I? And permit you to relax. No, just sit quietly. Allow me to think how best to retrieve the situation with your poor mama."

She did as he suggested. Now that she was with him, what she had done worried her: the servant would find the door unlocked and her mother would realize where she had gone, and why. It was the kind of thing that could cause a girl to be locked in her room for the remainder of the season, and if Arabella was as angry as she'd sounded . . .

If any of what she'd said was true! But surely—! Lucinda stirred, opened her eyes. It was dark here, and only one other carriage was about. "Richard? This is not the Strand."

"No. It's quieter here."

"But—" She swallowed. "Until we are betrothed, it's not permitted for me to be in such seclusion with you."

"Worried for your repute?" He laughed quietly. The horse had slowed; the other carriage was out of sight. There were lights, city lamps, but they seemed a great distance away.

She managed a smile. "But since it is the only one I have, of course I am." He was quiet; so quiet her heart began pounding again, as it had outside the closed parlor door. "Richard? What Mother heard—"

"Oh, that," he replied carelessly, and cast her a smile that was a gleam of teeth in the darkness. "I could say it is all slander, but that would not be fair to you, dearest Cinda." He waited; she opened her mouth but couldn't make words come. "I founded the Advocates, you see. We are quite exclusive, just thirteen. Fourteen, if you count the Master, but he comes only at certain times. For the Mass, you know."

"Dearest God," she whispered, and he laughed.

"Oh, not God, my sweet! We've all made a pact; it has a certain cost—"

"Just your immortal soul!"

"Exactly so. I see you're not entirely innocent! But the cost is more than balanced by the knowledge and the power one gains in return. I had heard from Mistress Bet, you know, about your mother; there are members of her family in London and others in Cambridge, and I've often wondered how well a blending of the two might work." Lucinda shook her head numbly. "I can easily sway mistress Bet—she adores me—and your father is such a babe in these matters, he'll accept me for my connections and my wealth—and of course, because you adore me, dearest Cinda." She shook her head again. "Well, but, you did, and you will again. After tonight, your mother will be no obstacle to my quest for your hand."

"You will not harm her—!" She caught at his arm with both hands; he shook her off easily.

"I will harm no one. But thirteen of us are to gather tonight, just north of London. A celebration, you see. You must meet my friends, and our Master. And it is said such ceremonies are best when the altar is graced with a naked virgin." He paused; Lucinda stared at him, stunned into a horrified silence. Outwardly, nothing had changed: his profile was still a work of art, his mouth still sweet; his voice held the same warmth that had won her. *How shall I ever trust any man again, after this?* "No one will touch you, sweet, if you feared it. True virgins are much too rare to waste. But you will surely not refuse me, knowing that I hold such a secret, will you? And your mother—"

Dear God, Mother. She felt ill. The carriage slowed again; for one mad moment, she considered leaping to the ground and running, but he would catch her in no time. Indeed, he had a hand on her arm already. "You'll not leave me, will you?" He drew the carriage to a halt and brought out a silver flask. "Here. You will drink this." She shook her head. "I'd not use force against you." She took it, sniffed gingerly. It smelled rather like fresh-cut trees but not as clean. "It's merely gin. You're overly excited, dear girl. This will relax you." When she would have merely touched it to her lips, he pressed it against her teeth and she swallowed deeply. The night swam with flecks of colored light and her ears rang. He poured another long drink down her throat, took back the flask, and edged the horse back onto the road. Lucinda watched the black shadows of trees go by, faster and faster, until everything blurred.

Later, she could not have said what was real and what was not: Richard swore a dreadful oath and the carriage swerved. There was a great, spinning light suddenly before them, and then overhead; the carriage tilted and she seemed to fall forever before hard ground shook her bones and drove the air from her. Richard was shouting again, this time surely in fear. The horse screamed and bolted. Lucinda fell back and let her eyes close; the rattle of wheels grew fainter; she heard what might have been a man's terrified shout and a splash.

She woke in her room two days later, aching, lethargic; for days after, she ate when fed, otherwise slept. Her mother sat by her bed; surely she must have slept, but whenever Lucinda woke, she was there.

Richard Coucey was dead, drowned, and she was too ill and exhausted to weep for him—or for the man she had thought he was. She was too ill to recall much of what he'd said, much of what had happened at the last, or to be grateful that somehow she had been spirited back to her Aunt Bettany's house without anyone knowing she had been in Richard's carriage that evening.

She managed to stay on her feet for his funeral; his sister Elizabeth, pale-faced and as beautifully golden as her brother had been, took his body home to Cambridge. There was considerable sympathy for Lucinda, but the season of course went on. It went on without her; Richard's loss had left a great void in her heart. And not long after his death, Arabella herself took ill. Even with her daughter's best efforts and the finest physicians Bettany could find, even with Elizabeth Coucey's attendance, and her own physician, a member of the Academy and a professor at Cambridge,

Arabella grew daily thinner and paler. She finally refused any further medical attentions. "Lucy darling, it's not anything medicine could cure; even my own skills are useless against it. It's—vengeance, I think." She refused to be more specific. Elizabeth Coucey, who had taken to Arabella as if she were an older sister, was greatly distressed by this, but Arabella—who had become at least as fond of Bess— would not confide in her either. "You must take care of my poor daughter when I am gone," was all she would say.

She died not quite a month later; Andrew came home from Italy barely in time to bid her farewell.

She stood against the ship's rail, eyes fastened on the gray distance the sailors assured her was land. Difficult to tell, with so much fog, overcast, gray water, gray and drizzly sky. She shivered down into the bright blue wool cloak and pulled the hood close over her dark hair: they must be near, though, for the weather was Boston as *she* remembered it.

Water sloshed halfheartedly against the planking bow; they must be near the Bay, perhaps within it. The Atlantic had been rough all the way from Plymouth. Fortunately, she still had her father's strong stomach, and a roiling sea had not bothered her at all. Lucinda bit her lower lip, remembering the crossing to London, three years earlier. Poor Arabella had been so ill, and all her magic hadn't been able to cure it. Lucinda set her lips together in a thin, hard line; dark brows drew down to form a single line across her forehead.

The family curse, her elder brother John called it. Perhaps John was right. Of course, he had disliked magic because it made their family somehow different. His protests that a lawyer could not practice sorcery were merely one way to avoid magic, because Arabella's brother, the lawyer who had sent John down to Harvard, certainly had no such qualms.

Lucinda leaned out over the rail to let her eyes follow the white spray coming off the bow of the ship, and sighed deeply. Poor Mother. Perhaps she had been unwell even before they left for England. It would have been very like her to hide it even from her husband and daughter. Lucinda frowned again. It was worrying, how she had shut those months away. She seldom thought of Richard, and just now could not even recall the last thing her mother had said to her. There seemed to be a haze between her and the real world, a haze that had grown up after Richard's death and continued to swathe her.

"Foolishness, it must be simple exhaustion from the journey home," she assured herself. But it had been only twenty months since Arabella's death. Still, that was long enough for her father to observe a decent year of mourning before he began to pay court to Elizabeth Coucey. Perhaps she should feel distress that her father should marry again. But she and Bess were like sisters, rather than stepmother and stepdaughter.

Lucinda bent her head and blotted a wayward tear against the dark, practical travelling glove, and forced her thoughts away from the past. She must not weep. She and Elizabeth had done all they could. And she did not wish to return home with her face swollen and blotchy.

She managed a faint smile. Poor Elizabeth hadn't done much better asea than Arabella.

The shore was suddenly there, beyond doubt—a dark line curving out to embrace the ship. The waves fell away even more, until she was reminded of one of the little rowing boats upon the Serpentine in London. Richard had taken her there one afternoon, not long after her arrival in England.

Oh, Richard. She couldn't think about him, even now. Dying as he did. And though she found it hard to recall that last hour, she could still taste that dreadful gin, hear his last words. *How could I ever have misjudged any man so?* It haunted her.

How odd that she should like Elizabeth, or that Elizabeth should like her. Richard's accidental death should have stood between them. Elizabeth's resemblance to Richard alone should have driven her away from the woman.

"Leave it be!" she ordered herself sternly. "Think of pleasant things!" She could not greet her elder brother with a tear-stained face.

The fog had lifted enough for her to make out one of the small shoreline settlements—a summer village for fishermen, if she recalled correctly. Small boats had put out near land and—wonder of wonders!—Was that a patch of blue sky to the north? Lucinda smiled and crossed her fingers under shelter of the blue cloak. She would take that blue sky as a positive omen.

Men were running barefoot back and forth across the plank deck, shouting orders, drawing in sails. Things creaked rather alarmingly. All the same, she heard the light patter of dainty, slipper-clad feet coming up behind her. Small Elizabeth's feet might be, and light on them she undeniably was, but Lucinda was always aware of her—by the stares of those around her, if nothing else. She turned and smiled; Elizabeth, muffled and furred to the tip of a rather pink turned-up nose, extended little gloved hands and caught hold of her stepdaughter's fingers tightly. "Ah! To think we have *finally* stopped rolling! They say we are very near landfall, Lucy dear, but I cannot see it."

Small wonder; Elizabeth's eyes were not strong. She peered in the direction Lucinda pointed, nodded dubiously. "Well! I shall see it all soon enough. Your father is still closeted with Captain Burke. I wonder he'll be out before we anchor!"

"I doubt he will, Bess." Lucinda laughed. "Though he'd have been able to tell you to the moment when we came into the Bay."

"Ah. He is welcome to his sea *and* his ships," Elizabeth retorted darkly. "I'll make my bed in this land and my grave, too, rather than take such a journey another time. I wonder you had the courage for it, Lucy! But I know, you have told me, it does not touch you, all this wallowing and tilting of floors under your feet!" She sighed deeply. "None of the new dresses I had made before we left London will fit, I have eaten so little this past fortnight." She gazed down dolefully at her muffled figure. "There *is* a decent seamstress in Boston?"

Lucinda laughed again and patted her stepmother's hands before releasing them and tucking her own into the fur lining of her cloak. "You will be agreeably surprised, Bess. When I left it three years ago, Boston was a proper city, and if my brother's letters do not lie, it has grown a good deal since then. We aren't savages here, you know!"

"If you say so," Elizabeth murmured. She didn't look convinced. She gazed toward the approaching shore in silence, and Lucinda watched her covertly, from under her lashes. But just as she began to think she must find something cheerful to say, to break the other young woman's low spirits, Elizabeth smiled and shook herself. "I have a few small items to put in my bag before we anchor. Are you coming down, Lucy?"

Lucinda shook her head. "I packed my cases at first light."

"Such enthusiasm." Elizabeth sighed and shook her head. Lucinda watched her hurry back across the deck. Several of the sailors turned to look as she passed them; Lucinda could scarcely blame them. Elizabeth, with her golden hair, the deep rose of her cloak setting off the pale cheeks, those huge, darkly blue eyes . . . And for all her last remark, and the age-envying-youth way she said it, Elizabeth was a bare five years her senior. Twenty-five was barely old if the lady in question were unwed; twenty-five and a wife, when one looked like Elizabeth, was surely the peak of one's beauty. *And how shall I look when I am twenty-five?* Lucinda wondered.

She shrugged the thought aside. She would still be unwed, of that she was certain. *I am done with men*, she told herself firmly. That aside, what was there for her to choose from here? Lads like that awful boy her father'd have wed her to three years before? If he'd done so—true, she'd never have met Richard, but she would not have been able to care for her mother through her last days.

Remember your promise to her, she told herself. Remember pleasant things: the opera, the dances. The water festival on the Thames with decorated boats and the barge carrying the King's musicians—that had been her second hearing of Master Handel's *Water Music*, the winter fest this past year, when the river had frozen solid.

She sighed, remembering. It was the music she would miss the most. Handel's music, Purcell's music, the hundred other

composers who were born in England or came there, seeking the freedom of London and the English Court. Music,
she remembered bleakly, found little fertile ground in the
Massachusetts colony. The Puritans did not permit it in their
churches; too few other churches had any means of creating
music save the voices of the congregation—and few of those
could carry even the simple tunes of the best-known hymns.
Of course, Harvard had a decent choir, and now and again
they ventured into the secular.

She shook herself. Another moment, she'd be weeping
for London. What a dreadful thought! London, after all,
was not an earthly Paradise—not with its bad water and
chill climate, with the oppressive smoke in winter, the
swamps and mosquitoes in summer, with dreadful poverty
everywhere and places even an escorted young woman dare
not go, for her repute—or worse, her personal safety. And
Richard Coucey—

How odd, how very odd, that a woman as sweet and kind
as Elizabeth should be related to someone like Richard.

"Again!" she told herself very firmly; a sailor hurrying by
with a handful of rope halted to glance at her inquiringly,
sped on his way when she shook her head and smiled
ruefully. *You promised yourself to let it all lie; there are
more important things this morning*! Such things as her
brother John, who had threatened not to meet the ship out of
resentment against their father's remarriage; such things as
the specially ordered glassware—two narrow-lipped flasks,
a long beaker, and an extremely high-temperature oil lamp
made particularly to replace old or broken items in the
hidden recess of her mother's herbarium. She'd wrapped
them very carefully—against discovery as much as against
breakage—in the linen sheets and the embroidered towels
she'd brought home for her wedding chest, and tucked the
whole under the wonderful rose and sky-blue quilt Elizabeth
had embroidered for her.

She wasn't entirely certain whether she intended to use
them or not: But it seemed so wrong to let Arabella's
beloved herbarium fall into disuse. And she had to have
some interest, since Bess would run the household. The

herbarium had provided her mother with income, as well as expanding her scientific knowledge. Andrew had seldom objected to Arabella's craft—her "tinkering," he called it. He knew of course she was circumspect, which silenced his greatest concern. After all, several members of her family *had* been accused of witchcraft. Lucinda wasn't certain he'd have that same trust in his daughter.

He didn't need to worry about John, she thought, and sighed. "And likely not for me, either. Why I bought the glass at all! Save that Mother intended to buy it from that particular artisan." And so she had the glass—and her mother's blood and her books, and something of her knowledge, too. And no heart to use any of it.

The ship let down anchor some time later; by that hour, the sun was high and much of the morning's cloud cover had blown away. Deeply blue sky, bright gold sun reflecting gold and silver on the choppy water. It looked much warmer than it was. Lucinda settled on the narrow wooden seat of the jolly boat and pulled the cloak snugly around her knees. The calendar and the sun might both say May; the wind said March, most emphatically, and her fingers, in the few moments it took to climb from the ship into the boat, were frozen inside her gloves. She felt the boat rock as her father stepped from the ladder, heard Elizabeth's faint cry of distress as he handed her into the unsteady little boat. She didn't look around; the wind was cold enough on the back of her head, even through the hood—and her eyes were fixed on the clutch of people waiting along the dock, only two or three ship-lengths away. John—Would he be there? His last letter to her hadn't given her much hope. He worried her. John had always been able to press their father's swift temper, and if he did today, he might well find himself disowned.

Three years had made a greater change in John than she could have expected. She felt his presence—the first-learned and simplest part of Arabella's dubious gift to her children—before she saw him, but until he began waving wildly and calling her name, she did not recognize him at all.

The sailors handed her and her traveling bag out first. She had barely set both feet on the planking when a man's sturdy arms pulled her close, hugging hard enough to drive the air out of her. "Lucy! Good Lord, Lucy, you left a child and came back a lady! Let me look at you!"

She pushed against his chest and he released her to hold her at arm's length. He'd grown considerably taller and broader at the shoulders. He'd had a neat beard when she saw him last; he was now smooth-shaven. His long coat and waistcoat were good, serious dark cloth, but only a little behind London fashion; his hose were unwrinkled and spotlessly white— something once unheard of. "You've grown yourself, John. And Harvard has apparently taught you cleanly habits."

He laughed. "No one will hire a reeky lawyer! But I won't fight with you—not today, at least." His gaze went behind her, and she turned to see their father standing on the dock, supervising the bags being handed out. "Not with any of you," John added firmly. "Before you ask."

"I'm glad," Lucinda said simply. Her own gaze traveled then, to take in the young man standing just behind John and clearly with him. Tall and lean, dark of face, black curls escaping from beneath his hat, black eyes shaded by thick brows, and a faint smile on well-shaped lips. Familiar . . . but who was he? John saw her look, and stepped back to indicate his companion with a slight bow.

"You surely remember Judah Levy, don't you, Lucy?"

"Judah—of course I remember Judah!" She extended both hands and he took them briefly. She wouldn't have recognized him, either; though they'd all known each other from early childhood.

"He graduated but a year behind me," John said proudly. "Imagine it, a Jew taking honors in sciences and graduating from Harvard! The founders are doubtless writhing in their graves."

"Nonsense," Lucinda said warmly. Judah merely smiled and shook his head. He was used to John's rather heavy humor after so many years of it, but he'd always shrugged off such comment in that way, ever since she could remember.

"And now he teaches and tutors, as I do," John went on. "Though of course my field is law and his the sciences." His eyes went beyond her and he waved vigorously. "Father! Here we are. Wait, I'll help with your baggage!" John pushed through the growing crowd, leaving Lucinda with Judah Levy. Lucinda smiled up at him, and received a rather shy smile in response.

John came back before the silence could grow uncomfortable between them, and—as Lucinda had always best remembered her elder brother—he was talking as quickly as he could form words. He was weighted down with almost all of the personal bags—most of them Elizabeth's. Elizabeth leaned on Andrew's arm, wide blue eyes taking in everything around them. Andrew was smiling at his son, and Lucinda didn't need any of the family extrasensory perception to realize her father was relieved at the way John was taking the remarriage and a stepmother almost exactly his own age.

John was of course still talking. "I live in rooms at the College, Father, but Mary and James Hazelton and the servants under them have kept the town house up for you. They should have tea laid when we arrive. I brought the carriage for you and one of the farm wagons for the luggage. The carriage only holds two in comfort of course, but I thought Lucy might . . ."

Andrew held up a hand for silence. "Bess and I will take the carriage, thank you, John. Lucinda may come with us if she chooses, or with you, if she'd rather. Who is this with you?—oh, of course, young Judah. How is your family, lad?"

"All well, sir."

"Good. Bess, your legs must feel strange, after so many days asea. We'll go home at once. Lucinda—?"

"I'll follow with John, Father. Thank you." Andrew nodded and followed John over to the small, open carriage. It took the two men to get a very tottery Elizabeth onto the seat; Lucinda could not hear what anyone said, but she could see her stepmother's deprecating gestures and blushes, heard both men laugh and shake their heads. Andrew patted her shoulder and John bowed over her fingers.

Lucinda had a sudden image of stern-faced old Increase
Mather, or his self-important and rather self-righteous son
Cotton, with a wife like Elizabeth—and had to bite her
lower lip to keep from giggling.

John and Judah Levy stowed the last of the bags; the
remainder would be sent on to the town house once they
were unloaded from the ship's hold. All the same, there
was a goodly pile in the back of the open wagon. Lucinda
let her brother hand her onto the high seat behind the two
horses, and slid over to make room for Judah. "Boston's
grown so much since I left."

"It has." Judah answered her; John had his hands full with
the horses and the wharf traffic. "Particularly the harbor,
though there are new shops everywhere, and plenty of new
houses."

"Don't let the size and the look of the town fool you,"
John warned. "Boston is no London. Certain forms of behavior and so on still very much apply, as I hope you will
remember."

"If you suggest I do not remember how to behave seeming-
ly . . ." Lucinda began warningly. John grinned and Lucinda
scowled at him. "For a man who does not wish to fight, John,
you are certainly pressing for one!"

"I merely spoke out of concern for you. Not even to speak
of things you did in London such as dancing and going to
theater! There are things which were frowned upon when our
grandpapa indulged in them, and the frown is still there—if
not quite so dark. In a word, sister, caution. By the by, is
our new mama religious? I hope she at least observes the
Sabbath?"

"She's Anglican, of course," Lucinda said.

"In times such as these, I fail to see the 'of course,'" John
replied crisply. "Anglican—well, that's safer than Catholic
in Boston." Judah laughed and John leaned across his sister to
smirk at his friend. "It is also safer than being Jewish, but our
Judah now attends chapel with me of a Sunday." He grinned
as his sister shook her head in confusion. "It assures Uncle
Increase has his place in Heaven, don't you agree?"

"John," Lucinda said sternly, "either you are babbling, or the voyage left my poor brain as unsteady as Bess's legs. Nothing of what you say makes sense, save that you'll get yourself in trouble yet with the men who wield power in this colony. Haven't you any wit at all?"

"He hasn't," Judah Levy said gravely. "But since he merely speaks, and that only in the frivolous manner you've just heard, why, no one takes him seriously. Such frivolity by itself might cause some to condemn him, but even your brother's detractors agree it's not as great a sin as lechery or strong drink. What he is trying to tell you is that I have converted."

"Converted? You—are Christian?" She stared at him blankly. "But why?"

He shrugged. "It seemed the sensible thing to do. My beliefs are my own, whatever I outwardly own them to be. And while my family has always been devout, they have not been extreme in their beliefs. Even my father, who would never do such a thing himself, had no quarrel with me for having converted. And quite frankly, my chance to attain a professorship is all the greater."

"Call it sensible, if you like," John said. "I personally think he did it mostly to silence the ministers, who preached to him daily for what seems years. Even so, it sounds quite cold-blooded to me. As cold-blooded as wedding a wealthy man twice your age and many times your wealth, even if it means leaving London . . ."

"Enough," Lucinda said firmly. "I know your feelings toward Bess; you made them quite clear in your last letters. I am glad *you* chose the path of sense today and didn't make Father cast you aside penniless. But I refuse to argue the matter with you. Elizabeth was a friend of Mother's, you know. And Father waited well over a year before he even spoke to her, let alone asked her hand! Has Mary kept the garden up?"

John twisted his lips, fetched a deep sigh, finally nodded. "Of course she has, though it's easy enough in a town this size to purchase whatever vegetables and fruit one wants. She kept Mother's herb garden up, too—for you, she said."

"Good."

John eyed her sidelong as he turned the wagon down a near-empty side street and urged the horses to a little more speed. "You aren't thinking of using Mother's herbalry, are you?"

"Herbarium, John. Perhaps." He looked unsatisfied with that terse and not very useful reply; Lucinda couldn't really blame him, considering Arabella's main use for the little hut at the bottom of the herb garden—a use that had only peripherally to do with tansy and sage, lavender and laurel. Considering his feelings on the subject of magic of any kind: black, sorcerous, white—or family.

She sat quietly a while, suddenly glad to be done with ships and open ocean. Glad to be home once more, glad to see familiar buildings, stone and brick and wood, familiar shops; to feel the well-remembered jostle of the stone-paved roads, the ruts and dust of the unpaved streets, and to smell odors that had been somehow different in London—fish from the harbor, hot metal and smoke from a smithy, flowers in someone's garden. The sound of American voices once again—Who would have thought there should be so much difference in accent and cadence, even the very words? After all, were they not all English?

The wagon moved slowly, particularly at first, for there was a good deal of foot and horse traffic, many other carts and wagons down near the water. Small carts, more people afoot—mostly women on the broad streets where the markets were held, where the shops were. Even away from the hub, though, there was more traffic than she remembered: there were paving stones on streets once thick with dust or mud, streets where there had been meadow or woods, and for one horrid moment, she thought herself completely lost, for nothing at all was familiar. Judah must have noticed; he touched her hand and nodded his head to the right and a little ahead of them. "There is the Dancey house, do you remember them?"

She stared at it as they went by. "Not possible! They were at the very edge of town—!"

"On the road itself," he agreed and smiled faintly. "You'll need a guide when you venture out."

"Are you volunteering yourself?" John demanded.

Judah shrugged. "It wasn't my meaning. But—well, yes. Why not?"

"Why not?" Lucinda echoed. For one awful moment, her heart sank; Richard had made just such an offer, her first days in London. But then she smiled back. Judah was a friend, a boy she'd known since they were children together. It was not at all the same thing, was it? The awkwardness which had come between them at the wharves vanished as if it had never been. "I'll accept that offer," she said. "I've Father's talent for riding a seagoing vessel but none of his gift with charts."

"I shall speak to him, then," Judah said. "And ask his permission." She opened her mouth to protest. Permission? But, then, they weren't children any longer, and even though his offer was the kind of friend's gesture she'd expect from Judah Levy, the rules had changed.

John pulled the wagon around a corner and drew up with a flourish. "And here we are," he said.

The house seemed smaller, darker and rougher, but she'd missed it, and welcomed everything, from the familiar odors of Mary's kitchen to the board just inside the doorway that creaked at the lightest step—even Elizabeth's, she noticed with amusement. To the way the light shone on Mary's table, and Mary herself brushing meal from her hands and apron to welcome them in.

Hours later, she found herself alone in the tiny loft room that was hers, next to the box-room, across the staircase from her parents' large room. She was tired, full for the first time in years, of food that tasted just right. Judah Levy, John, and James had carried in bags and trunks and boxes, and Judah had obtained Andrew Greene's rather amused permission to escort Lucinda about town when his studies allowed. Now she wanted nothing but sleep, hours of it, as much as she could fit between now and the early hours when the household would bestir itself. First though: she moved between various bags and parcels until she found the heavy

wooden box done up with thick rope that concerned her
most, just now. The knots were stiff but finally yielded
to a softening spell. Bess's gift-quilt needed airing but
there were no stains on the fabric, no snag in the thread.
Lucinda drew a sigh of relief and suspended the rose and
blue coverlet across the end of her bedposts. In the morning
she'd spread it out over the lavender hedge down in the
garden. Beneath it in the box, the sheets and other cloth
items were only a little musty, and the glass pieces they'd
held were unbroken.

At the very bottom, her fingers encountered the thick
leather cover, hand-bound on the left side: her mother's
book, copied from her own mother's. Unless John chose
to accept his heritage, there would be no need to copy the
book until Lucinda's children needed it—but no, she would
never wed or have children. She sat on the edge of her bed
and gazed at the cover for some moments, finally shook
her head and laid it back in the box. The glassware went
in, loose, atop it. Perhaps she'd have James take it down
to the little hut at the bottom of the herb garden tomorrow.
Then again—perhaps she'd wait. She gave the rose and blue
coverlet an affectionate pat and began unpinning her hair
for the night.

Her dreams were unsettling: an enormous, black-clad
figure in a foggy place spoke to her in riddles—or so
they seemed when she finally woke. *I know you are there,
Arabella's daughter. But I can barely touch you and only in
your sleep. Something stands between us; someone blocks
me. Find and destroy the barrier before it destroys you!* And
then a swirl of white across black-covered shoulders, pale
eyes fixed on her accusingly. Something very bright owned
those eyes—Willow, she realized with a pang. Willow, the
will-o'-the-wisp who had served Grandfather Amer, and
eventually her own mother. *Where is my Arabella?* a small
voice demanded. *Why can I not see her, and why can I not
touch* you? She could see more, then: the workshop that
had been her mother's on the family farm, south and west
of Boston. She had played there with John, and with Judah,
whose father's land adjoined theirs.

There might have been more to the dream, but she woke, chilled, and could not remember. She pulled Bess's comforter over her shoulders and slept soundly. The dream, and memory of it, faded.

Somehow, time slipped away from her: two days, then three—a full week, two. The glass retorts and beakers remained in their case, the case wedged between wall and the chest that held her sheets and towels.

There had been callers, a few very quiet parties, services on the Sabbath, where Elizabeth had been much stared at. There had been visits to old friends, shopping trips to the market, to the wharves, others with Elizabeth. Judah, true to his word, had come calling twice and taken her around the City, until she again felt at home.

Once or twice, she again woke from unsettling dreams, but she could not recall them.

Other times she would waken and remember very clearly: *Willow—I should be able to bespeak her now, I should search the book to see if it tells a reason why I cannot—or ask my uncle; he might know. I have new equipment to set up in the herbarium, old equipment to polish; surely Mary did not bother with that place. Chemicals to account; many must have lost potency, or dried out, in so long a time.* Why did she only see this late at night? During the day, she never thought of the sturdy little building at the foot of the garden, hard against the herb beds. Or if she did, the very thought made her so very tired that she let it go. It was too much to deal with, and somehow, it was so hard to concentrate on these things, though she was certainly not unwell. She had plenty of energy for other things.

Later. There would always be time—*That is what Arabella thought,* Willow's late night voice told her accusingly.

Unease finally sent her into the herbarium, nearly five weeks after her return home. Not the nagging in her dreams, however: John was worrying her.

He had always been impatient and headstrong so he had suffered his share and more of childhood hurts. Even now, his knees and shins were constantly bruised because he moved too quickly about his rooms or simply did not watch where he walked. But though he'd been accident-prone, he was not clumsy, and he had always ridden as though he were part of his horse. In the space of three days, he had twice fallen down stairs on his way to class—falls that might easily have killed him, had he landed wrong or struck his head. And his favorite mare had thrown him.

Lucinda worked the stiff lock and pulled the heavy bar aside. "Perhaps he has become clumsy; he cannot ride as often as he did. He might have misjudged the mare or the crossing," she told herself, but she wasn't at all reassured. She flung the door wide, wrinkled her nose as she stepped into the herbarium: the chamber was overly warm and stuffy, the air thick with sage. She stifled a sneeze, picked up the heavy black case, and carried it inside. The door could remain open while she cleaned and arranged shelves; it was only when she actually began work that she must use extreme care.

A cool little breeze slid across the low ceiling, setting hanging bundles of very dry plants to rustling and clattering. The worktable was against the black wall—regular herb preparation on the near side, the more esoteric workings behind, nearly invisible behind the kettles, boxes, cloth bags, and wooden bowls. The smell of itch salve was very strong here.

The table was not as dusty as she might have expected; perhaps Mary had cared for the herbarium as well as the house? Lucinda wondered for the first time whether the indentured servants knew about Arabella's alchemic and sorcerous pursuits, or how they might feel about them. No one had ever said anything about it—but then, the subject certainly wasn't an open one. She pushed stray hair from her brow, tucked it into the clean white kerchief, and pressed her sleeves to the elbow.

All at once, she wanted nothing more than to sleep. She stifled a yawn, blinked to clear blurring vision. Not surprising, really; she'd worried about John much of the previous night. Tired—she felt so sluggish; it suddenly seemed such an effort to set things up. Her mother's book felt so, so *heavy*. Somehow, she hoisted it onto the table. *John*, she reminded herself firmly. "John," she said aloud. The name seemed to clear her mind, a little. "You worked it out last night, what to do. Do it now."

It was one of three things, she had decided: truly accident, threat from a personal enemy of John's, threat from an enemy of the family. Their grandfather Amer had made enemies aplenty, in particular that Salem coven. A protective spell would take care of any of those threats, but John might very well refuse one. Well, he would never need to know she had created one for him. Not if she'd worked it out right.

Lucinda reached into the pocket hanging from her chatelaine, fingered the fine brass buttons, and smiled. She had bought them for John in London; they were the latest mode and fastidious; fashion-mad John would adore them. She'd bought the silk for the waistcoat, too; it was nearly completed. The buttons would simply undergo a little ceremony—a protective baptism, as it were—before they went on. Buttons protected would protect the waistcoat, and thereby the wearer. The wearer, once so protected, would remain protected. *Thank Heaven for Grandfather Amer's dedication to knowledge,* she thought fervently. *And that my refusal to use that knowledge for so long did not preclude my using it forever!*

An hour later, she dropped heavily onto the stool at the table's end and let her head fall into her hands. It was impossible! She could not think, she could not concentrate! "This is no great problem, it is all set out step by step in Mother's book and *still* I cannot do it! What is wrong with me?" she mumbled into her palms. There was of course no answer.

A tap at the outer, still open door finally roused her; she let her hands fall and pushed to her feet, half expecting Elizabeth had come in search of a shopping companion, or that Mary had come to summon her to eat. The figure silhouetted against the sunlit garden was much taller than either, and crisply curling hair gave him away. "Judah," she exclaimed. "I had not expected you."

"May I?" he asked, and at her gesture stepped inside. He clasped his hands behind his back, as though fearing to touch anything, and gazed about with interest. "So this is your mother's famous distillery. My grandfather always swore by her green liquid for bad stomach. Are you thinking of making it again? I know he at least will buy."

"I—I'm not certain," she stammered. He nodded thoughtfully. There was a silence, a rather pleasant one, while he looked around the small chamber. To her surprise, Lucinda did not worry about what he might see, or resent his presence, even when he leaned across the table to study the various objects there.

"I came to ask if you would like to go for a ride," he said finally. "I see you are busy, however, and so we can postpone that. I also wished to ask—well, that also can wait. I am worried about John."

"Oh?"

"Truly worried," he said. "I know him; he does not like upsetting folk, and so I doubt he's told you about certain distressing events—"

"Two unpleasant falls," Lucinda said as he paused and looked at her inquiringly. "And Milady threw him into the stream. He might not have mentioned them, but the bruises were quite visible and he had to explain the limp."

"He's not told you everything," Judah said quietly. "Though *I'd* not heard of his horse. He was ill last week; they said bad shellfish, though no one else went sick of it. That, and—enough other unpleasantries that one begins to wonder what person or force John has offended of late." He paused again; she shook her head and gestured to him to go on. "He would not appreciate my telling you; you know he thinks himself invulnerable and you both younger and female and so doubly useless. But, I thought—" He stopped speaking abruptly and Lucinda thought he was blushing; it was difficult to tell for his dark skin and the poor lighting. Oddly, she understood what he was trying to say.

"It's all right. We've been friends for so long, Judah. You know about Mother's—gift, don't you?"

"Crafter blood," Judah replied softly, and she heard the relief in his voice—relief, she thought, that he would not have to continue to toss heavy hints in her direction. "I was not certain if she used this place also. I knew of the workshop on your farm."

"I didn't know she'd told you."

His color went a shade deeper. "About John," he said finally, and very firmly.

"John," Lucinda agreed, and found she was also relieved to get back to the subject, though she did wonder what Judah knew about Arabella's previous workshop—and how he'd come by the knowledge. Snooping, likely. Children did, after all. She fumbled a button out of the pocket and explained what she had in mind. "If I can work the spell properly, he'll be safe from anything short of a full coven's joint displeasure, wearing the waistcoat or not. Though I do wish he weren't so hidebound about such things," she added angrily. "It would be much simpler to just protect John, without using a Contagion spell." She ran a hand across her forehead, partly dislodging the no-longer-white kerchief, and sighed. "I must be too long out of practice, Judah my good friend, for I cannot even seem to find the concentration to complete preparations. I cannot concentrate on any of this at all, and indeed I cannot recall the last time I could."

He turned to look at her, and for the first time unclasped his hands from behind his back. One touched her shoulder lightly, the other came to rest against her forehead. He leaned forward to peer at her rather anxiously. "How odd," he said softly. "Until a moment ago, until you said that, I would not have thought you different at all. There *is* something wrong. Have you been ill?" She shook her head. "But that is wrong, for there was nothing like this when we last talked together." He dug into his pockets, coming up with a much-folded piece of paper and a stub of charcoal which he rubbed to a point against one of the iron herb kettles. "Give me, please," he said crisply, charcoal poised, "the date of your birth, your father's and his new wife's if you know them. John's I have."

She did. He set them down in an impossibly small hand given the medium he had for writing. Lucinda found herself suddenly sharply aware of him—the rather pleasant, warm smell of his skin, his intense eyes, the taut set of his shoulders. Somehow, it lent her an intensity of her own. *Help him*, she thought, and went in search of the box that contained powdered ink, horn, and several sharpened quill pens. She mixed ink powder with water from one of her new glass vials and pushed the horn of black liquid and a pen under his nose. He dropped the charcoal without looking up, mumbled an absent "thank you," and continued to scribble. Numbers, more numbers, odd symbols filled the sheet; he waved it in the air to dry it, turned it over and continued to work until the back was covered with more symbols, numbers.

Gooseflesh crawled over her arms; she nearly exclaimed aloud. *Cabala*! Judah was working a numeric spell. Someone had spoken of it in her hearing just once, years before: it was a Jewish thing, a purely learned sorcery—unlike hers which was learned and inherent both. Or like Richard's, requiring a pact with the Devil—*How can you think of Richard at a time like this*? she asked herself angrily.

He had stopped writing somewhere in the past moments and had gone around the long bench. He hesitated, long fingers clasping a squat, narrow-mouthed retort. "May I?" She nodded blankly, and came around to watch closely what he did. With the glassware in his hands, he suddenly became authoritative. "A hair, please." He held out a hand. "From the root, if you will." She separated one from under her kerchief, just above her ear, and laid it across his palm. He nodded, set it in a box of white, dry sand, and turned his attention to the boxes and bottles ranged in a shelved box behind him. She looked down at it in sudden dread, and wondered for one brief, wild moment if she could simply tell him to leave it alone. *What is it I fear he will find?*

"Have you rearranged these, or renamed them?" he asked.

"No."

"Good. I believe I remember your mother's system of organization, since it's similar enough to my own." He pulled a cloth bag from the bottom shelf, sniffed gingerly at the pinch of yellow powder he brought forth, nodded and dropped it in a beaker, adding an even darker yellow liquid from the bottle next to it. He handed it to her. "Place your palm over it, please, and shake it vigorously. Excellent. Pour it down the length of the hair now—" She drew a steadying breath and did as he told her. She cried out in surprise then, and nearly dropped the beaker: The sand under the hair was smoking; a thick curl of blue smoke rose and hung in the air above it. Judah took her hand in his, took the beaker away from her, and set it back on the bench. "Don't be startled; the color will fade."

"My hand!" Lucinda gasped. The palm had turned a deep, horrid blue where the liquid had touched it. She was shivering violently; Judah wrapped his arms around her shoulders and she leaned back into him, grateful for the warmth of his woolen shirt.

"It will fade," he said again, reassuringly. "It tells us what I feared, however; someone has enspelled you, Lucinda."

She twisted around so she could look up at him. "Enspelled *me*? But why? And for what gain?"

"Anything is possible, though I suspect it was to keep you from this chamber, from using your talent. For I saw nothing untoward in you until I came into this hut. As to why, I cannot yet tell. That will take more effort on my part and yours both, and only if you wish to know. As to who, however— stand very still." He dipped both index fingers in the yellow liquid and touched them simultaneously to her temples.

Lucinda shut her eyes and swayed. She felt as though someone had torn a thick comforter from around her. Someone *had* put a spell on her, a very selective spell that had damped her magic—not only the talent itself. She had been blind to other things related to it: her illness after Richard's death, her mother's illness. Those last moments in Richard's company. . . There was something unclean about all of it, something that went beyond Richard's talk of covens and altars. She glanced swiftly at Judah and pushed that thought away from her; it made her feel fouled; he must not know of that! But for the rest, there was a blanket of magic over all of it. When had she last thought so clearly, unless it was an ordinary thing such as dinner, or what color thread to use in her sampler, or whether to buy new slippers?

Judah touched her shoulder lightly and indicated the blue smoke which still hung before her. There was movement there: tiny, distant figures. She could not tell where they were, when, who—except for one. She herself had said it so often: she would always know Elizabeth. "What does it mean? Can you see what I see also?" she asked Judah, her eyes still fixed on the smoke. She sensed rather than saw him shake his head. Suddenly, she knew what he had done, what he had used to strip Elizabeth's spell from her; how to enhance his magic with her own. "This vision is too faint; let me." She moved around him and began taking items from the cupboard, rapidly mixing half a dozen seeds, a tiny pinch of the yellow powder, a foul-smelling clear liquid from a small brown clay jug. "Stir it with your smallest finger." He did; she took it to stir herself, turned her gaze back to the smoke.

It had dissipated slightly, but that merely made a larger space for what the malodorous liquid now showed them: a group of thirteen black-clad people—hooded and cloaked, all; it was impossible to make out sex, age, or any other feature. The amorphous shadow of a fourteenth in their midst cast a darkness over them all. It faded, most of the circle faded, until only two remained. Lucinda was not at all surprised when one flung back his hood to reveal Richard Coucy's handsome, once-beloved face. Nor was she any longer surprised when his sister Elizabeth tilted her head back to look up at him, letting her own hood fall back. "Witch," she whispered.

"I wondered," Judah said quietly. "But I also wondered why you showed no sign of distress in her presence."

"But why has she done this to me?" Lucinda poured the liquid into the sand; the single hair sizzled, leaving behind the smell of burned hair and rapidly fading smoke.

"To avoid detection?" Judah shrugged. "But why against John?"

"She cannot—" Lucinda stopped abruptly. It was foolish to say Elizabeth could not be plotting against John for some unknown reason. And she remembered that quarrel between Aunt Bet and Arabella: someone feeding her mother a dose. "Oh, dear God," she whispered and bent over the table. Judah spun her around and held her close; she leaned into him for comfort and warmth. "Dear friend, how can I thank you?"

He laughed—a rather odd laugh, she thought, for there seemed to be little humor in it. "Ah, well. Friends—they need not thank each other. Lucinda, pull yourself together; someone is coming." She shivered and squared her shoulders; Judah let his hands fall and gestured for her to precede him away from this corner of the little hut. There *was* movement along the path, familiar, light footsteps coming toward the herbarium, and then Elizabeth's shadow filling the doorway.

"Here you are!" she exclaimed, and stepped gingerly into the little hut. "What a dreadfully thick smell, Lucy dear! I had thought you might accompany me to the glover's, I want new gloves to match my gray gown for the Governor's party, and—ah, Mr. Levy, I did not see you." She inclined her head in a rather cool fashion. "Perhaps you would care to drive us both?"

"It would please me," he replied. "But I came only to speak to Lucinda a moment. And to give her this." He turned back and slipped something cool over Lucinda's left hand. She held it to the light and caught her breath: a silver cuff bracelet, very plain except for the ropelike twisted gold wire framing it clasped her wrist. "I hope you will have it as a betrothal gift," he added. "It belonged to my father's mother. Of course, I must speak with your father, Lucinda. But since we have known each other so many years, it seemed only right that I give this to you beforehand, and to make certain that you were not averse."

"Ohhhh. It is lovely, Judah." Had he chosen such a moment deliberately? she wondered. Either to distract Bess—or perhaps to assure that she would not flatly refuse him? But that last was surely an unworthy thought. *We are friends,* she reminded herself. *Even if I do not wish to marry anyone . . .* He turned away from Elizabeth and gave Lucinda a warning look; his lips framed the words: *Go with her.*

"How very exciting," Elizabeth said. She didn't sound at all excited. "And how sudden! My husband will be at home this evening, Mr. Levy, should you care to speak

with him then." She took another step into the herbarium.
"So this is Arabella's workshop. The air is quite stuffy; it
would give me a terrible headache. Of course, I prefer my
distillations ready-made; the preparation is so hard on one's
hands. And there is always the chance of accident." Her eyes
slid sideways to meet her stepdaughter's. "Don't you agree?
You must be careful indeed, Lucinda. I should hate for any
accident to befall you."

"I am always careful," Lucinda replied. She managed a
faint smile; Elizabeth's words seemed suddenly quite ominous, full of various unpleasant meanings.

"I am so fond of you, Lucy dear, it would be terrible
if you were as prone to accident as your poor brother."
She dabbed at her cheek with the back of one hand. "Or
my own."

"Oh," Lucinda said evenly, "I am not nearly so adven-
turous as either of them, Bess." She held out a hand.
"Come, I'll go with you. It is much too warm in here,
and I am certain you will never find a decent match for
your gray gown without me." She somehow managed not
to shudder as Elizabeth's fingers closed over hers, but
turned and held out her other hand to Judah. The bracelet
shone warm in the afternoon sun. "I shall expect you this
evening, Judah. You are certain you cannot come with us
just now?"

He smiled, shook his head. "I need to discuss certain
matters with Father, and that entails a ride out to his farm.
I'll lock up for you here, shall I?" She met his eyes, nodded.
They understood each other, he and she: he would first
remove Arabella's book to safekeeping.

The silver cuff was heavy, but a reassuring presence
against her wrist. She doubted it bore any spell—there was
none she could sense at any rate. Her mind was busy as she
followed Elizabeth: he must have planned this, else why
carry the bracelet? Did he love her? But that was no true
basis for marriage, was it? Common sense ruled Judah's
actions; common sense and practicality. Well, she was a
practical person herself, these days. Herself and Judah—
perhaps. They were friends. More importantly, they had

worked like a well-ordered team this afternoon. It would be nice to have such a partner.

It would silence Andrew—who spoke increasingly of a desire to see his daughter wed; and it would remove her from Elizabeth's domain.

She eyed her stepmother sidelong as they settled into the small carriage and James set the horse moving toward the shops. Why had Bess done this to her? To keep her stepdaughter from knowing she had been part of that coven? But, then, why John?

All the same, she did not like the little smile on Elizabeth's lips, and she wondered she had never before noticed the expression in Elizabeth's eyes. Like her brother's, they promised mischief.

Judah came that evening; at the end of a late supper, she found herself a betrothed young woman, with a marriage to take place in early autumn, and with what seemed to her a tidy dowry indeed, a dowry that included the farmhouse she'd grown up in, with a portion of its land to adjoin the land given Judah by his father. It would help support a wife; even a full professor made very little money, and Judah was some years from such a position.

She had a few minutes alone with him that evening, between the door and the gate where he'd left his mount. "Your mother's book is safe. I took the liberty of removing it and other of your stores to her room on the farm, since it will be yours. Remember to search your bed for anything Elizabeth may have put there. The protection I gave you this afternoon will not last long if she has put a Contagion spell on you. You are certain you do not object to marrying me?" Suddenly, he looked so uncertain, so young and worried, her heart turned over; she stood on tiptoe and kissed his cheek.

"Oh, Judah. How could I possibly mind? We have been friends for so long. How many who marry can say that?"

"If that is all—"

"It's better than merely love," she replied. "I know. Don't look so downcast, Judah. Perhaps the two things together, love and liking—"

"I see," he said quietly; he smiled and his fingers tightened on hers. "It's something to think about, isn't it? Remember what I said, about your bedding." She nodded; she had already folded the rose and blue coverlet away and put it in the box-room. "We'll speak tomorrow. Tell your father I want to take you out to see Grandfather. Father has no objections, but Grandfather is not entirely certain I should choose a bride from among the *goyim*." He smiled again. "Forgetting as he does that I myself am one, by conversion. But he has always liked you, Lucinda." She nodded again; he leaned over to kiss her forehead, and was gone.

He was late the next morning, and grave-faced when he arrived. Lucinda was waiting for him at the front gate. "Elizabeth went to the wharves with Father; she's awaiting a box of fabric from England. I'd hoped to be gone before she returned."

"I'm sorry to have kept you waiting. John's laid up with fever. The doctor thinks it not serious." He handed her onto the horse's withers and climbed into the saddle.

"Fever," Lucinda echoed. She clasped her hands about his waist as the horse started down the street.

"*I* think"—Judah turned to glance back at her before he urged the horse to a faster walk—"that you had better prepare those buttons right away. Grandfather is not actually expecting a visit right away. The workroom at the farm is dusty but everything is in place. I saw to that much yesterday. I hope you've no objection to my simply arranging these things?"

"None," she replied as he hesitated. "You anticipated me, and I am glad for it. I shall feel much safer away from town and Bess."

"The buttons . . ." he began. She freed a hand to delve into her pocket, and held one up in front of him. "I brought them. You said everything was at the farm, and I hoped you would mean for us to use it today."

There wasn't much conversation after that: Judah concentrated on riding as quickly as he dared down the narrow and rather rough-cut path that led to the old Greene and

Levy farmsteads, while Lucinda concentrated on keeping her seat—no easy task, seated sideways on a rough-gaited beast, with no platform for her feet. *We will need a cart, if not a carriage*, she thought. At the very least, they might get a proper pillion seat for her.

The farmhouse was old, all a single room, taken up at one end by an enormous fireplace and two high-backed settles, and at the other end by a huge bed. Improvements had been made during the years when she was growing up here, however: a ladder near the bed led up to a narrow loft, windows with aging oilpaper flanked the main door; and there was a window made of two dozen tiny diamond-shaped glass panes (she'd counted them as a child) next to the bed. A door next to the fireplace went into the barn and wood storage; another in the back wall led to a scullery and, beyond it, a low-ceilinged, windowless room with a beaten dirt floor. Judah had scattered fresh-cut grass to keep down the dust, and there were two oil lanterns to illuminate the tall workbench. Boxes, bags, vials, oddly shaped containers lined the far wall. Her fingers closed about a familiar one: an eight-sided box with richly carved sides. Inside was Willow's globe. She'd wondered when she was a child whether the sprite was contained in it, or merely drawn to it once it was opened. Her mother had given her some long and confusing reply that made no sense at all, and she still didn't understand. She drew the box from the shelf and set it on the bench; perhaps once the real work was done, she'd open Willow's box, and introduce the sprite to Judah. They would need to know each other.

Another bench to one side held a cupboard—the very cupboard from her mother's city herbarium, Lucinda realized. A place had been scrubbed clean for Arabella's book, and she warmed to Judah again for such thoughtfulness. The glassware alone was largely unfamiliar.

"Some of it is mine," he said when she touched a wooden rack of slender glass tubes and looked a question. "And some here when I came." He stepped back and drew up a stool. "Will you mind if I watch?"

"Please," she said. He smiled and braced open the door between the house proper and the scullery, to provide day-light and fresh air, then seated himself at the end of the bench. She had already shed her gloves and pressed her sleeves up, one hand questing for the narrow-waisted bottle that held the main ingredient for her spell. She laid the brass buttons in the fold of the book. "Particularly if you don't mind sharing the work with me once again."

"I—of course."

"Then, if you'll make a flame for me, I'll begin at once."

She worked in silence for the next hour, vaguely aware of his interested gaze, of growing warmth that was partly the little oil burner that set a nasty-looking liquid to boil and partly midday sun beating down on the low roof, partly a growing inner warmth that was, she finally decided, pure-ly pleasure in his quiet company. He made no attempt to amuse her, did nothing to distract her—he was there when she needed him. Twice, he neatly anticipated her need for things—tongs, to pull the glass tube from its metal brace and away from the burner; a cup of chilled well-water to cool it in and another for her to drink. He held the tube upright while she dropped the buttons into it, one at a time. She finally took the tube and held it up to the light coming through the doorway, sighed with relief. "They are absorbing it; good. I hadn't been certain—but when the liquid is gone, the buttons will carry a full spell, and I'll sew them on the waistcoat tonight. But I brought a scrap of cloth to make a small herb sleep pillow for him."

Judah nodded approvingly. "Very sensible. He may not feel well enough to wear the waistcoat for some days."

"What a pity," came a sweet voice from the doorway, "that he will not receive *either* gift." Lucinda nearly dropped the tube as she whirled around; only Judah's steadying hand kept it from sloshing precious liquid. Elizabeth stood in the scullery, leaning against the open doorway and blocking the light. There was a sulfurous odor that accompanied her—faint but strong enough to overcome the liquid soaking into

John's brass buttons. "It really *is* a pity; I have nothing personal against John, or you. Even though I know John does not truly like me." She sighed, rather dramatically. "But there it is. Andrew is a wealthy man, but divide that between you and John and me, and it would not be much wealth at all. I do intend to present him with children and I should truly hate to see them grow up poor."

"Andrew's wealth is not static," Judah said, when it became clear Lucinda was incapable of speech. "Given a few years, he will certainly replace what he gives his daughter as a dowry, or his son to start a household. And John has no plans yet to wed."

"You killed Mother, didn't you?" Lucinda said suddenly. "You killed Mother, because of Richard." She was aware of Judah staring at her but her whole attention was for her stepmother—for Bess, and to keep herself from moving. If she touched the woman in this moment, she might murder her. If she could touch her at all, of course.

Elizabeth sighed again. "Richard wanted you. Not simply for your, let us say, purity, though that initially figured in the matter. He had been ordered to perform a full Mass, and once I was fully initiated, there were no more virgins in our circle. And as he surely told you, it is difficult to know when a young lady is a virgin, and when she merely says so. Our Master does not like it at all if he is thwarted—or cheated. Richard also liked the idea of your father's wealth, though he did well enough with his own funds, and he was an excellent gambler. He did find you attractive, if that matters to you."

"It might have, once," Lucinda said.

"Yes." Elizabeth cast Judah a chill glance. "Well. Unfortunately, Arabella was a problem; she distrusted him from the first, and he was obliged to use a potion to dull her magic—you'll know about *that*, of course, won't you? And then, when she discovered it, as we knew she eventually would—Well, we underestimated her."

Lucinda shivered. It was all coming back, suddenly. The taste and smell of Richard's flask, the swirl of light and sound that sent her flying from the carriage, and the horse running out of control down the darkened path. "That was—"

"That was a spell of your mother's." Elizabeth smiled; it was a most unpleasant smile, and Lucinda shivered again. "It weakened her." She shook her head impatiently. "I didn't murder her, you know! Though I could have done it, I had no need. What she did to my brother took so much of the life force out of her, she could not regain it."

"Particularly," Lucinda said evenly, "with your potion to keep her from knowing how to rebuild."

The smile slipped. "No. There was not enough of her left to do that!" She drew a deep breath and brought her chin up to glare at her stepdaughter. "Think rather that *you* yourself caused her death, by running to my brother when a decent girl would have hidden in her room!" She glanced quickly at Judah. "You may wish that bracelet back, Mr. Levy."

Lucinda didn't dare look at him. His voice warmed the chill that was threatening all of her. "Oh—I doubt that, very much so."

"As stubborn as she, aren't you? You'll suit each other very well—or you would have, given the chance," Elizabeth finished ominously. She stepped back into the scullery, beckoned. "I truly see no need to remain in this airless, grubby little hole while we talk, do you?"

"No need," Lucinda whispered, and let her shoulders sag. She turned aside to set the glass tube in its wrought-metal base, and with her free hand picked up Willow's globe. It stretched her fingers, but was still small enough to slide down into a fold of her skirts. Elizabeth must not have seen; or perhaps she was so confident, she felt no fear of anything Lucinda might do.

Maybe she had cause. Lucinda had no idea, herself, what she would do. Something stirred deep in her mind: *she will not harm another person I love!*

The main chamber was awash with afternoon sun, drowsy with the sound of flies exploring the fireplace and the stoop before the open front door. Lucinda let Judah seat her on the edge of the bed; her feet dangled. He leaned against one of the headposts; Elizabeth drew up a small cushioned stool and fastidiously brushed dust from it.

She'd changed; or perhaps she no longer felt the need to hide behind the guise of respectability. Her hair fell in golden curls across bare shoulders, and the pale violet gown swung loose from the low, lace-edged throat to wide skirts. To Lucinda, she looked infinitely beautiful, desirable. As Richard had. But Judah showed no sign of desiring her. He crossed his legs at the ankle and folded his arms across his chest as Elizabeth spoke. "My brother was at least as interested in what kind of combination could be worked with your sorcery and ours. Did he tell you that? Your cross-ocean magic is nearly as hard for one of us to see as our witchcraft seems to be for you. Arabella certainly never realized what *I* was, and it took her a very long time to see through Richard, and to realize how he had tricked her." She paused; Lucinda motioned her to go on. "I *was* sorry when she became so very ill and I saw she must die if I did not reverse the dampening spell. But if I had, it might have cost me *my* life: they hang witches in England also, you know. And my Master would not have liked it. Besides"—she shrugged—"certain things *must* be. To let a brother die and not avenge him—"

"You might remember that, Bess dear," Lucinda said gently. *I should hate her,* she thought wearily. *I can only feel sorry for one so misguided.* Elizabeth laughed, showing neat, white teeth.

"You found the seeds in the comforter I stitched for you, didn't you? Well, they kept you inactive nearly long enough. And you're no match for me, Lucinda Greene. I joined Richard's coven when I was thirteen, you know. I was given enough knowledge then to bury you and John—and your Levite betrothed as well. Now: Well, I've not wasted the years between, Lucy my sweet."

"I don't doubt it," Lucinda said. "But I was born with my skills. Nor am I an ocean away from my roots as Mother was. Bess, be warned, I have no desire to hurt you, but I won't tamely wait for you to do harm to me and mine." She paused, studied the other woman's face intently for some moments. "But *I* don't believe you really want to." She snatched the little globe from under her skirts and flipped the lid away with her thumbnail, throwing the contents across the room.

Elizabeth shrieked and leaped back, sending the stool flying. Fine white powder filled the air; her heel caught on her wide-flung skirts and she fell, sneezing repeatedly. Judah was ready to throw himself on the fallen witch, but Lucinda caught his arm. "No—wait!" Elizabeth drew a wheezing breath and then another, rubbed her streaming eyes with her fingers, and let out a sharp cry as she gazed up. Directly above her, hovering midair in the cloud of white powder was a pale blue light—almost human in shape, extremely tiny. Pale, intense eyes caught and held the witch's.

"Madam . . ." The voice of the will-o'-the-wisp was not deep but somehow it vibrated Lucinda's bones, and Elizabeth's teeth were suddenly chattering. "It has come to my attention that you did harm to my mistress when I could not be with her." Silence. "Madam?"

Unwillingly, Elizabeth nodded.

"And now you plan more harm. Is that your intent, madam?"

"Beware," Elizabeth replied in a faint, panting voice. "Whatever you are! My Master will—"

"Your Master cannot see you while the contents of this box are floating on the air, and *I* can keep them there a goodly while, madam. Even if he did see you, he would not come to your aid. That is not his way. He did nothing to save your brother's life, did he?" Elizabeth moaned and covered her face with shaking hands. There was another, deep silence. "Daughter of Arabella, do you wish her dead?" Elizabeth moaned again; Lucinda shook her head.

"No, Willow. I have no more taste for vengeance than did Mother. You know that better than any," she added meaningfully.

A deep, rumbling noise shook the pot hooks in the fireplace and rattled the glass panes; Arabella's invisible companion was sighing. "My Arabella was too soft-hearted," she said accusingly. "So are you."

"You had better get used to that," Lucinda said tartly. "If you intend to serve me."

Willow sighed again. "But I suppose it has become a habit, serving your family. Woman," she addressed Elizabeth again. "You have a choice to make, here and now: your life or your calling."

Elizabeth looked up, and her eyes and the set of her mouth were bitter. "You'd have me abjure? You know that isn't possible."

"Who said that? The Prince of Lies, or your brother, who wanted you under his thumb? It is possible. A woman cannot serve two husbands. Choose between them."

Elizabeth shook her head. "I can't—!"

"You can," Lucinda overrode the other woman's rising hysteria. "But I think you already have." She crossed the room and knelt to take the other woman's hands in hers. "Oh, Bess! If you truly wanted to kill John, *or* me, you'd have done it before now. You've been dabbling, haven't you? You're fond of Father, I can see it whenever you're with him. I know you're fond of me, Bess." Reluctantly, Elizabeth nodded. "As I am of you. Bess, I should hate you for Mother's death, but I can't. I know how persuasive Richard was, and I only knew him a few short months and I wasn't part of his—his Advocates. I can't believe you would have actively harmed anyone, if you'd been let alone. Give it over now, Bess, now you've seen a different way. You've a good life and a happy one here; you don't need to stay committed to such evil."

Silence. Elizabeth looked up at her uncertainly. "I can't. Richard said—when a maid chooses at thirteen, as I did—"

"He lied, to tie you to him and to his way of life. To keep you from happiness of your own, Bess! But you didn't choose—he chose for you, didn't he?"

"I—oh, Lucy, I can't!" But there were tears in her blue eyes, and her lip trembled.

Lucinda glanced up at the waiting will-o'-the-wisp. "A bargain, Willow. She will do no further mischief against us; you will watch her but do no mischief against her so long as she is idle. Bess, think, I beg of you! Don't simply accept what you were told without wondering why the words were said. Think of Father, and how much he cares for you!" She drew a deep breath. "Think about the bargain I've offered you. And—in case you think to carry out this fool's plan of vengeance and greed before good sense saves you, know that Willow is watching, and will know what your decision is as soon as it is made."

"I don't doubt it," Elizabeth whispered. She glared up at the hovering form and sneezed again. Then pulled herself together with a visible effort and drew her feet in under her skirts, smoothing them down in an attempt at dignity. "I see no point in remaining here any longer. Lucy, your father expects you and Mr. Levy to dinner tonight. We shall see you then." And she vanished as suddenly and silently as she had arrived. Arabella's—now Lucinda's—companion went whirling after her.

Lucinda picked up the little box and closed it carefully, then turned back to find Judah Levy watching her, wide-eyed. "Will you always surprise me like this?" he asked.

"I surprised myself," Lucinda admitted. "But—do you mean Willow, or that I didn't simply loose the will-o'-the-wisp on her? I meant what I told her, you know. Poor Bess. Imagine making such a dreadful pact at such a tender age! She cannot have known anything else, certainly very little pleasant, until she met Mother. No wonder she was so fond of parties and balls when she had her London season. It must have been the first real pleasure in all her life."

Judah closed the front door and led the way back through the scullery. "You think she will abjure, then?"

"Say, rather, I hope it," Lucinda said. "She is intelligent, and like me—like you, Judah—she is practical. But enough of Bess for now." She stood in the doorway and looked around the sunlit room. "Tell me, since I foresee we will both spend much time in this house, should the working room not be larger, and should we not add a window, perhaps a door? Certainly another, larger bench, since two people will use it so often together." She turned back to take his hands. They were large, warm hands, and unlike certain other hands, she expected strength of these. Judah brought her fingers to his lips. "I think Bess will realize, with no effort at all, that there is a good deal to be said for happiness."

Anno Domini 1773

THE SUMMONING

by Katherine Kurtz

The old man sat on a stump beside the frozen river, watching black water race past a hole in the ice. It was twilight, the last day of the year 1773, and the bone-chilling cold of the coming night was descending; but the old man only wrapped his cloak more closely around himself and waited—watching, willing—as the last weak rays of sunlight finally retreated from the ice-rimmed hole and left the surface a black mirror.

"Now show thyself to me," he whispered, sketching the sign of the Dragon in the air before him, centered over his blackened mirror. "Show thyself, who shall come at the appointed hour to accept thy destiny. Show thyself. . . ."

Sitting back then, he waited, eyes fixed on his mirror, summoning the image of the one who would come. Absently his hand sought the silver chain around his neck, his thumb caressing the coin-sized medallion with its image of a knight confronting a dragon. Slowly the image came—of a tall, commanding figure in a full-cut black cloak with shoulder capelets, striding along a snow-covered street.

A smart tricorn hat crowned reddish-brown hair pulled back in a queue. Well-polished boots with spurs showed below fawn-colored breeches as he set one toe in a polished stirrup and swung up on a tall, raw-boned grey. The gloved hands that gathered up the reins were big, almost a little awkward, the thighs gripping the grey's sides thick and powerful.

The old man nodded as the image wavered and then faded, touching the silver medallion to his lips and bowing his head in thanks for the Vision. Very shortly, he was roused from his meditation by the crunching footfall of someone approaching from behind him in the snow.

"Yes, daughter, I know what time it is," he said, even as he turned to greet her. "I was just ready to come in. Is all in readiness?"

The girl was just eighteen, small like her mother had been, with hair of a rich bronzy-gold pulled up in a loose knot at the crown. Her cloak was a deep forest-green, the gown beneath it the saffron hue of marigolds or sunflower petals. The eyes that gazed at him adoringly were a clear, startling blue. He had named her Amanda, for the mother she had never known. Today's Amanda bore a wreath of fresh laurel leaves in her slender hands, looking very much as her mother had looked at a similar age, so many years before. The radiance of her smile made it seem that the sun had turned backward in its path, bringing the dawn once more.

"Well, this is done, at any rate. I hope it's what you wanted," she said, displaying the wreath hopefully. "I only took slips from young laurel trees, as you suggested. That helped to keep everything supple, and made the weaving easier."

"Did you remember to take from thirteen different trees?" he asked, arching an eyebrow.

"Of course!" she replied, drawing the wreath away momentarily in mock indignation. "And also asked permission before I cut them. Whose daughter do you think I am, to forget something that important? Seriously, though"— she flashed him a smile and offered the wreath again— "will it be all right?"

He took the wreath from her and held it up for inspection, breathing deeply of the pungent, familiar scent. He was white haired and bearded, with a nobility about his bearing that recalled gentle origins in the Old World—and indeed, he had been born noble, though castles and lands and titles had been left behind with his wife's grave, across a broad ocean that he knew he would never cross again.

Nor had he any desire to re-cross it. That phase of his life had closed with Amanda's death. Here, he was simply Jakob, sometimes referred to as the Hermit of the Ridge. There were others of his kind farther along the Wissahikon, some of whom had banded together in a semi-monastic community—and others, still, who had abandoned the pretense of Christian façade and pursued their ancient skills more openly—and more precariously. But though a younger Jakob had considered both options, he had deemed neither course suitable for the father of a young son and infant daughter.

Accordingly, in the nearly two decades since his arrival in these Pennsylvania woods, he had carved out a sheltered and solitary life for himself and his children, diligently setting himself a routine of study, work, and prayer, teaching his children to reverence the same, bequeathing them a richness of spiritual freedom that was not possible in the Old World, with its hypocrisies and religious intolerance. One still must be careful, even here—distant cousins had burned in Salem, less than a century before—but the old man's pious demeanor and willingness to help anyone in need, and the reassuring little chapel, with its simple cross of iron, had long ago disarmed any local suspicion or resentment.

"The wreath is marvelous, my dear," the old man murmured, bending to kiss the top of her burnished head. "Exactly as I envisioned. Now, what about your brother? Has he finished at the chapel?"

Her face clouded briefly at that, but she made a brave attempt at a new smile and nodded. "Of course he has, Father. You know that you have only to ask, and either Ephraim or I would do anything for you, but—"

"But?" he repeated, smiling gently and caressing her cheek with one veined hand.

She hooked her arm in his as they started back toward the snug, sod-walled blockhouse that was their home, sighing as she scuffed her little boots along the snow-encrusted path.

"I wish I had your confidence," she said, searching for the words. "I know what the prophecies say, and I respect our ancient ways. But how can you be so certain he will heed the Call? He is not one of us. The Dragon's breath does not stir his lungs. The blood of the Dragon does not run in his veins."

"No, he is not kin to the Dragon," the old man agreed, "but nonetheless, he will play a vital role in the New Order. Besides, this is not the Dragon's land—though it is meet that the Dragon should find refuge here. The one who is to come is kin to the Eagle, I suspect—though perhaps the Dragon may help teach the Eagle to soar. But doubt it not, he will come, my darling. I have seen his visage, and he will come."

They reached the blockhouse then and went in, and the old man sat beside the well-scrubbed table and contemplated the laurel wreath while the girl built up the fire. She was drawing the curtains at the front windows to shut out the gloomy forest and the falling night when her brother returned with an armload of wood, cheeks red from the cold outside, eyes blazing with his news. He was a tall, handsome youth, as dark as Amanda was fair, with the same guileless blue gaze that all three of them shared. The graceful hands were callused from honest work, but every line of his slender form confirmed his gentle breeding.

"I ran into Caleb Matheson, when I went down to chop the wood," he announced, depositing his wood in a sturdy basket beside the fire and throwing off his heavy cloak. "Do you know what's happening up in Boston?"

As he sat himself eagerly on a stool opposite his father, the old man nodded slowly.

"A little over a fortnight ago, in outraged and righteous protest against scandalous new British taxes, a great deal of tea was flung into Boston Harbor," he said blandly. "So that it would appear that Red Indians were to blame, the perpetrators blacked and painted their faces, and communicated by means of grunts and 'ugh-ugh,' and exchanged the phrase 'me know you,' as a countersign.

"In truth, however, the plan was hatched in a tavern called the Green Dragon, by Bostonians of several different radical groups and Masonic Lodges, united by the resolve that the tea should not be off-loaded and the tax should not be tolerated. It is believed that some of the participants foregathered at a meeting of the Saint Andrew's Lodge—which was adjourned early, there being few members present—ending their night's escapade at a chowder supper hosted by the brothers Bradlee. What came between Lodge and chowder, few will own openly, but the names of such notables as Dr. Joseph Warren and Mr. Paul Revere have been mentioned in connection with the affair, and it is certain that some three hundred forty-two chests of tea ended up in Boston Harbor, to the value of some eighteen thousand pounds sterling. Rumor also has it that old Mother Bradlee kept a kettle of water hot, so that 'the boys' could wash off their face-black and war paint, afterwards."

Young Ephraim's jaw had dropped as his father's recital became more and more specific, and he shook his head as his sire finally wound down. At twenty-two, he was sometimes inclined to believe that his youthful agility gave him an edge on gathering news; but somehow his father usually managed to know about important events long before the local grapevine carried it to Ephraim's ears.

"You knew!" he blurted, half-indignant. "How in the world did you know? I only found out the details this afternoon."

The old man only smiled, touching a fingertip lightly along the leaves of the laurel wreath and watching his son. The smile was infectious, and Ephraim soon broke into his own perplexed grin.

"It's clear that I still have a great deal to learn," the youth said amiably. "I suppose you've also heard that it's feared the British will close the Port of Boston in retaliation, and make them pay back the eighteen thousand pounds?"

The old man raised one eyebrow in question.

"You hadn't heard?" The young man's delight was palpable. "Well, Caleb had it from his father, who heard it in Philadelphia. Apparently the State House is all a-buzz with talk of a blockade, once Parliament finds out what's happened. The Virginia Burgesses are calling the threat an attack made on all British America, and wondering who'll be next. In fact, all the Colonies are supporting what Boston did. There's even talk of a Continental Congress in the new year."

The old man drew a deep breath as the youth finished, lowering his eyes in contemplation, and a silence fell around the little table. When he raised his eyes to them once more, the fire of his calling smoldered in their blue depths, and he carefully folded his hands on the table before him.

"It all is coming to pass, even sooner than I dreamed," he murmured, shifting his gaze into the circlet of the laurel wreath, focusing beyond the scrubbed pine of the tabletop. "The events in Boston have already triggered the change. No more shall the Old World extend its wickedness to the New. Those who revere the cause of freedom shall enshrine it upon these shores, and hereon the footsteps of kings shall never tread. God has spoken and it is so. Say Amen!"

"Amen," his children repeated softly, not daring to gainsay him.

There would be no supper tonight, for fasting would hone and focus their energies for the night's work. Bread and water only would he allow, though he made of this sparse fare a sacrament, as he blessed and broke the bread for them, then blessed and passed the cup filled from the sacred spring outside their door.

Afterward, when they had spent an hour in meditation, threesome hands joined around the table, Amanda silently helped father and brother pull on the ritual garments set aside for their most important work—white hooded robes sewn from nubbly virgin wool, carded, spun, and loomed by her virgin hands. The scarlet cinctures they knotted about their waists had been plaited of more of the wool, each one the prayerful work of the individual who should wear it, dyed with the last of the precious cochineal Jakob had brought with him twenty years before. Amanda donned her robe as well, but she did not go with them to the chapel; her place was to keep watch here in the house, adding her prayers to theirs, and to join them when he had come. She set a candle in the window as they went out, sinking to her knees to focus on the flame.

The two men did not speak as they made their way across the snow, Ephraim carrying a lantern and his father bearing the laurel wreath, both wrapped in cloaks over their robes. The chapel was a small, round building made of sod, but with a good thatched roof and a chimney thrusting skyward on the right. A little wooden vestibule guarded the doorway, and as Ephraim opened the door, light from the candles left burning on the altar streamed out across the snow. The night wind swept a flurry of snow inside and stirred the white cloth adorning the altar, and Ephraim shut the door before setting the lantern squarely in the center of the little chamber.

The walls and floor were planked with pine, with a modest brick fireplace built into the wall on the right as they entered. A large cross of iron hung above the altar, clean-lined and simple, centered on a hanging of nubbly white wool. As Ephraim went to feed the fire back to life, his father carried the laurel wreath to the altar and laid it beside a slender silver flagon and a large, richly bound Bible. The latter had been a family heirloom for nearly two hundred years, bound in crimson leather and stamped in gold, the corners and clasps fashioned of silver-gilt, but the old man paid it only passing interest as he shifted its bulk a little nearer the altar's front edge. For beyond the book and the wreath and the flagon, almost invisible in the angle between surface and wall, lay a naked sword of an earlier age. And in the nearer angle of quillons and blade lay three smooth-polished quartz pebbles that had not been there earlier in the afternoon.

Blessing the messenger, the old man smiled and bowed his respect to the altar, touched his fingertips to his lips and to the crossing of the sword hilt, then scooped up the pebbles and closed them in his hand before turning to face his son.

"The one we have awaited will come at the third hour after midnight," he said quietly. At his son's look askance, he repeated, "Doubt it not, he will come. At the third hour of the new year, as the clock concludes its strike, he will come through yonder door to take upon himself his sacred mission. All is prepared for his coming. We have only to keep our faith, to continue the Call, and he cannot but come."

He and his son knelt in prayer then, while behind them, close beside the door, the ancient grandfather clock that usually graced a corner of their sitting room ticked off the minutes and the hours. At eleven, the old man extinguished the lantern and moved it aside, throwing open the door to the winter night and beginning to pace back and forth across the width of the chapel. His son fed the fire again, remaining nearer its warmth to continue his prayers. The altar candles filled the little chapel with a softer glow than had the lantern, spilling a golden path onto the snow outside—a beacon to anyone approaching.

The old man paced on, head bowed and hands clasped in prayer. When the clock finally struck twelve, ushering in the new year, Ephraim lifted his head and glanced toward his father, compassion welling up—for though the appointed time was yet three hours away, youthful impatience worried that the old man might be wrong.

"Father, what if he doesn't come?" he whispered, tottering unsteadily to his feet to flex his knees, stiff after kneeling so long.

The old man glanced back at the open doorway, at the path of candlelight streaming out onto the snow, then turned back to the altar and the sacred objects it held.

"He will come," the old man declared. "At the third hour after midnight, the Deliverer will come."

Silently he resumed his measured pacing; and as Ephraim watched and listened, he realized that the steps and his father's breathing had fallen into an engaging rhythm. The pattern was at once compelling and reassuring, weaving its own call in counterpoint to the ticking of the clock.

Renewed in spirit, the youth knelt once more near the fire, out of the direct draught of the open door, and resumed his meditations, letting himself fall into the rhythm of the spell, lifting his spirit to soar with his sire's call, searching out the one who was to come. Detached from physical perception, he quested outward, casting in an ever-widening net.

By one o'clock, the altar candles had nearly burned down. Carefully, reverently, the old man changed them, inserting fresh tapers in the pewter candlesticks, making certain they stood straight, that everything was as it should be. The honey scent of beeswax continued to fill the little chamber with its sweet incense as he again resumed his pacing.

The clock struck two. Now the old man stood before the fireplace, bowed head resting on the hands clasped to the edge of the pine mantel, shifting to a different sort of concentration, never ceasing to send forth his call. The wind had risen with the turn of the year, and the candles danced in the breeze, the altar cloth billowing along the front edge and ends. The stillness in the tiny chamber became more profound, each tick of the clock carrying father and son deeper into concentration, strengthening the spell.

When the clock at last began to strike the hour, the old man slowly raised his head and turned to face the open door, his white head cocked in a listening attitude. And as the third stroke hung and died away on air suddenly gone very, very still, there came hesitant footsteps in the little vestibule, stamping snow from boots; and then a tall stranger of majestic presence ducked his head to enter the room, grey-blue eyes sweeping the little chamber in respect and wonder.

"Pray, pardon my intrusion, friends, but I seem to have lost my way in the forest," he said uncertainly, removing his tricorne and making the old man a courteous bow. "Can you direct me to the right way?"

"I can, if thou wouldst find the way to thy destiny," the old man said, catching and holding the gray-blue eyes in his compelling gaze. "Come in and close the door. The winter night is cold, and we have waited long for thy coming."

The stranger's eyes widened, but he turned without demur and closed the door, coming in then to the center of the chamber, to stand unresisting before the old man's inspection. The red-brown hair was powdered now, the linen at his throat more formal, the line of his dark blue coat more stylish than the image the old man had seen in his black water mirror.

But the gloved hands were the same, and the black cloak with its several shoulder capelets, and the spurred black boots—though the latter now were caked with snow. A smallsword hung at his side, its silver hilt just visible through the parting of the cloak.

"It is late to be out on such a night," the old man said.

The stranger nodded, fingering his hat a little nervously, his expression suggesting that even he was not certain why or how he had come here.

"Yes, it is."

"And some desperate burden lies upon thy heart, to bring thee to this place at this time," the old man continued softly. "Is it not thy country's welfare?"

Looking a little startled, the stranger gave a cautious nod.

"And it troubles thee, does it not, that a subject might feel bound to raise his hand against his king?"

"How do you know that?" the man demanded, staring at the old man in amazement. "Who are you, to know what troubles me?"

"I am but an instrument, sent to prepare thee," the old man said. "Thy calling comes from One far higher than I. Put aside thy sword and kneel before this altar. With thy right hand upon the Volume of Sacred Law, pledge thy faith; and having pledged, receive that threefold confirmation which shall sustain thee in the times to come, as future deliverer of a nation's freedom!"

A little dazed-looking, the stranger complied, laying his hat aside and letting the youth divest him of his sword, which then was laid reverently upon the altar. Of his own volition he stripped off his gloves as he sank to one knee, stuffing them distractedly into the front of his coat as he set his bare right hand upon the Bible. Throughout, the grey-blue eyes remained locked on the old man's blue ones, the craggy face still and expectant.

"Know that before half a year has passed, thou shalt be called to lead thy fellow countrymen to war!" the old man said, both admiring and pitying him. "Soon shalt thou ride forth to battle at the head of mighty armies. Soon shall thy sword be raised as a shining beacon to those who shall help thee win a nation's freedom!"

As the stranger's face went a little paler, the old man laid his own hand atop the one resting on the Book, though no compulsion accompanied the questions he now put to the chosen one.

"Dost thou promise that, when the appointed time doth come, thou shalt be found ready, sword in hand, to fight for thy country and thy God?"

Without hesitation the answer came, the voice steady, the grey-blue eyes clear.

"I do."

"Dost thou promise to persevere through defeats as well as victories, knowing that both shall have caused thee to send good men to their deaths?"

The stranger's "I do" was softer this time, but no less determined.

"And dost thou promise that, even in the hour of victory, when a nation shall bow before thee, thou shalt remember that thou art but the instrument of God in achieving this Great Work of a nation's freedom?"

"I do promise," came the answer, clearly and firmly.

"Then in His Name Who hath given the New World as the last altar of human rights," the old man said, taking up the flagon from the altar, "I do consecrate thee its Champion and Deliverer."

Moistening his thumb with oil from the flagon, he slowly and deliberately traced a cross and then a circle on the stranger's brow, sealing the vows and imparting his blessing with the sacred symbol. A shiver went through the stranger at the other's touch, and the eyes half-closed. His breathing deepened as the old man replaced the flagon on the altar and took up the laurel wreath, and he bowed his head and clasped trembling hands in an attitude of prayerful reverence as the old man lifted the wreath above him.

"In times ahead shall come a victor's crown," the old man said, his gaze flicking expectantly to the door. "But let it be no conqueror's blood-stained wreath—though blood thou shalt shed. Rather, this brighter crown of fadeless laurel."

But before he could place it on the stranger's head, wind gusted through the suddenly open door, billowing the altar cloth and setting the candles to guttering, and Amanda was standing in the doorway. She had wrapped her green cloak over her robe to make her way from the house, and her loosened hair floated on the wind like a tawny halo.

The old man paused as he saw her, her brother's eyes also turning in her direction. Then the old man lowered the wreath and made her a profound bow.

"Come to us, as *la Déesse de la Liberté*," he said. "For it is fitting that a nation's Champion and Deliverer should receive his crown of laurel from the hands of a stainless woman."

Lifting her head, she drew the door closed behind her and let fall her cloak, at the same time assuming the psychic mantle he had bade her take upon herself for the office to which she was called. As she came softly to her father's side and took the laurel wreath from him, the stranger's eyes lifted to hers, not comprehending; but as she willed him to see past the merely visible, the grey-blue eyes widened—not in fear, but in profound recognition.

He was trembling as she lifted the laurel wreath above his head, and a shudder went through his body as she placed the leafy crown on his powdered hair—a shudder stilled by the touch of her hands upon his shoulders, and by the kiss she pressed gently to his forehead, atop the imprint of the sacred oil.

Then, as she straightened and backed away a step to stand beside her father, her brother moved before the altar, unsheathing the stranger's sword and laying it nearer the front edge, moving the antique sword close beside it. The scabbard and belt he gave into his sister's keeping, sparing only a brief glance at his father before extending his hands flat over the antique blade as he had been taught, closing his eyes.

His lips moved silently in prayer; the stranger watched numbly, the big hands still clasped loosely at his heart in an attitude of reverence.

Then the young man's eyes opened and the hands slowly were lifted, drawing an ethereal, ghost-image of the antique sword out of the physical steel to float a hand-span above. A gesture of his left hand held the image steady while his right hand traced the Dragon sign over the ghost-hilt, severing the connection with the original weapon.

Slowly he drew the ghost image to overlap the stranger's sword, superimposing the energy of the first over that of the second, pressing the image into the second sword's steel, making of the stranger's blade a magical implement akin to the first. Blue sparks arced as his hands touched the steel of the stranger's sword, startling even him.

But then he took up the weapon by its hilt, touched his lips to the crossing, and sheathed the blade in the scabbard his sister offered, letting the ends of the sword belt dangle free as he shifted it to his left hand, grasping it below the hilt, and turned to give the stranger his right hand. His eyes locked with the other man's, compelling his attention, ensuring that his words should be engraved on the other's memory for all time as he raised him up.

"Rise now, Champion and Deliverer of a people. To thee I give the hand of loyalty and service, which shall be a sign for the hands and loyalties to come, to sustain thee in thy mission. I know not thy name," he went on, releasing the other's hand, "yet on this Book I swear to be faithful to the cause you have made your own, even unto death."

He touched the fingertips of his right hand briefly to his lips, to the sacred Book, then bent to buckle the sword to the stranger's side. When he had finished, he stood back and made him a little bow. It was the signal for the girl also to bow, after which the three of them, in unison, made the stranger a sign of respect.

The stranger looked at all of them a little dazedly—and at the altar, at the Book, at the iron cross witnessing all— then raised his chin in growing confidence, the laurel wreath resting like a royal diadem on his noble head.

"I know not whether I wake or dream," he whispered, "but this I vow, by all that is sacred—I shall be true to the charge you have set before me."

So saying, and taking his example from the young man, he touched the fingers of his right hand to his lips and laid that hand flat on the Bible for a moment, his eyes closing briefly.

Then he was turning to stride out of the little chapel without a backward glance, blindly taking the hat that the young man pressed into his hands. The sound of his retreating footsteps mingled with the moaning wind as he opened the door and passed into the night of the new year, taking their magic with him.

When he had gone, the girl and the young man turned to their father.

"Will he remember what has happened here tonight, Father?" Amanda asked.

"He will," the old man replied. "It may be but the whisper of a fleeting dream, when the time is right—sparked, perhaps, by the scent of mountain laurel—but he will remember."

"And he will, indeed, take up the sword?" Ephraim persisted.

The old man nodded, his aged eyes staring far beyond the path of candlelight still streaming onto the snow outside.

"He will take it up," he whispered. "By the Dragon, he will become the Deliverer. It is his destiny."

Anno Domini 1845

UNHOLY ALLIANCE

by Morgan Llywelyn

The rich aroma of crisping, crackling flesh permeated the hall. A suckling pig was roasting in the vast stone fireplace. When Michael turned the iron spit, small globules of fat slid from the meat and dropped, hissing, into the fire.

Michael Crafter's mouth flooded with saliva. Wait, he told himself. Be patient. Perfection cannot be rushed, old Amer had written, whether it be perfection in cookery or . . .

His eyes slid toward the great oaken sea chest in the far corner of the hall. Within its sturdy timbers and brass bindings the Book was safely hidden, and better so. Ireland would not welcome a volume of arcane wisdom from the New World, Michael knew. Too many versions of belief were at war in Ireland already.

Michael sighed. Even behind the stone walls of the manor house, his hypersensitive nerves were abraded by the conflict of dogma between the Roman Catholic priests and the followers of Protestantism, the doctrine that had been imposed upon the Irish by the conquering English. Anglicanism was the state religion now; the Papists only ministered to the peasantry.

In the year 1845, Ireland was a seething mass of troubles. Even a Crafter was not immune. "Perhaps you made a mistake in coming here," Michael remarked aloud to a portrait on the wall. The likeness of a dark-visaged man with curled hair and dancing eyes stared back at him. Eben Crafter, Michael's great-grandfather, who had fled America to escape the restrictions of Puritanism and eventually settled in Ireland to make a fortune, just as the English were doing there, by exploiting the conquered natives.

Somehow Eben had gained the confidence of the English power structure in control of Ireland, and been able to claim lands and amass considerable wealth. His Crafter kin back in America were horrified to learn that he was taking such advantage of the natives, selling their produce for high prices in Europe while forcing them to a life of bare subsistence on the land that had once been theirs.

But for many years, Eben had not seemed to care what others thought of his success. As his fortune piled up he had built himself the huge manor in which Michael now lived. Then, in old age some incident occurred which Eben never divulged, but which had changed him drastically. He had set about trying to make reparations to the peasantry he had cheerfully exploited. He built better housing for his tenants, he gave them a share of their produce, he saw that their medical needs were met and their old age provided for. He even obligated his descendants to do the same, with the result that the fortune Eben had acquired was slowly but surely dissipated over the years in one family's attempt to better the dreadful lot of the peasantry in their district of western County Clare.

By the time Michael reached adulthood all that remained of the Crafter wealth was the house, which was slowly succumbing to the Irish weather, and Eben Crafter's sea chest, containing one copy of *The Science of Magic*.

On his deathbed, Michael's father had assured his son, "There is enough in the Book to support you for life, if you dare to use it. But I warn you—it takes a brave man. I myself have never been forced to employ it. You might, however. There are hard times coming. Hard times." He broke off, coughing.

"How do I make use of the Book?" Michael had wanted to know. But his father was already beyond words. He died of consumption the next day, leaving his only son alone in a huge and echoing house. There was no longer enough money for servants.

Michael had approached the chest containing his heritage with some trepidation. The magical sciences of Amer Crafter were a family legend. He took his first look at the Book, a large volume bound in leather, filled with tiny lines of crabbed writing in fading brown ink, then put it back in the chest and fastened the lock. I do not need it yet, he thought with a sense of relief. There was something intimidating about the Book. He could live simply; he need not rely upon spells and sorcery.

He had not touched the Book again until the coming of the Famine.

A loud pop reminded Michael of the pig on the spit, which needed to be turned before the meat burned through and let the precious food fall into the flames. How many in Ireland would eat so well this night? Michael wondered.

A distant sound reached his keen ears. Michael froze. Then he heard a timid scratching at the door.

He glanced at the pig. Its fragrance must have escaped through the chimney and reached the nose of some nearby starveling with a brood of famished children. And it was hardly enough to last Michael two days.

The scratching sounded again, beseechingly.

With a sigh, Michael crossed the cold flagstoned floor to the archway in which the door was set. Once there would have been a liveried servant at that door, welcoming titled guests to glittering entertainments, filling Crafter Hall with laughing men and ladies with gleaming, naked shoulders.

All gone now. All changed now. Only a gaunt shell of a house left, with a gaunt and lonely man in it, watching his youth being swallowed by shadows and silences, yet loving the land too much to leave as another might have done.

The massive entry door creaked open on rusty iron hinges. Beyond, on the top stone step, Michael saw a figure dressed in rags. It might have been human, a stooped and shrunken human. Then it moved, and its eyes caught and held the light of hearth and candle emerging from within the house.

"Is it meat ye be having?" a thready voice inquired.

The creature must be hungry indeed, Michael thought. It was not like the Irish to ask any question so directly. They preferred to circle around and around, coming up on the point only gradually and with indirection.

"It's a small piglet only, the first meat in this house in a fortnight," Michael said apologetically.

"Yer own stock, would that be?"

Michael almost laughed. "We've had no livestock here for years. I trapped this in the woods yonder."

"In the Cratloe Wood? A pig?" The man's voice quavered with excitement. Michael expected him to break and run, hurrying to tell his people so they might descend in a ravenous pack on the woodland. At once Michael regretted his lie. It was too easy to imagine the disappointment of the starving folk who would expect to find a sow and her litter, and get nothing for their pains but a few acorns to eat.

In some places, people were being found dead of hunger with their mouths stained green where they had tried to subsist on grass.

"There are no more pigs left in the wood," Michael said quickly. "This was the last."

"Ah." The man's face fell, but he took a step forward. "Ye have the one, though? Enough to feed a few? Meself and me woman? In the old days, a hungry woman would never have been turned away from this door."

That was all too true, Michael reflected ruefully. But was this one of the Crafter tenants, the folk his father and grandfather had cared for? He stared hard at the man, yet could not recognize him. But all the people were so changed. Since the Famine had come.

Michael sighed. "You are welcome to what I have," he said. "Bring your woman in." He stepped to one side with grave courtesy, as if welcoming a prince to Crafter Hall.

Turning, the man beckoned to someone crouched in the shadows. When she stepped into the light, Michael's jaw dropped.

He had never seen such a woman.

Like the man, she was slight in stature and slender of form. Her clothing owed nothing to any known style, being a wrapping and overlapping and skillful draping of what appeared to be dozens of bits and pieces of multicolored fabric. The man, Michael now realized, was clothed similarly.

But it was the woman's face that arrested attention. She was white. Not pale, but white. Like snow, like milk, like a swan's breast. Her face and uncovered throat glimmered in the firelight with a luminosity that made Michael think of the light sometimes seen on the crest of the waves at night, by the seashore.

One hand was clutched to her bosom as if holding her rags together and it, too, was of a dazzling whiteness. Her hair was a pale yellow, clinging in tendrils to her temples and cascading down her back. As she walked past Michael he saw sticks and leaves caught in its locks, as if the woman had recently been lying upon the earth.

Without a word, she went to the fireplace and stood gazing at the roasting pig. She was so still she might have been a statue.

"The meat will be cooked soon," Michael offered lamely. He wanted her to turn and look at him, but she did not. "You would not want to eat it half-raw."

"There's those in this land who would eat it still alive and squealing if they could," the man said. "Since the crop failed . . ."

He left the thought unfinished, glowering at Michael as if it were somehow his fault.

But it was no one's fault, and it was worse than a simple crop failure. The English had introduced the potato—ironically a New World vegetable, Michael reflected—to the Irish peasantry to serve as their staple food, thus releasing the crops and livestock the peasants grew to be shipped to England to grace English tables. This was the same trade upon which Eben Crafter had built his original fortune. Had the old man somehow used the Book to give him access to the English aristocracy, enabling him to purchase land in Ireland? No one knew; his secret had died with him. Only his guilty conscience seemed to have survived, compelling his descendants to try to make reparation.

Meanwhile the Irish peasants had learned to live on potatoes and buttermilk and little else, farming land that had once been their birthright, seeing their produce loaded onto ships and carried away. There should have been anger and rebellion, but the Irish chieftains who would have led such a rebellion had long since been killed, or driven from the country. Only the peasants remained: gentle, pious people who had no choice but to accept their lot and make the best of it—or see their landlords pull down their huts and set fire to them.

So they had worked, and survived by eating the lowly potato. Until one morning Ireland had awakened to the stench of rot. A blight had attacked the crop. In the fields, the green vines that had seemed so promising the night before lay shriveled and dying. When the people dug up the potatoes from the soil beneath they found the tubers blackened and slimy with rot.

In the wink of an eye, Famine came.

The merchants continued to ship all other Irish produce, which was quite unaffected, abroad. The Irish priests, fearful of their own position under the conquerors, urged the people to remain law-abiding and try to survive.

Then the next season the same thing happened again to the potatoes, and now the Irish were dying.

"I have tried to help," Michael said, uncomfortable before the small man's accusing stare. "But our lands have had to be sold off, over the years. My father and his father before him enjoyed living well, you see, plus they were always generous to those less fortunate . . . our wealth is gone. . . ."

"Ye have the pig," the man reminded him.

At these words, the woman turned and fixed her gaze on Michael. Her eyes were fever-bright and seemed to penetrate the secrets of his soul. "You have the pig," she echoed.

"We can eat it now, if you like," Michael heard himself say.

The long oaken table had not served a proper feast in years, but Michael spread what he had upon it. The roast piglet was swiftly carved, with the joints and sliced meat piled upon a pewter platter that had come from America with Eben. From a cupboard Michael produced a loaf of brown bread and a bottle of wine, and gestured to his guests to seat themselves on the benches beside the table.

With infinite grace, the woman did so. He could not take his eyes from her. *I have lived alone too long,* he told himself. *But who could I ask to share my fate? To whom could I even explain who and what I am?*

His guests fell ravenously upon the food.

Michael made himself eat more slowly, watching the woman to be certain she had all she wanted. When nothing remained but gnawed bones and a few crumbs, she smiled at him.

"My name is Aisling," she said, pronouncing it *Ash-ling* in the Irish way. "The word means a vision, a dream."

Michael nodded. "I know it."

"You speak the Irish, then?"

"A bit. And you speak the English."

It was her turn to nod. "A bit."

"Many of your people do not."

She narrowed her eyes. "Who do you think my people are?"

"The peasantry." He hesitated, suddenly afraid he might have offended her. Yet the peasants knew their class; they had never been offended by the description, so far as he knew. Still, somehow it did not seem appropriate, applied to this woman.

"The natives, you mean," Aisling replied. "In that sense you are correct, *sasanach*. I am a native of Ireland."

"You call me *sasanach*—Englishman—yet I am a native as well. I was born here, in this very house," Michael told the woman. "My ancestors came to this land from America, not England."

She flared her delicate nostrils. "Saxon. You are Saxon in your bones. Where were your ancestors before they went to the New World?"

The atmosphere in the hall writhed with ancient hatreds. Michael felt the skin prickle on his scalp. "I love this land," he said defensively. "And I have never done any harm to any Irish person."

"You are a landlord," she said, her tone making the word an epithet.

"I told you, I hardly own any land now, aside from that under this house. Most of it was sold before I was born. I don't know who collects your rent now, but it is not I, not my agents."

The woman exchanged a look with her ragged companion, who was running his finger around his mouth to collect the last of the grease, which he then sucked avidly from his finger.

"No one collects rent from us," she told Michael.

"Where is it you live?"

"Not far from here."

"But I have never seen you in chapel."

"You are a brave man to be going to chapel yourself, Michael Crafter," the small man said unexpectedly.

"I go to pray!" Michael burst out. He thought of the long hours he had spent on his knees on the stone floor, head bowed over clasped hands, begging God to give him the ability to help the people dying all around him. Begging God to forgive the sins of his fathers—and the magic, if that was a sin—and somehow work a miracle through Michael to help the people of Ireland.

But no miracle had occurred. And in despair he had opened the Book and tried to find, within its pages, another way to help, yet been frustrated even there. Whatever gifts old Eben had possessed for using the Book did not seem to have been passed through blood to his great-grandson, at least not with enough strength to enable Michael to work the ancient magic.

Afterwards, he had returned to chapel with shaking hands, afraid the priest would somehow know what he had attempted.

As this small man seemed to know, looking at him so keenly. Reading his soul.

Who were these people?

"Which God do you pray to?" the woman asked. "The god of the Roman priests, or that of the Protestants?"

"I believe it is the same God."

"In this land you are almost alone in that belief," she replied. "And what else do you believe in? What belief, for example, did you draw upon to produce that pig when everyone knows there has not been a pig in the Cratloe Wood for these two years or more?"

Michael was so startled, he could feel his face grow pale. Unintentionally, he glanced toward the brass-bound sea chest.

The little man gave a crow of delight. "I told you he had something, Aisling! They've all had something, they brought it with them! How else did they get the English to accept them and allow them to buy the land?"

Michael tried to protest, but suddenly they were standing on either side of him, their small hands pressing firmly on his shoulders. "What is it?" Aisling hissed. "What have you in yonder chest? Where did you get the pig? Is there help in it for the folk of Ireland?"

Even as he tried to protest his ignorance, Michael realized it was no use. This strange pair knew something and had guessed more. No accident had brought them to Crafter Hall.

"Is this how you repay my hospitality?" he managed to say, trying to sound outraged.

The woman laughed. "We did not come here for your hospitality—at least, not directly. We merely came to see if you had something to offer. We are not those who have been accustomed to receiving bounty from your clan in better times."

In Aisling's voice, Michael now recognized an unmistakable note of authority. Whatever she and her companion were, they were not starving Irish peasants. "What is this about?" he demanded to know. "What more do you want from me?"

She smiled a disarming smile, which somehow made her seem all the more dangerous. "Brocc and I want nothing from you. Not for ourselves. But we had to eat the meat to be sure."

"Sure of what?"

"That it was magicked, Michael Crafter."

Michael went cold all over. "I know not what you mean."

Aisling laughed; a tinkling, silvery laugh. "Ah, but you do."

"Who are you?" He noticed Brocc had lost his accent.

"Not of your breed," Brocc interposed smoothly. "But there is a fragment of talent in you akin to talents we possess, and it called to us. We recognize you as one musician knows another."

"What . . . breed . . . are you?" Michael asked in a whisper.

Aisling laughed again. "In Ireland there are several names for us. You would know some, but not others. It does not matter. What is important is the Famine, Ireland's enemy."

She waved one white hand toward the fire on the hearth, and for one heart-stopping moment Michael thought he glimpsed a face there. A hideous face, inhuman. Huge. Skull-like, with famished eyes.

"Famine," Aisling said again.

Michael's defenses collapsed. "I can do nothing," he admitted. "Do you not know I have tried? But I am one man only."

"A man with a talent. A gift."

He shook his head. "I inherited a few arcane secrets, that is all. But I have not the skill to make use of them to any great degree."

"Then where did the pig come from?"

Michael's shoulders slumped. He half-turned his body so he would not see that monstrous face if it appeared again in the flames. The face of the enemy.

"I made one last attempt," he said in a voice so low it could hardly be heard above the crackling of the fire. "But all I was able to produce was that one pathetic piglet. My earlier attempts were not even edible."

Aisling leaned toward him. "How did you make something from nothing?"

"I did not make something from nothing. What I did is to apply a form of science. Do you know the word? I took some of the solid substance of which the world is made, and I rearranged it into a new pattern."

"Magic," said Aisling firmly. "I told you so, Brocc."

"And did I not agree? Did I not?" Brocc was speaking deferentially, Michael noted with surprise, as if power lay with the woman. How strange!

"If you could do even that much, why have you kept it hidden?" Aisling wanted to know.

"Surely you understand. If it became public knowledge that I practice any magic at all, the priests would have me stoned and the Protestants would have me burned."

"So your fear the Christ-men."

"I—I suppose I do."

"Yet you go to chapel."

"Our family have always worshipped. We were of the Protestant persuasion; I daresay that helped my ancestor, Eben Crafter, when he was starting to build his fortune here under the English. It is only in recent years that I have begun very quietly attending services in the Catholic chapel in the woods. I do so only because it is . . . the faith of the people. And I like to think of myself as one of the people."

"If the authorities knew you were doing that, your few remaining holdings would be confiscated," Aisling said. "They hate one another, these men of the New Religions. Protestant condemns Catholic. What is sacred to one religion becomes blasphemy to its successor. I assure you, Michael Crafter, our own race has suffered more than you can possibly imagine for that very reason. Now we are reduced to hiding in mounds in the earth." Her voice rose, quivered with passion. "Yet it is still *our* earth! And it cries out with the agony of the people starving upon it! We are not left in peace, dreaming away the centuries in our hiding places. So we must seek help, and we come to you."

If it had not been for the Book, Michael would have found this whole evening incredible. He would have thought he had gotten hold of some bad poteen and tried to curl up to sleep it off.

But he had read the Book. He knew that the sum total of reality is contained in the Unknown, not the Known, which is but a minute particle of that reality.

Whatever else they might be, Brocc and Aisling were real and they were in his hall, demanding his help for the victims of Famine.

Looking at Aisling, Michael thought to himself, *Amer Crafter was reputed to have a creature called Willow. Do patterns repeat?*

Was Willow as lovely as Aisling?

Aloud, he said reluctantly, "You must try to understand. I have hardly any gift for . . . for magic. I only followed directions set forth in a book. I attempted to produce a huge herd of wild pigs, which the landlords could not claim, and which would be enough to feed the people of this district. But my best effort only resulted in one scrawny piglet, and that contained little sustenance, for already my belly growls again. People cannot be fed on thin illusion."

Aisling would not be dissuaded. "If you could do even that much, surely you can do more, with our help. You are not a coward. A coward would not go to a chapel to be with the commonfolk, although he knew it could mean dire punishment. You spoke of a book. Show it to us."

"I keep it locked in yonder chest. If it were known I possessed such a thing, it could mean my death."

"There are worse things than death," Brocc remarked.

" 'Death can be a friend'," Michael quoted Amer Crafter, and the other two nodded in understanding. "Can either of you read written words?" he wanted to know.

Aisling's chin lifted. "I can even read the patterns birds make in the sky," she assured him.

Michael found himself on his knees beside the great oaken chest, fumbling with the lock. The lid creaked open. Michael thrust his arms inside and lifted out the Book. A smell of old leather rose from it, and tiny bits flaked off as he carried it to the table and opened its cover.

Aisling and Brocc crowded against his shoulders, peering down. He was intensely aware of Aisling.

"Hen scratchings," Brocc observed of the spidery writing.

Aisling asked, "What language is that?"

"I thought you said you could read."

"I can!" she flared. But Michael could tell that the writing conveyed no more to her than it did to Brocc.

"The language is English," he explained, "or rather, English as it was written in the Colonies in the olden days."

"And what does it say?"

"This is a recipe for reshaping. It is the one I used in molding the pig. I began with a handful of earth, some fungus, and a scrap of pigskin from a ruined pair of gloves."

Aisling clapped her hands together with delight. "Magic!"

"The Science of Magic," Michael corrected her.

She shrugged. "Whatever you call it, you were able to create a suckling pig."

"I did not create it. The gift of Creation is beyond human ken. What I did was employ certain physical agencies to make matter assume a different form." His stomach interrupted with a loud growl, and he laughed in spite of himself. "I cannot feed everyone on earth with a pigskin glove, though. So even this book is not proof against Famine."

As he spoke the word, he saw Aisling look past him, toward the hearth. In spite of herself he followed her glance.

The face of Famine appeared again in the flames. This time, however, it was not an amorphous vision, but as solid and real as Aisling and Brocc, a malign embodiment drawn to the hall as they had been drawn to the hall.

Touching the Book, Michael Crafter's fingers tingled.

Aisling turned her back on him and raised her doubled fist, shaking it in front of the hideous spectre. Every line of her body was rigid with defiance. "You are not welcome here!" she cried. "This is an ancient land and a rich land; she has always fed her children!"

From the face in the fire came a hollow, echoing voice like one emanating from the void between the stars. "No more," it wailed. "No more. I am here now. I am here now. . . ."

"NO!" screamed Aisling, hurling herself toward the hearth. In one desperate leap, Michael caught hold of her just before she threw herself bodily upon the spectre. It took all his strength to hold her. She was shaking with rage.

He pulled her back from the hearth. Her slim body began to shake with sobs. "The richest of all lands," she was saying, weeping. "In the old days, when the gold sparkled in the streams and the apples bloomed on every hillside. Ah,'twas Tir-na-nog then, the Land of the Young! And we danced!"

She twisted in Michael's arms, torn with grief.

With Brocc's help, he got her seated on a bench and forced her to take a sip of wine. When at last she recovered herself, she looked at Michael with a tear-stained face. "Will you help us?" she asked in the softest of voices.

Born and raised in Ireland, Michael nevertheless had Crafter blood in his veins, good solid New England stock, people who never admitted defeat. With Aisling's eyes upon him—beautiful, strangely disturbing eyes—he could not admit defeat now. "I'll do what I can," he promised.

Brocc put one hand on his arm. For the first time, Michael realized just how small the other was, almost like a child. A child with great flaring ears so thin that light showed through them, and pointed features that were not really human at all; *kinder* than human, somehow.

"If you cannot feed the people yourself," said Brocc, "can you find magic in that Book of yours to change the hearts of their oppressors?"

Michael considered. "I do not know of any form of science that will soften hearts."

Aisling said, "Then is there some charm we can work upon yourself that will give you the power to lead the people in a rising? Encourage them to refuse to give the landlords the produce of their fields and herds?"

Michael tried to imagine himself becoming such a leader. He shook his head. "The magic in the Book is not designed to change human nature, I fear. These are gentle people, as I am myself. There is no spell I could cast, no enchantment I could summon, that would turn them into an army, or me into its leader."

Brocc lost his temper. "Then what use is that Book of yours? Throw it in the flames!"

"Stay!" Aisling commanded. "There is magic; the pig is proof. It only remains for us to find a way to use it."

Until this very night, Michael had always thought of the Book and its contents as treasure. Now he must consider its limitations.

Science would not create a herd of pigs, nor magic change human hearts. What good was either, then?

Yet Aisling's compelling eyes were fixed on his as if she *knew* he could do something.

He began turning the pages of the Book. Spells, potions, incantations, protective symbols . . .

Michael paused. "Ireland is filled with symbols," he said, thinking aloud. "Symbols left behind by all the people who have inhabited this island since the beginning of time. The great stone forts of the Fir Bolg, and even older things, the images left carved in stone by vanished races . . ."

His fingers took on a life of their own, seeking among the pages. Suddenly they stopped. Alone, in the center of an otherwise blank page, was a single form.

A triple spiral. Three swirling shapes combined into one.

Aisling drew in her breath in a hiss. "I have seen that before," she whispered in Michael's ear. "There is a forgotten stone chamber under a huge mound of earth, with that sign at its heart. It is the rarest and most sacred of symbols from the ancient times. How did it come to be in your Book?"

"My ancestor knew many secrets," Michael told her.

"Including a sign that has not seen the light of day for thousands of years?"

Michael could not answer.

Brocc spoke instead. "When you mentioned science, Michael Crafter, you said the word as if we did not know what it meant. But we do know. You are not the only being with ancestors. My people understood science long before yours first glimpsed the concept. In the forgotten times when we dwelt in the lands of Lemuria and Atlantis and Mu, we used that which you call science to fashion the Sword of Light and the Stone of Destiny. The triple spiral was ours then.

"But people forget with time, and magic grows weak with disuse. As you know. Those ancient secrets have been all but lost. Yet the fact that your ancestor knew enough to put the triple spiral in this Book tells us he met one of our people, or one of his own ancestors knew one of ours. . . . There are links, Michael Crafter. There are links, and they have closed now.

"We can work together. Aisling is the most gifted of us, but I have my own abilities, as you have yours. You need only believe. If we combine our forces—your New World vigor and our ancient wisdom—perhaps we can use the spiral once again to help the people of this island. Are you willing, Michael Crafter? Whatever the outcome?"

There was an ominous undertone to his words. Even though he would not let himself look toward the hearth, Michael knew the head of Famine was there again, watching him with ravenous eyes, eager to suck the life from him as it was sucking life from the Irish. By opening himself up to magic, was he giving that monster access to his inner self?

As if she heard his thoughts, Aisling said, "We will challenge an evil thing, Michael. The face of Famine hides appalling horrors. If we try to use the power of the spiral we may put ourselves at unimaginable risk, for the spiral has always been dangerous. The power it represents is beyond mortal control. It comes from the stars."

"Amer Crafter thought he could control it," Michael told her, his eyes scanning the next page.

Aisling's lips curved in an irresistible smile. "Good. Then read aloud to us from his words."

She folded her legs and sank gracefully to the stone floor, sitting at Michael's feet. Brocc planted himself on the nearest bench, elbows on knees, body canted forward in a listening posture. With the Book open before him, Michael began to read everything Amer Crafter had to divulge about the symbol of the triple spiral. The attention paid by the other two was so intense it seemed to suck the words out of his mouth.

Late into the night he read, until the words blurred before his eyes, but each time he tried to stop they made him go back and read again from the beginning, until the wisdom of the Book was carved into their three memories as if carved into stone.

All the while the fire on the hearth writhed and twisted without any additional fuel, as if the malign life in it was watching them, listening to them, pitting its will against theirs. The flames of Famine gobbled their hunger, and spat and cackled obscenely, as Michael tried to keep his entire attention focused on the message in the Book.

As the grainy light of a watery dawn seeped in through the long windows, Aisling sighed, stood, stretched. "We shall come back to you tomorrow night, Michael," she said. "It is the night of moondark, best suited to our purpose according to your book. Be ready then."

She plucked at one of the tattered bits of cloth that draped her lithe body, and unexpectedly tossed it toward Michael. The fabric clung to his face, blinding him. When he pulled it away, they were gone.

Michael stood in his empty hallway and wondered why he had not felt a draft from the open door as Aisling and Brocc went out.

Silence clamped around him. He looked toward the hearth. There was no flame upon it, only cold and stinking ashes.

Ireland seemed to be holding its breath. With infinite weariness, Michael returned the Book to its chest and made his way to bed.

They came to him when the moon was dark. As before, he was alerted by a scratching at the door. As before, he felt a certain tension, as any mortal man would do when in the grip of strange forces. But Amer Crafter's blood flowed in his veins. Michael opened the door to admit Aisling and Brocc.

A silvery light suffused the hall as they entered. On this night, they did not look shabby. Clad in rough brown clothing, Brocc looked like a gnarled tree trunk whose knots and whorls formed an almost human face.

Aisling seemed to have attired herself in rainbows.

"Are you certain you even need me?" Michael had to ask.

"We do indeed," Aisling assured him. "Your powers are

not great, but you provide the link with the wisdom of your ancestor, which we mean to draw upon. The three of us working together will be mightier than three. You can interpret the magic in modern form; we understand it in ancient ways. But it is all the same magic. As the god of the Protestants and the Papists is one with the Creator whom we recognize in tree and stone and river. Swirling and swirling around a center, the spiral turns," she murmured, using Amer Crafter's own words from the Book. "Take my hand, Michael."

He took her hand. Aisling's tiny white fingers were as insubstantial as fog, yet surprisingly strong.

The three left the old Crafter mansion and made their way through the Irish night, soft and dark and thick with mist. Aisling led the way, her small feet finding paths Michael had never known about. They threaded a sure route through bog and marsh, up hill, down glen. Michael had a sense of vast time passing, eons passing.

At last Aisling stopped. "Here is the first place we shall use. It is an old ring-fort, long forgotten, with crumbling banks and collapsed stone walls. Once it sheltered three hundred against Viking raids. It can surely shelter some of Ireland's children now against Famine. Let us begin the protections."

The abandoned fort was, like all its kind, built in a circle. Aisling moved into the center and lifted her hands, nodding to Brocc and Michael to join her. She was easy to see in spite of the lack of moonlight; she glimmered like a will-o-the-wisp in the darkness.

"Call out in your head to your powerful ancestor," she told Michael. "Reach him through your blood; request him to help us."

The three linked hands and began a slow, measured dance, following the spiral patterns described in the Book. Michael threw back his head and closed his eyes. In a deep voice, he began chanting the names Amer Crafter had once written in connection with the symbolism of the spiral.

"Bootes and Canes, provide!" he exhorted. "Aries, Camel-opardalis, Cancer, Cygnus, Delphinus, Equuleus, Pisces,

Serpens, Taurus, Ursa, Vulpecula . . ." Names known to
the science of astronomy.

Their feet beat an ancient design on the earth as Michael
called to the stars. Swirling and swirling, the three danced,
summoning, invoking, drawing down the powers of the
cosmos.

The names Michael called upon changed. "Perseus, Orion,
protect!" he cried. The pattern of the dance also changed,
mirroring different configurations in the sky. Michael felt as
if his strength were being literally drawn from him, pulled
into the earth. His knees trembled with weakness. At last
he staggered to a halt, but Brocc's fingers pressed his like
iron, and Aisling's voice demanded, "Not until you say the
final words from the Book!"

And so he did. Using the incantations Amer Crafter had
discovered long before, Michael wove a spell in the ring-fort
that night, a spell to alter the very nature of time within those
crumbling walls. He and Brocc and Aisling rested a brief
while afterward, then moved on to another site. And yet
another.

Each night for three nights, they met to repeat the ritu-
als. Each night for three nights, Michael was left totally
exhausted; yet he felt a growing sense of elation as if his
flesh and bones knew their effort would succeed. He felt
the gift of magic growing in him with practice; he felt doors
opening inside himself.

During the day he travelled far afield to visit the pathetic
hovels remaining to the surviving Irish peasants in the district. Though the peasants considered Michael a *sasanach,*
his ancestors had indeed been kind to them and the people
had not forgotten. They listened to what he had to say and
a faint light of hope began to illumine their faces.

"Take shelter in the old ring-forts," he told them. "There
you will be under the protection of . . . the Good People.
No harm will come to you within the walls, and while you
are there you will not feel the pangs of hunger. Time is
stopped there; you can stay as long as you like, until the
awful Famine has passed from the land, and you may then
emerge still alive, though thousands have died."

When he invoked the name of the Good People—the *sidhe*, the fairy folk—he saw fear leap in his listeners' eyes. Some crossed themselves and would have nothing further to do with the idea. Some would tell their priests, who condemned the plan in the most shocked phrases. But some, who knew the Crafters as decent people, believed. They followed Michael's instructions, making their way to the old and long-abandoned ring-forts, and hid there amid briars and nettles while Famine stalked through Ireland.

When at last it was over, they emerged, no thinner than when they went in, to slowly repopulate the land. The legend of the fairy forts came with them, to be told in whispers down the years, each telling more wild and wonderful than the one before, until a great aura of superstition attached itself to the 'fairy forts' and it was believed—as it is to this day—that to harm or desecrate one was to bring the direst of punishments upon oneself. So many an ancient ring-fort stands unscathed in the center of an otherwise plowed and productive field, a field once belonging to the native Irish, who have taken back the land where their ancestors suffered and starved.

As for Michael Crafter, who used New World magic in the Old World, no man knows his fate. During the worst of the famine he was seen throughout the west of Ireland with two strange companions who let no man get close to them. It was rumored they danced in ring-forts by the dark of the moon. Then, when the Famine faded at last, Michael was seen no more. His great house stood abandoned to the elements, tenanted by wind and rain, sinking back into the earth.

In time the Christ-men in their churches began accusing Michael Crafter of having formed an unholy alliance for unspecified purposes. They said the collapse of the once-powerful Crafter line was proof of evil, an evil not mitigated by the acts of charity Michael's predecessors had performed. *Michael Crafter's soul now burns in Hell*! they assured their flock, *and the same will happen to you if you surrender to pagan superstition*!

Protestant and Catholic alike, they condemned him most heartily.

But there is a song still sung in the district of Cratloe

Wood, in the county of Clare, where the wild wind comes wailing across the Atlantic from the next parish, which is Boston. The song tells of a lonely man with a gentle nature, a man who did the best he could, and loved the land where he was born. This man went off with the fairies, according to that ballad. He followed a beautiful vision into the hidden halls underneath the earth, and he lives there still. Lonely no longer.

The song celebrates him as being a man of magic and science, though science is not a word often used in the county of Clare.

County Clare, one of the worst hit by the hideous spectre of Famine. County Clare, where an incredible number of people somehow survived.

EPILOGUE

Jeffrey Ambrose Crafter was exhausted, yet exhilarated. He had seen what he could do, what had to be done, and he had done it. He smiled as he hurried through the grey, damp Moscow dawn, the briefcase containing the leather envelope and velvet bag held tightly in his hand. Around him the stolid citizens of the U.S.S.R. made their weary way through the icy streets. On the other side of the world, he knew, the citizens of the U.S.A. were ending their work hours. There were going to be some changes soon for them all, he hoped.

Later that afternoon, the acknowledged protégé of Yuri Andropov sat in his limosine as the chauffeur drove him to his dacha, and considered the amazing events of the day. First his mentor, and then President Brezhnev himself, had called into question years of propaganda, years of data analysis. They had voiced aloud, had *dared* to voice aloud, criticisms of the state of Mother Russia, forced into decline by the moribund bureaucracy of the Party. They had, they both agreed, awakened that morning with an astonishing clarity of vision and a new sense of purpose.

They had voiced, in fact, thoughts that the soon-to-be

Premier of the Soviet Union and Chairman of the Communist Party had privately held for some while. Extraordinary. But then, Mikhail Gorbachev thought, these were extraordinary times. . . .